Murder on Thin Ice

Also by Laurie Cass

The Bookmobile Cat Mysteries

Book 'Em, Eddie
No Paw to Stand On
A Troubling Tail
The Crime That Binds
Checking Out Crime
Gone with the Whisker
Booking the Crook
Wrong Side of the Paw
Cat with a Clue
Pouncing on Murder
Borrowed Crime
Tailing a Tabby
Lending a Paw

The Victorian Square Mysteries

Dead, Bath, and Beyond

Murder on Thin Ice

A BOOKMOBILE CAT MYSTERY

Laurie Cass

CROOKED LANE

NEW YORK

Published in the United States by Crooked Lane Books, an imprint of
The Quick Brown Fox & Company LLC.

Crooked Lane Books and its logo are trademarks of The Quick Brown Fox & Company LLC.

Library of Congress Catalog-in-Publication data available upon request.

ISBN (hardcover): 979-8-89242-699-2
ISBN (paperback): 979-8-89242-700-5
ISBN (ebook): 979-8-89242-701-2

Cover design by Sam Hadley

Printed in the United States.

www.crookedlanebooks.com

Crooked Lane Books
34 West 27th St., 10th Floor
New York, NY 10001

First Edition: October 2026

The authorized representative in the EU for product safety and compliance is eucomply OÜPärnu mnt 139b-14, 11317 Tallinn, Estonia, hello@eucompliancepartner.com, +33757690241

10 9 8 7 6 5 4 3 2 1

In memory of Darlene Ryan
(aka Sofie Ryan, aka Sofie Kelly),
an all-around wonderful person.
You are missed, my friend.

Chapter One

After thirty-five years of living on Planet Earth, most people have gathered enough experiences to stop being surprised all the time. Me? Not so much.

Case in point was that particular sun-drenched February morning. All around, snow crystals sparkled with a hundred million colors, reflecting and refracting the bright light into a kaleidoscope of winter. Though you'd have thought there wouldn't be anything except blue and white, somehow there was every color. It was—

"Minnie."

My ears woke up and recognized that what I'd heard was the not-so-patient tone of someone who'd used my name more than once.

"Hmm?" I asked. But I continued to gaze through the bookmobile's windshield, a sappy smile on my face.

It was ten o'clock on a Monday morning just after Valentine's Day. There'd been a six-inch overnight snowfall, and thanks to the dedicated snowplow drivers, the main roads were clear and dry. It was almost twenty degrees already, a flat-out gorgeous morning, and there was absolutely no reason to worry about anything, and that included whatever it was that Julia Beaton, one of my two part-time bookmobile clerks, was suddenly so impatient about.

She poked at my shoulder with her index finger. "You're going to wind up with a stiff neck if you keep doing that."

I gave the endless blue sky one last look and sat back against the support of the driver's seat, wiggling my shoulders to loosen the tension that had accumulated while I'd hunched myself over the steering wheel and cricked my neck to peer upward. "Yes, Ms. Beaton," I muttered as I turned the key, starting the engine.

"What was that you said?" Julia put a mittened hand to what would have been her ear if her head hadn't been covered by a brightly colored knit hat. "Thank you for watching out for me, Ms. Beaton?"

I grinned, dropping the transmission into drive, easing us out of the library parking lot and into the quiet back streets of Chilson. "Exactly."

"Hear that, Eddie?" Julia tapped her boot toes on top of the cat carrier that was strapped to the passenger floor. "Your momma finally appreciates me."

I'd always appreciated Julia, and she knew this because I said so on a regular basis. How could I not? Julia, now in her mid-sixties, had grown up here in Chilson, a small, sleepy resort town. The day after graduating from high school, she'd loaded up her Chevette hatchback with all her worldly belongings and hightailed it out of town for New York City with the single-minded aim to become the world's biggest supermodel.

That had worked out about as well as you'd expect, but her second career choice of acting had given her a bucketful of Tony Awards, a comfortable though not luxurious lifestyle, and a contacts list that would knock your socks off.

When Julia retired from the bright lights of Broadway, she and her husband had moved back to Michigan. A handful of weeks later, her loving spouse had mildly told her to find something to do with herself or they might end up divorced. She subsequently became part of the bookmobile crew, and that's how we ended up with an world-class actor as our primary storyteller.

"Mrr."

I nodded in the direction of my cat, because he was obviously following my train of thought. Our other part-time clerk, Rila Shutleff, didn't have Julia's storytelling skills, but as a former international soccer player whose career had been cut short by injury, she had a plethora of personal stories about people and places from all over the globe. Rila, not yet thirty, was new to the bookmobile. Though she was freshly divorced and still working out what she wanted the rest of her life to be like, she seemed content working on the bookmobile. Just as important—Eddie liked her.

"Mrr!"

Julia craned her around to look in through the cat carrier's wire door. "Yes, my lord and master?"

"He's still mad at me," I said.

Just after Christmas, my new husband and I had zipped over to London for a slightly delayed honeymoon. We'd returned replete with fine food and the sights of two thousand years of human occupation to a cat who wouldn't talk to us. My aunt Frances, who'd taken over cat care in our absence, has sent us numerous Eddie-related text messages and photos, but none of what we'd read and seen while strolling through Regent's Park or down Baker Street or in Soho had given us a hint that we'd be treated to a sulk that was lasting weeks.

"Let's see if we can jolly him into a good mood." Julia bravely stuck her fingers in through his wire door. "He-llo-ooo-oo," she called out, stretching the short word into thirty-seven syllables. "Too-dle-ooo, young chap!"

My coworker had a habit of putting on accents at the drop of a sentence. And, given her many Shakespearean stage roles, her default was British. Though Scots, German, and Scandinavian snuck in every so often, along with various flavors of American, her go-to was the cut crystal of expensive English boarding schools.

I gave my furry friend another glance. "That accent could be making things worse. It could be reminding him of where we went when we abandoned him for almost two whole weeks."

In truth, I didn't think any such thing. Though Eddie was a cat of many talents, I was a hundred and ten percent sure that his mental capacity didn't stretch to making connections between Julia's vocals and where his minions—that would be me and Rafe—had traveled.

But Julia nodded. "Good point. I could try Italian. Or Australian. Or . . ." She sat up and I could feel her squinting into the distance. "How about a brand-new accent?" she asked thoughtfully. "Rooted in time and place?"

"Um." I flicked on the turn signal and steered the thirty-one-foot-long, twenty-odd-thousand-pound bookmobile—laden with its three thousand books, magazines, board games, and miscellaneous items such as ice fishing paraphernalia, ukuleles, and bread makers—onto the county highway that would take us to the first stop of the day. "How would that be different from regular talking?"

Julia launched into a discourse about the origins and evolution of the human language. I tried to pay attention, but when she got to the cuneiform tablets of Mesopotamia, my mind wandered off to something a little closer to hearth and home.

My furry friend. My pal. Eddie.

I slewed a glance sideways. He'd rotated himself so his back was facing me, a sure indication of feline displeasure.

With a small sigh, I wondered if it was time to take him to the vet. I'd mentioned the possibility to Rafe the other day, and his response had been, "Okay, but what are the symptoms? He's eating and drinking like normal. Using the litter box like normal. Shedding like normal. What's Dr. Joe going to do, exactly?"

"There's something wrong," I'd insisted, but I hadn't yet made an appointment, because Rafe was right. What would I tell Joe? That Eddie was being mean to me?

The thought made me smile. Eddie had adopted me just shy of three years ago, back in the time when I'd been living with my aunt Frances in her rambling boardinghouse in the cold months, and on my adorable little houseboat during the warmer times.

On that fateful April day, the weather had turned unseasonably warm and sunny. I should have been cleaning the houseboat, but I'd decided that particular chore could wait, and had instead wandered through the local cemetery, enjoying the view of the twenty-mile-long Janay Lake and the horizontal blue line of Lake Michigan just over the hills to the west.

My quiet walk had been interrupted by a black-and-white tabby who had materialized next to the gravestone of Alonzo Tillotson, born 1847, died 1926. Knowing nothing about cats due to my father's allergies, I'd assumed he had a home and tried to wave him off. Instead, he'd followed me, much to the amusement of passersby.

The "Found Cat" notice I'd run in the newspaper had gone unanswered, the local veterinarian, Dr. Joe, had said my new friend was hale, hearty, and about two years old, and Eddie and I were now pals for life.

Or at least I'd thought we were. Could our heretofore unbreakable bond have been broken during my ten-day absence? Could he have decided he didn't like me any longer? Had he decided he didn't like sharing me with Rafe? Was this why he'd been a stray three years ago—he'd decided to move on from whoever he'd been with?

"No," I murmured. It wasn't possible. Eddie loved Rafe and me, and we loved him. If he'd decided to hate us he wouldn't be sleeping in our bedroom at all, albeit underneath the bed instead of snuggling on top like he usually did.

Maybe it was the weather. The temperature had been running ten to twenty degrees below average for weeks, and we'd hardly seen the sun since November. Lots of people suffered from seasonal affective disorder. Maybe cats did, too.

I made a mental note to ask the Internet—no need to bother Dr. Joe with a question that might get me a look of disbelief and an answer that felt like a pat on the head—and went back to listening to Julia. She, however, was going on about Chaucer and Middle English, so I went back to my own thoughts.

Since I'd decided on a course of action regarding Eddie, I moved on to the next topic on my mental agenda, titled *What Am I Going to Do With the Rest of My Life?*

I hadn't thought much about this particular item in years. Partly because I'd been too busy, and partly because I'd more or less achieved the biggest things I'd wanted to do.

One, become assistant director in a small-town library.

Check!

Two, find a way to live in the wonderful world of Up North, also known as northern lower Michigan.

Check!

Three, grow a solid group of friends, coworkers, and colleagues for whom I'd do almost anything, including driving them to the Traverse City airport for the early flight.

Check!

That I'd achieved all three of those things by the time I'd reached thirty-five was astonishing not only to me but also to my parents and brother. Dad and Matt were both engineers who did things I'd never understood, and Mom was the presentations coordinator at the historic open air museum Greenfield Village in my hometown of Dearborn.

My family loved me and I loved them, but they'd assumed I'd follow their corporate steps and had smiled tightly when it had become clear that I was more inclined to follow the career track of the black sheep of the family, my dad's sister Frances.

"The only thing we all agree on," I murmured, "is that there was absolutely room for both Rose and Jack on that floating door."

"Mrr."

I looked over. Eddie had squished himself against his door hard enough to make his fur stick out the wire squares. If it stayed like that, the kids at Moulson Elementary were going to spend a lot of time trying to smooth it down. "Hope you're up to it," I said, mostly to myself.

Julia stopped her monologue, which might or might not have had something to do with the root differences between Chinese and Korean. "What was that?" she asked. When I didn't instantly respond, she sighed and leaned forward. "Master Edward, I fear your mother hasn't been listening to me. In fact, I believe that she won't retain a single thing from my scintillating lecture on languages."

"Mrr!"

"Exactly," she said. "So glad you agree with me."

"You sound sure that's what he was saying." I flicked on the turn signal and put my foot on the brake.

"I am fluent in Eddie," Julia said.

"Great. I'll call you at three in the morning when he's howling for no apparent reason."

"I am," she said, "fluent in Eddie during bookmobile hours only."

Laughing, I brought us to a slow stop in the unloading zone. The school had a library, but since they hadn't had a librarian in years, the room got little use. Worse, the books were sitting there, unread. The principal, Sarah Schrader, and I had sat down late last summer to brainstorm how the bookmobile might be able to fill the gap. After spitballing a handful of good ideas and a lot of bad ones, we'd decided to run a pilot trip and see how things went.

The whole thing had not been a success straight out of the gate. Though we'd gone into classrooms and said what we could to make the bookmobile sound fun and interesting, only a handful of kids got up out of their seats to come aboard. However, that handful had been engaged enough to encourage a few more to join the next time, and now we had so many youngsters participating that we needed to break them into timed groups.

Half an hour into the third set, Julia clapped her hands and said, in her most dramatic voice, "Five minutes, my young friends."

The immediate disjointed chorus of "But we need more time," "I haven't petted Eddie yet," and "I want to stay" warmed my heart and reminded me, once again, that I had the best job in the world.

"Five minutes," Julia said, uncompromisingly. "And in six minutes we'll be in the library for story time."

"What story?" a small girl asked, her nose in *The Baby Who Stayed Awake Forever*. "It can't be better than this."

Such a statement was a direct challenge to Julia. "Good, better, best," she said, "is not important. You, my dear, can read that book at the time and place of your choosing. But how often am I here? That's right, once a month. Do you really want to miss hearing the story of the girl and boy—twins—who were stranded on a boat in the middle of Lake Michigan? With a dragon?"

The girl's eyes narrowed. "How big was the dragon?"

Julia returned the narrow-eyed look. "How big do you want it to be?"

With the lure of an imminent dragon story, herding the kids back into the building was a relatively easy task. As Julia and the teachers lined up the small humans, I pulled a slip of paper out of each book they wanted to check out.

"Bye, Ms. Minnie!"

"Bye, Eddie!

After waving them off, I went up front, unlatched the driver's seat, turned it around, and locked it down. Then I rotated the small piece of wood that secured a countertop, lowered said countertop, and pulled the laptop out of the newly revealed hidey hole. As soon as the computer found the school's Wi-Fi, I started entering the books, which I did by scanning the QR codes printed on the slips of paper.

The motions were so automatic that my brain didn't feel the need to pay full attention to them, so I started a one-sided conversation with Eddie.

"That went well, don't you think? The only problem with that is every other elementary school in the county might want a bookmobile stop, too. Well, not Chilson Elementary, because they still have a librarian, but—"

I heard a noise I couldn't identify, which was rarely a good sign. When the kids had been aboard, Eddie had been temporarily brought out for gentle (supervised) pets and then reinstalled into the carrier. The high activity level during the visits meant Eddie's sleep patterns were disrupted, and now was usually the point at which he started snoring.

But his yellow eyes were wide open and staring at me, so he was out as the culprit. Silly me, thinking that the past ten thousand Eddie-related noises in a row had created any sort of precedent.

I looked around and saw a small piece of wood on the floor. What the . . . "Oh." I recognized it as the bit that held the countertop vertical when we were driving. "That's a problem."

But not a major one. One of Rafe's Christmas presents to me had been a small red Swiss Army knife. When I'd opened it, I'd pasted a bright smile on my face and started to thank him politely.

"Yeah, I know what you're thinking," he'd said. "How can you carry a pocketknife when you go to so many places that don't allow knives? Look." He'd opened it up. "No blade. Just that little pair of scissors and the multi-function tool. Bottle opener, screwdriver, and wire stripper. See?"

Though I couldn't imagine a situation in which I'd need an emergency bottle opener, let alone a wire stripper, he was so happy about the gift that I promised to carry it with me always. And now, here it was, coming in handy. I pulled it out of my coat's inside pocket, picked up the chunk of wood, which happily still had the screw inside, and stood to do the quick repair.

Eddie was watching me with a critical gaze that was saying *I could do better*, something that would normally have been annoying, but today was welcome because at least he wasn't ignoring me.

"You know," I said, "this should teach me to pay more attention to things. If I had been earlier, I would have noticed that screw being loose."

"Mrr," my cat said.

He could have meant many things by this, ranging from "Time for a treat" to a snarky comment that there was no way to tighten the loose screws in my head, but I chose to interpret it as agreement and nodded.

"Like Mom always says, if we know better, we can do better." It had been a phrase that hadn't sat well with me at ten years old when I'd done a poor job of making my bed, but now I was glad I'd had that kind of parenting. And maybe someday I'd tell my mom so.

"Doing better is always a goal, I suppose," I mused as I tightened the screw. "But it's almost too vague to be useful. Maybe it's more like a mission statement, and then you develop action steps. Sort of like—"

This time the odd noise I heard was indeed the snuffly noise of a snoring cat. Smiling, I shook my head and went back to beeping through the mound of paper slips. I'd just finished when the door opened and Julia came in with a burst of cold air.

"Mission accomplished," she said, saluting.

I saluted back. "At ease, soldier. Dragon status satisfactory?"

"Gentled and working as a heat source for the town." She plopped into her seat and flipped her long strawberry-blond braid, often used as a prop during story time, over her shoulder. "What's next? Housebound stops or the township hall?"

One of the services the library's outreach program offered was dropping off and picking up books for folks who couldn't leave their houses, whether temporarily or permanently. The length of the list varied by season. Not so many people on it during the summer, but it was way longer in the winter months with the cold and snow and ice. The only growing demographic in Tonedagana County was our senior citizens, and we wanted to serve them as well as we could, but there was a logistical complication in that we had many seniors with friends and family who came up in the spring, summer, and fall to help out; not so much in the winter.

"Some of both," I said. "Two quick drop-offs, then the township hall, then Gerald is last." We often did housebound deliveries by car, but we occasionally delivered via bookmobile.

"Hear that, Eddie?" Julia tapped her toes. "We're going to see Gerald. You get a treat, and the humans get fresh coffee, complete with real cream."

Something that was not a snore emanated from the carrier.

Julia's eyes went wide. "Is he growling at me? What did I do wrong?"

"Welcome to my world," I said, putting away the computer. "I told you, he's been off since we got home from London. Fine one minute, cranky as all get-out the next."

"Hmm." Julia pulled her hat and mittens from her capacious coat pockets and tossed them onto the wide console. "Maybe he needs a kitty girlfriend."

"Not likely." My aunt's husband, Otto, had an adorable little gray female short hair. When Aunt Frances had volunteered to take care of Eddie when we were gone, we'd taken him up the hill to their house for a visit before we left. I'd tried to purge the memory from my brain, but images of flying fur, sharp teeth, and horrific hissing continued to plague my dreams.

The rest of the afternoon, Julia continued to offer ideas to bring back the old Eddie. All were interesting, but none hit the trifecta of realistic, affordable, and likely to work.

"Well," she fake-huffed as we pulled into Gerald Arnhold's driveway, a lane so long, winding, and tree-lined that his house wasn't visible from the road, "that's it for me. If you don't think getting him to wear a pirate costume will help, I have nothing else to offer."

"Keep trying," I said, coming to a stop on the concrete pad in front of Gerald's garage. "You never know when inspiration will strike."

We clicked our seatbelts open. I stood to grab Gerald's books, and Julia picked up Eddie's carrier. Gerald, an octogenarian, had signed up for housebound delivery after he'd been told by his eye doctor that his driving days were over. He lived alone, and we'd never seen any signs of wife, children, or grandchildren. Food was delivered for a small upcharge by a local grocery store, and everything else he ordered online. Which included cat treats, because Gerald was a big Eddie fan.

"Mrr-RRr-rrr."

Julia hurriedly put the carrier on the console. "That's not the *about-to-hurl* howl, is it?"

"No, that was more the *I-hate-this* noise."

"Huh."

We peered in through the wire door. The cat glared back. After a few moments of silence, I shrugged and took the handle. "He looks fine. If he starts making weird noises, we'll bring him back out."

Julia picked up Gerald's big bag of large-print books and we headed out. Gerald, even though he'd sold his SUV months ago, kept his long driveway—and the big turn-around that made bookmobile deliveries possible—free of ice and snow. His isolated ranch-style house was perched on the edge of a low bluff that overlooked a shallow lake too small to have a name. Built in the sixties, back when a 1,200 square foot home with three bedrooms and one full bath was all most families aspired to, its single story was compact and efficient, just like its owner.

As we'd been told to do months ago, we came through a side door into the now-empty garage, knocked three times on the inside door, and turned the knob.

I frowned. "It's locked."

"Are you sure?" Julia reached out and tried it herself. "He must have forgotten to open it for us."

We waited, but no shuffling Gerald footsteps approached.

I glanced at Julia, who was looking at me. Gerald had told us—and probably umpteen other people—where he kept the spare key, but we'd never used it. I tried to quiet the tumbling feeling in my stomach. "I'll get the key," I said quietly, and felt around the outside door's jamb until I found it hanging from a nail.

After unlocking the door and putting the key away, I pushed the door open to a seemingly normal kitchen.

"Gerald, 'tis us!" Julia sang out. Well, not *sang*, because early in her stage career the quality of her singing voice had had her kicked out of the background chorus of an off-Broadway musical, but she definitely used a singing-ish tone. "Are you decent?"

Usually by this time, Gerald had already seen us coming up the drive and had his coffeepot going. But this afternoon the kitchen was dark and empty, though the wooden table with its knobby legs was covered with an assortment of small, tidy piles of paperwork. This meant that Gerald, a bookkeeper who still kept his hand in, had recently been working on his personal finances. "Clients in the office," he'd told us. "Kitchen for me. Keeps things straight."

"Hello?" I called.

Silence.

Julia and I exchanged a glance.

"I'll go," I said quietly. I put Eddie's carrier on the floor and made sure my mental assistant librarian hat was firmly on my head. There were three likely scenarios. One, that Gerald was sleeping. Two, that he'd taken sick. Three . . . my mind shied away from that sad possibility as I walked through the house.

"Gerald? Are you here?"

He wasn't in the living room where we sometimes found him sitting next to the fireplace, all cozy with a crackling wood fire, plaid wool blanket, and shiny brass fireplace tools. He also wasn't in the master bedroom, or in the bedroom he'd converted to an office for his bookkeeping business, or in the third small bedroom that was a guest room, or in the bathroom.

After a moment of deep breathing to gather my courage, I opened the basement door and descended into creepy land. But the only things down there were a workbench, a drill press, a table saw, and a few boxes with printed labels. Christmas decorations, fishing lures, and so on. Normal stuff.

Puzzled, I climbed the stairs. "He's not down there."

"Ohhh." Julia's shoulders sagged. "Good. I mean . . ."

I nodded. "But where could he be? I don't see anything to make me think he got sick or hurt and had to call an ambulance. Everything is organized and tidy, just like always."

Julia looked around, and her gaze settled on the pegs next to the door that led to the garage. "His coat is gone."

I whirled. She was right. Gerald, with his deteriorating eyesight, had started to buy bright clothing, and in November he'd showed us his new and shockingly red winter coat with its matching hat.

My stomach clenched. This meant he was outside. In the cold. Maybe injured, maybe . . . "Okay," I said, as calmly as I could. "We'll leave Eddie here."

"MRR!"

"Sorry, bud, but we have to. The humans will go outside and look for him, you stay here and keep watch." I looked through the kitchen window, out at the wide expanse of white. "If we don't find him within a few minutes, I'll call for help and—" My words clogged in my throat.

"What?" Julia's voice was tense. "What's the matter? What do you see?"

I kept staring at a tiny wooden building sitting in the middle of his iced-over lake. His ice shanty. "Keep your phone on," I said, and hurried into the garage and out its back door.

Gerald being Gerald, he hadn't done what normal people did and simply waded through the snow out to the ice. Instead, he'd used his snowblower to clear a nice wide path, and then used a shovel to scrape the path down to the brick pavers that he'd patiently laid himself, one by one by one.

"Hello?" I hurried down to the frozen lake. "Gerald? Are you there? Are you okay?" But there was no cry for help, no tapping noise, nothing other than my own footfalls. My own breathing.

I reached the edge of the lake and hesitated, which was silly because with the cold we'd been having the ice had to be two feet thick, then kept going. "Gerald?" I half-walked, half-slid across the ice. "Gerald?"

When I reached the ice shanty, I called his name a final time and pushed aside the canvas tarp he used to keep the cold out. Inside was an overturned five-gallon bucket, an ice fishing rod, and a bright red hat.

The one other thing to see was the only thing I was seeing—a large, round hole in the ice.

My fingers didn't want to work, so it took me a few tries, but eventually I was able to dial the three numbers.

"Central dispatch, what is your emergency?" asked a calm voice.

I pulled in a deep breath and said, "I'm calling about a possible drowning."

Chapter Two

It had taken four sheriff's deputies, the undersheriff, a dive team, the sheriff herself, a medical examiner investigator, a warming tent, portable lights, and a tremendous amount of mysterious and expensive-looking equipment, but five hours after I called 911, Gerald's body was pulled from the water and gently placed on a stretcher.

At least that was what Detective Ash Wolverson told me late that night. After the undersheriff had arrived and Julia and I described the afternoon's events numerous times, he'd told us we could go home, and that we'd be contacted when there was news.

"Sorry, Minnie," Ash said. "I know you were hoping for a different ending. That maybe he'd walked over to a neighbor's house."

It hadn't been much of a hope, as Gerald was a serious stay-at-home kind of guy, but still. "Thanks for stopping by." I sighed. "I'll call Julia."

Rafe, standing next to me, shook his friend's hand. "Thanks, bud. Appreciate it."

Ash gave us a nod, hesitated, then said, "I'm sure Mr. Arnhold would have appreciated how concerned you were about him. Knowing that you cared would—"

"MRR!!"

Ash flinched, Rafe winced, and I shook my head. "Sorry about that." I leaned down and scooped the noisy cat into my arms. "He's been weird for weeks, and even weirder today." It had been Eddie's decibel level that had made me look out Gerald's kitchen window in the first place.

Rafe eyed me, clearly saying without a word that Eddie's level of weirdness was perpetually high.

"Yeah?" Ash reached out and patted Eddie's head. "He looks pretty normal to me."

I wasn't sure the words "normal" and "Eddie" belonged in the same sentence, not without some kind of modifier, but I didn't have the energy or desire to enter into that kind of discussion. Instead, I snuggled Eddie tight and buried my face in his warm fuzzy fur.

"Well." Ash cleared his throat. "Unless something happens, we're still on for Friday night. See you at what, six?"

Rafe put his arm around my shoulder. "Sounds good."

Ash went out into cold darkness, and I stood there, breathing in Eddie-scent. Just that morning, I'd been texting Chelsea Stille, Ash's fiancée, about weekend plans. Their wedding was in less than three months, and since Rafe and I were the master and mistress of ceremonies, there were things to finalize. For Rafe, it was mostly making sure there would be backup beer at the reception, for me it was the timeline, and for both of us it was making sure Ash's law enforcement pals didn't play some prank that would not be funny, at least not to the happy couple.

Right at that moment, though, Friday seemed very far away. Almost as far away as that morning, when I'd looked forward to the cup of afternoon coffee that Gerald always insisted on brewing for me. "It's something I can do," he'd said over and over. "As long as I can see that smile on your face when you take a sip, I'll keep making it."

I sighed. It had been wonderful coffee, and I'd told him so every time, even though he'd always shaken off the praise. "I'm going to miss him," I whispered to Eddie.

"Come on," Rafe said gruffly. "Time for bed."

After the tragic end to the day, I expected to have a night filled with tossing and turning and haunted dreams. But thanks to a husband who held me close and to an Eddie who'd unexpectedly given up his sulking-underneath-the-bed sleep patterns and jumped up to curl, purring, against my tummy, I slept like the proverbial rock, not opening my eyes until Rafe nudged me.

"Wakey wakey," he said. "If you get up now, we have time to eat at the Round Table."

I shot out of bed and into the shower, towel-dried my stupidly curly hair as best I could, jumped into my standard winter library clothes of dressy pants, turtleneck, and blazer, and kissed a blinky Eddie good-bye.

The clientele at the diner on a mid-February weekday morning was a handful of regulars—older men sitting at the large table for which the restaurant was named—and us. Rafe and I nodded at the men as we slid into our favorite booth and turned over the white coffee mugs to accept the life-giving liquid that Sabrina, the Round Table's forever waitress, was bringing our way.

"Minnie Niswander," she said, filling my mug. "Rafe Niswander. Any reason we're seeing you on a Tuesday?"

"What, we need a reason to see your smiling face?" Rafe winked at her.

With one hand she pulled a pencil from her bun of silvery hair, with the other she pulled her order pad from her apron pocket. "Save the charm for someone who might take it seriously. Minnie, you look like you need bacon this morning. Crispy." She flicked me a glance, shook her head, and continued to order for me. "Scrambled eggs, and sourdough toast with orange marmalade." She slid her pad back into her pocket.

"Hey!" Rafe sat up straight. "What about me?"

"You'll get what you're given." She sniffed and headed to the kitchen.

Rafe watched her go. "Why is it we keep eating here?"

"Because it's the only place in Chilson to get a full breakfast this time of year."

"Oh. Right."

"Plus the food is good, priced for locals, and you order the same thing every time."

"Not every time," he protested.

"Okay, you've had the same breakfast order since you turned twelve."

"There you go."

He grinned, and my heart went a little mushy inside. After two decades of friendship with Rafe, developed during the youthful summers I'd spent with my aunt Frances, I'd finally realized that I loved him deeply. Though his good-ole-boy banter could be irritating, and his habit of acting far stupider than he was annoyed me no end, he would do anything for his friends and family. And that smile did something to me, every time.

"Are you going to tell me about yesterday, or what?"

I looked up. Sabrina was back, hands on her hips. "Um . . ."

"They just said"—she tipped her head at the geezers in the back of the room—"the bookmobile found that Gerald Arnhold drowned out ice fishing. Bookmobile. That's you."

Rafe looked at me, then turned in the booth to face Sabrina. "Minnie doesn't want to talk about it. Can you just leave it for a day or two?"

I touched the back of his hand. "No, it's okay." Sort of. He was right, I didn't want to talk about it, but I also knew people would be asking me about it all day, so I might as well get used to it.

So I gave her as concise a summary as I could, ending with, "It's just so hard to believe. Gerald was so careful about . . . everything. I didn't know you knew him."

"He was a regular," she said. "Long time ago. Two eggs, fried, sausage links, rye toast, no butter. Black coffee." She rapped her knuckles on the edge of our table. "Your order will be up in a sec."

I stared into my coffee, thinking about Gerald. Remembering him. He'd taken the news about his gradual blindness with a calm courage that had made me respect him even more than I already did, and I wondered for the zillionth time why he'd never married. He was such a nice man. Had been such a nice man.

Sabrina slid our plates in front of us. Rafe and I forked in our food, talking idly about our upcoming days. Rafe's would be full of his typical middle school principal tasks—meetings with teachers, meetings with parents, approving invoices, reading emails—and mine would be full of having to tell everyone at the library, employees and patrons alike, about what had happened to Gerald.

"It'll be all right," Rafe said as we stood in the entryway, zipping up our coats and pulling on gloves (Rafe) and mittens (me). "Two days from now you'll never have to talk about yesterday."

"Something to look forward to," I said, trying to smile.

"Want a ride to the library?"

I shook my head. "The walk will help clear my head."

"Then I'll see you tonight." He leaned down and gave me a soft kiss. "And if you're good," he whispered, "I'll make that recipe Kristen sent us, the pappardelle pasta with the olives and burrata cheese."

Super good, my chef friend had written, *and so easy that even Minnie can do it*. "Promise?" I asked.

"Cross my heart."

We walked out together. I watched as he roared his pickup truck to life, waved as he exited the parking lot, and made a mental note to remind him for the thirty-fourth time to make an appointment to get a new muffler.

The sky had returned to its February default of low gray clouds. I tried to be grateful for the one full day of blue sky that we'd had. It was more than we got all month in some

Februarys, so yes, I was appreciative, but that didn't mean I wasn't still longing for sunshine.

I stood on the sidewalk, hands in pockets, and sighed. Mid-February. No matter what that groundhog in Pennsylvania did, we stood a good chance of getting snow for two more months. We wouldn't see many daffodils until the end of April, and the trees wouldn't start leafing out until the middle of May.

"Living year-round Up North isn't for the weak of heart," I murmured as I started walking and trying to find pleasure in my surroundings. But Janay Lake, normally a lovely blue on all but the grayest of summer days, was a dull icy white. Our hundred-year-old Shingle-style house, renovated in bits and pieces by Rafe out of its chopped-up apartments and back to its original glory, was a hop, skip, and a jump from the lake and not far from downtown, but it was out of my sight and getting further away.

Scuffing my boots a bit, I walked on.

Downtown Chilson, if I paid attention, would perk up my spirits. The few blocks of retail stores and restaurants, mixed with an occasional insurance or real estate agency, was a happy blend of old and new construction. Take a bunch of early 1900s two-story brick and story-and-a-half clapboard buildings, sprinkle with an oddball metal or stucco-sided building, add a dash of new three-story buildings that were mostly windows, and you ended up with an organically grown downtown that would never have been concepted in a planner's office but which defined Chilson perfectly.

I passed Corner Coffee, the toy store, Gennell Books & Goods, Benton's General Store, Hoppe's Brewing, the jewelry store, Henika's Candy Emporium, and my friend Pam's store Older Than Dirt, and I caught a glimpse of the Lakeview Art Gallery down a side street. It was all nice enough, but my mood didn't change until I got a whiff of the scents wafting out of Tom's Bakery.

Doughnuts, with a hefty side dose of chocolate chip cookies.

I pulled in a deep breath, and a slow smile spread across my face. Who could be sad when there were smells like this? Cheered, my feet started moving at a more normal speed, and soon I was walking through the back door of the library.

As I did every time I remembered to do so, I slowed to admire the amazing building in which I worked. A few years back, just before I was hired, the taxpayers generously approved a short-term millage to renovate a shuttered elementary school into a new library.

The building I had the pleasure to work in had high ceilings, oak beams, and a multitude of details in the Arts and Crafts architectural style. There were dark brass fixtures, metallic mosaic tiles, and massive pendant lights hanging in the old gymnasium turned main stacks. It also had a reader's fantasy come to life: a reading room with a gas fireplace and a deep, upholstered window seat.

As it was two hours before the library opened its door to the public, everything except the red emergency exit signs was dark. Some people might find it unsettling, but I loved the feeling. It was like a stage before the curtain went up. You never knew what was going to happen, and it was almost certainly going to be fun.

I was in the break room, waiting for the coffeepot to do its thing, when my boss came in. Graydon Cain, the third director I'd worked under, was by far the best, and I hoped he'd stay forever. Or at least until I was ready to stop driving the bookmobile and think about becoming library director myself.

"Hey," he said.

I eyed him. His morning greeting was usually more enthusiastic than that. "Something wrong?" I asked.

"Maybe. Not sure yet." He took a random mug from the cupboard and filled it. "Come up in half an hour and I'll let you know."

He left before asking about the events of yesterday, and I stared at the vacant doorway.

Well, that was more than a little odd. I'd called him from Gerald's house while we were waiting for law enforcement to show up, and he'd been understanding and supportive and had told me I could bring him up to speed first thing in the morning. Which was now.

Huh.

I tried not to assume the worst, then started thinking about what the worst might be. He'd been diagnosed with a horrific disease. Or his wife had, or one of his kids. Or maybe a library board member. Then again, another horrible thing would be an employee termination. Could it be me? Julia? One of the bricks-and-mortar clerks? My friend Holly? Donna? Kelsey? It couldn't be our maintenance guy, Gareth. And certainly not our IT guy, Josh. We couldn't operate without either of them. Any of them. No one was quitting, were they? The library was a tight ship. Everyone fit. Remove one of us and the whole thing might—

"What's the matter?"

I blinked. Holly Terpening was walking into the break-room, a plastic tub in her hands. "Brownies?" I asked. Holly, a few inches taller than my efficient five foot and with lovely straight brown hair, was close to my age. Her husband worked out west doing some lucrative thing with massive mines and was home maybe two weeks out of every eight. She also had two young children, Wilson and Anna, ten and nine respectively. How she had time to bake her legendary brownies was yet another mystery of the universe.

"Heard what happened yesterday." She plopped the tub on the table and pulled the top off, releasing the aroma of warm brownies. "You get first dibs."

I'd had a big breakfast. I wasn't hungry at all. "Are there chocolate chips in there?"

"No," she said. "But there are chocolate chunks."

My hand, which had been withdrawing, dove into the tub and withdrew a square of warm, moist, chewy goodness.

"Hey!" growled a low voice.

I ignored the comment. It was Josh Hadden, our IT guy and another coworker about my age. It might have been our similar ages or it might have been that the three of us had started at the library at roughly the same time, but whatever the reason, we had a relationship that was very sibling-like.

He approached the brownies, looked them over closely, and took the largest one. A corner piece.

"Knew you'd take that one." Holly rolled her eyes.

"Well, why wouldn't I? It's the best."

As he bit into the gooey goodness, I took a look at him. His dark hair looked even more tousled than usual, his cargo pants looked as if he'd intentionally added wrinkles to them, and his eyes had those shadows of sleep deprivation underneath.

I bumped him with my elbow. "You seem a little rough around the edges this morning. Everything okay?"

Holly snorted. "Probably stayed up until three playing some new video game."

Though that was definitely possible with Josh, it had been more likely before he'd married the wonderfully intelligent Mia. Another thought clutched at me, matching it up with Graydon's oddness. "Please tell me the library's servers are okay."

"What are you talking about?" he asked, a crumb of brownie dropping out the side of his mouth. "They're fine. Least they were five seconds ago. I'd get a phone alert if something was wrong." He slapped a pants pocket.

"Then why are you so tired?" Holly asked. "You look worse than you did after that all-nighter when you were downloading anti-ransomware updates."

A smile curled up one side of his mouth. "You'll never guess."

Holly stared. "No way. You have got to be kidding."

I looked from one to the other and back. "What are you talking about?"

"Mia's pregnant," Holly said.

I blinked. "She's . . . what? How can you know?"

"Hah." Holly pointed at Josh. "He has that look. Brian had it. Most new dads get it when they hear they're going to have a kid. Like they did something special."

I looked back at Josh. "Is she right? Mia's going to have a baby?"

Josh's goofy grin got even bigger. "Hate to give Holly credit, but yeah. Mia's at about ten weeks, the doctor said yesterday. We were up half the night, talking and planning and stuff."

Holly's fake-harsh demeanor broke, and she launched herself at Josh, giving him a huge hug. "You are going to be the worst dad ever. I can't wait to tell you what you're doing wrong. This is going to be so much fun!"

Laughing, he hugged her back, did the same to me, and the two of them went straight into pregnancy and baby preparation discussions. I didn't have a whole lot to contribute, so I topped off my coffee mug, murmured a few words that they paid no attention to, and headed upstairs.

Graydon's was the only office on the second floor. He had an outstanding view of downtown Chilson and Janay Lake, and easy access to the boardroom and smaller conference room, but I'd always thought it must be lonely up there.

I knocked on the door frame. Graydon, in his mid-forties, was going gray and losing his hair at the same rate—a race to the finish, he'd joked more than once. He looked up from his computer and smiled.

"It hasn't been quite half an hour," I said, "but . . ."

He waved at the chair across his desk. "Have a seat."

That didn't bode well. Not wanting to get too comfortable, I sat on the chair's front edge. "What's up?"

"Remember the strategic plan from last year?" He shook his head. "Of course you do. You wrote most of it. Anyway, you know how a newly designed website was a key action item. A complete redesign. To push out more information, to invite engagement, and above all, to be easy to use."

I nodded patiently. Each one of those had been a bullet point in the plan. I'd also worked on the request for proposals for a website designer, helped advertise it, helped choose the firm we recommended to the library board, and helped set the timeline. Why he was reciting all this, I had no idea. "I got an email from Collins yesterday morning," I said. "He's sending the final concept in a couple of days. Everyone is super excited about it."

A few weeks ago, Donna, one of our part-time clerks, had laughingly suggested a website reveal party. The idea had caught on, and planning preparations were well underway.

"You're going to have to postpone the party," he said, sighing. "I just got off the phone with the company's owner, Erik. They fired Collins yesterday. Erik didn't say why, and I didn't ask, but since Collins was the lead designer on our project, they have to push everything back."

"Oh." I sat back. "Well, it's disappointing, but not the end of the world. What's another week or two?"

"Glad you think so, because I have to take a leave of absence, starting tomorrow."

I suddenly couldn't move. Couldn't speak. Could barely breathe. "Is it . . . okay to ask why?"

He smiled easily, and air rushed back into my lungs. "Of course you can. And you don't have to look so stricken. My parents are moving to Missouri, is all. They bought a house with an April move-in date, but things shifted." He sighed.

"The sellers moved out last week, so I need to help my parents sort through forty years' worth of stuff, help them pack, then go to Missouri to help them settle in. At the pace they move," he said glumly, "it'll take me weeks."

"And then," I said, "you'll want to sleep for a week to recover."

"Sounds about right. I just talked to the board members." He gestured at his desk phone. "They have complete confidence in your ability to keep the plates spinning while I'm gone."

"Oh. Right." I'd acted as interim director once or twice, back before Graydon had started. I looked around. "Um, I don't have to work up here, do I?"

He laughed. "You can work anywhere you like. Just leave me something to do when I get back."

Graydon scheduled an impromptu afternoon staff meeting. We'd sent a quick text to any employee not scheduled to work that day, offering overtime pay if they attended anyway. I don't know if it was that or the note at the end of the text that Holly had baked brownies that morning, but either way, almost everyone was there. I manned the front desk while Graydon broke the news about the website and his upcoming absence.

Afterward, Holly told me that, though everyone was concerned about Graydon, Josh was clearly more upset about the website.

"I'm sure that's not true," I said.

"No? Ask Graydon. He was looking right at Josh."

I laughed. "Josh was messing with him. He may act like he doesn't have an emotional bone in his body, but you saw him this morning, all dopey happy about being a dad."

"Maybe. But—"

Whatever Holly had been about to say was cut off by the ring of the library's landline. I picked up the receiver. "Good afternoon, Chilson District Library. This is Minnie, how can I help you?"

"By answering your phone."

It was Ash Wolverson. Detective Wolverson.

"Sorry to disappoint. I'm doing a shift at the front desk. No cell phones allowed."

"That's a silly rule."

I kept my eye roll internal. It had been a policy for which I'd advocated. "Anyway," I said. "What's up?"

"What time do you get off work?"

"Today?" I turned to look at the wall clock. "In half an hour. Why?"

It turned out that he wanted me to stop by the sheriff's office, which I found interesting. It had been less than twenty-four hours since . . . since the events of yesterday. There was no way a toxicology report had come back, let alone an autopsy. In the north, all that stuff had to be sent downstate, and results could take days, and sometimes weeks.

But attempting to pry information out of Ash ahead of the meeting would be a waste of my time, so I told him I'd be there soon. Accordingly, in less than an hour, I walked into the sheriff's office, where Chelsea Stille greeted me with a friendly smile and led me back to a small interview room, where I sat in what I tended to think of as my chair.

"Can I get you anything?" Chelsea asked. "Coffee? Water?"

I looked up at Ash's fiancée. With her silky brown hair, smooth skin, and facial features that would have made her a top candidate in any beauty contest around, she was an excellent physical match for Ash's remarkable good looks. He and I had briefly dated a few years ago, but there'd been no spark. It had been like going out with my brother.

"Thanks," I told her, "but I'm good. Although I am wondering why the sheriff's office manager is here with me instead of a detective."

"They're with the sheriff, but they should be in as soon as they can."

I unzipped my coat and tried not to sigh at her use of the word "they." Ash would have said if the sheriff had wanted to talk to me, so the other part of the "they" would have to be—

"Afternoon, Ms. Niswander," Detective Hal Inwood said, as he sat his lanky self across from me. "Detective Wolverson will be in directly."

I gave Chelsea a beseeching look, one that clearly begged her to stay and divert some of the ire that was sure to come my way, but she vanished, leaving me to my fate.

"We should probably wait for Ash," I said, and inwardly cringed at the hopefulness in my tone. I was a grown woman. I did not need a man, or anyone else, to protect me. I was perfectly capable of dealing with Mr. By the Book and Only By the Book With No Room for a Single Shade of Gray all by myself. I'd done it before, and I could do it again.

I looked him straight on. "But why waste my time and yours? Let's get started."

The detective flicked me a glance over the top of the reading glasses he'd just put on, took a small notebook from his shirt pocket, and flipped through pages noisily until he found the right one. "Our report regarding Mr. Arnhold's death," he said in a voice that lacked any vocal inflection, "will state that it was a sad accident. We have found no evidence to suggest that it was foul play or suicide."

Hal droned on, citing the many steps the investigation had already gone through and the many steps that remained, including talking to neighbors, relatives, and friends, but my attention veered away from the one-sided conversation and to Gerald.

Gerald, who replaced his smoke detector batteries at every time change.

Gerald, who never made a new purchase without doing hours upon hours of research.

Gerald, who, in his driving days, always checked the air pressure in his tires before going anywhere.

Gerald, who had a chain ladder rolled up in his bedroom closet for use in case of fire, even though his house was only one story.

Gerald, who always put a bookmark in any book he was reading, even if it was a used paperback.

I put my hands flat on the table. "No way was it an accident," I said, and prepared myself for Hal's reaction.

He did not disappoint.

"Ms. Niswander," he said, sighing heavily. "We have been here before."

"And I've been right every time."

"There is a vast difference between—"

I waved off whatever he was going to say. "Gerald was a cautious and careful person. Taking any kind of risk was absolutely not in his wheelhouse. And honestly, how careless did someone have to be to fall in through a hole that size? I mean, it couldn't have been much bigger in diameter than . . ." I swallowed. ". . . than he was."

Hal looked tired. "It happens. Every year."

"There's no way." I could hear my own stubbornness but couldn't back off. "Something's not right. Something happened out there, and you should be figuring out what it was, not tying up your report with a tidy bow."

I stood, shoving my chair back so hard it banged against the wall. It had been an accident, I hadn't meant to be so physical, but Hal Inwood had a gift for bringing out the worst in me.

"Whoa." Ash was easing into the room. "Minnie, why don't you sit down and we can—"

"If anyone wants to hear a number of very good reasons why I think Gerald's death couldn't have been an accident," I said as calmly as possible, which wasn't very, "I'll be happy to help."

The two men exchanged a glance, and Hal flipped his notebook shut. Ash looked at me, shrugging.

Fine.

With a sharp nod at the air between them, I left the room.

Chapter Three

"I have no idea how Hal and Tabitha have managed to stay married for so long," I said to Rafe over dinner.

My husband, who had heard me ask this particular question more than once, shrugged. "Different strokes for different folks," he said, twirling his fork into the steaming pile of cheesy pasta.

I attempted one last time to imagine the life that Hal and Tabitha led. Hal, tall and thin enough that I was sometimes concerned about his bone density, was dour, private, and never wasted any energy on smiling. Tabitha, with her springing white curls, was irrepressibly cheerful, perpetually upbeat, and had never found a good reason to frown.

They'd moved north a few years ago after they'd retired from downstate jobs, Tabitha from a legislative policy analyst job with a respected nonprofit organization, Hal from a detective role in a large city. Not long after they settled into their new life, Hal saw a posting for a vacant position at the

Tonedagana County Sheriff's Office. Tabitha encouraged him out the door, and he was still working and giving no indication of a final retirement date.

"I love him to the moon and back," Tabitha had once confided in me, "but if that man doesn't have somewhere to go every day, he gets downright morose."

Since I thought Hal was permanently in the sullen and ill-tempered category, I questioned Tabitha's implication that he could get worse, but she'd known him a long time. As Rafe said, different strokes. After all, there were probably people who were puzzled at the successful Rafe and Minnie combination. Sure, we'd been married less than six months, but I'd known marriages that had ended in less time than that. And every long-term marriage was once a new one. We'd get there; it was just a matter of time. Speaking of time, this could be the perfect time to introduce a new topic.

I kept my head down, focusing hard on rearranging my fork contents so I had some noodles, cheese, and an olive balanced across the tines. "What do you think about us writing a personal plan for our marriage?" I asked, then shoved the too-big bite into my mouth.

"A what?"

We were sitting like grownups at the dining table, in a space that was more library than dining room. Rafe had built bookcases on almost all of the wall space, and the shelves were filling nicely with books that I'd brought as my dowry, with Rafe's books, and with a happy collection of books we'd bought together. It was a room that gave me a deep sense of satisfaction every time I gave it a long look.

Rafe's face, which had been wholly blank of expression after I'd asked my simple question, remained so throughout my chewing and swallowing. It was possible that he was on to my stalling technique. It was also possible that he had no idea what I was talking about. And it was also possible that he hadn't been paying attention to what I was saying and needed a repeat. All three possibilities had approximately the same chance of being correct.

"A personal plan," I said again. "For our marriage."

His look didn't get any less blank.

"Remember the library's strategic plan I worked on last year?" He nodded, more or less, so I went on. "We're starting to implement it. I think it's really going to help take us to the next level, and I was thinking maybe we should do the same thing. For us. For our marriage."

The idea had popped into my head somewhere between the sheriff's office and our back door. I had no idea what had triggered the notion, but the more I thought about it, the more I liked it.

"Just think." I put my fork down and stared off into space, near the bookshelves that held Rafe's collection of graphic novels. "We could have multiple versions. A five-year plan. Ten-year. Maybe a twenty-five or thirty to get us to retirement. And then forty and fifty to make sure we're staying active and involved as we get old." The idea was exciting, and I started to make a mental list of things to include.

"Speaking of plans," Rafe said, "if Ash and Hal Inwood aren't going to look into Arnhold's death, I assume you are?"

I blinked away from my list and focused on the present. "Starting tomorrow. Unless you think I shouldn't?"

He gave me a long look. "Trying to keep my wife from righting wrongs sounds like a waste of time. Just . . . be careful, okay?"

* * *

The next morning, even though I wasn't scheduled to be at the library until noon, I showered and dressed at the regular time. Since my usual routine on noon start days was to stay in bed an extra hour, snuggling with our furry friend, Rafe's eyebrows went up when I slid into a seat at the kitchen island.

Rafe filled my mug with coffee and just the right amount of cream—he really was the best of husbands—and slid it across the counter to me. "Thought you didn't start work until noon."

"I don't. This is the start of my Gerald investigation." I frowned, not liking the title, then shrugged. I'd figure out something better later on. "One of Gerald's neighbors is a bookmobile patron. I thought I'd drop by."

"And do what, exactly?" Rafe asked. A tiny line appeared between his eyebrows, which indicated one of two things. Either he didn't understand what was going on, or he had concerns. In this case, though, I figured it might be a combination of the two.

"You don't need to worry about me," I said, reaching across the island to pat the back of his hand. *Pat, pat, pat.* "Betty Hahn is ninety if she's a day, and she's shorter than I am."

"Yeah, but how is she at martial arts?"

He asked the question with one side of his mouth curled up, so I knew he was joking, but it was still in my mind when Betty opened her front door. I hadn't seen her in a few months—she didn't get out as much in the winter—but she looked the same as always. Thin as a broom handle, white hair braided up like Heidi, hands nearly crippled from arthritis, and gray eyes that twinkled merrily. She wore a long sweater that might have been cashmere, black leggings, and fleece slippers that sported pink bunny heads.

"Well," she said in a deep and gravelly voice that didn't fit her looks at all, "if it isn't the bookmobile cat librarian. To what do I owe the pleasure?"

Before I could answer, she ushered me inside. I'd been standing on the porch of the fieldstone farmhouse that had been in her family since they'd hauled the stones out of the fields themselves in the late 1800s. Betty herself had moved to Chicago soon after she'd graduated high school. She'd made her way through college, not an easy task for a woman in the 1950s, landed a finance job with a fancy accounting firm, married, had zero children, worked hard, got promoted to a top spot, eventually retired, got widowed, and moved back north to care for her parents. After they passed away, she decided there wasn't anywhere else she wanted to live, so she stayed.

"Boots off," she commanded. "Coat, too."

I hadn't planned on staying long enough to warrant doing either one of those things, but I wasn't about to argue with Betty, so I did as I was told and was soon sitting at her kitchen table, stocking feet propped on the rung of a pine chair, wrapping my hands around a thick mug filled with the stuff of life.

"Half hazelnut, half decaf," she said. "That way I can drink it until midafternoon. What do you think?"

I thought it was wonderful and said so. I also thought her house was wonderful—plaster walls, wooden maple floors, wide oak trim around the doors and windows, and large area rugs to keep the chill off. The furniture was an interesting mix of ruffled upholstered, which had to have belonged to her parents, and city slick leather and chrome, which she must have brought up from Illinois, but it was all balanced by a proliferation of plants.

I nodded at the massive Boston fern hanging in the kitchen window. "If Eddie ever stops in, he'll think that's a cat toy."

Betty laughed, deep and rich and thick. "Cats think the whole world is a cat toy. And they're probably right. My kitty, she's a tuxedo, is around here somewhere, but you know how cats can be." She looked at me sideways. "I know how you can be, too. You're here about Gerald."

"Sorry, but yes."

"Don't apologize, young lady. Your odd penchant for finding dead people is well matched by your terrier-like tendency to find answers for their loved ones. Nothing there that requires an apology."

Betty had been a bookmobile patron from day one, and she'd been an avid follower of our escapades, especially the ones that didn't have anything to do with books.

I took a sip of my coffee. "How well did you know Gerald?"

"Shouldn't you be asking if I killed him?" she asked.

"Did you?"

"Of course not. How could you ask such a thing?"

I laughed, making tiny waves in my mug. "Silly me."

"The youth of today." She sighed ostentatiously. "As to your first question, Gerald kept himself to himself. I'd wave if I saw him on the road, and vice versa, and he picked up my deliveries if I was out of town, but that was about it. We were neighbors, not friends."

When I asked if she'd seen any cars the day Gerald died, she shook her head.

"Not a one. But then I wouldn't have. I was in the kitchen all yesterday. Baking day, you know."

"Were any of your other neighbors friends with him? Or at least friendly with him?" It was a sparsely populated corner of the county, something that usually meant one of two things. Either everyone in a three-mile radius knew everything about everybody, or they knew nothing.

"Now, that's an interesting question." She pursed her lips, creating thin vertical lines around her mouth. "I've seen Gerald and Bob from down the road at the diner in Dooley together. Breakfast. Coffee. Like that."

My ears perked up. "Bob? Do you know his last name?"

"Starts with a C. Crunch? No, that can't be right." She snapped her fingers. "Cruchley. Bob Cruchley. He and his wife are big golfers. They have a putting green behind their house."

"They live down the road? How far?"

"From late April to mid-October, half a mile." She pointed to her left. "But it's February, dear Minnie, and they're golfers. They're in Florida."

Naturally.

We chatted a while longer. Betty couldn't remember seeing anything unusual on the day Gerald had died, or in the days leading up to it. She also couldn't think of anyone else that Gerald knew or might have confided in.

"Like I said, he kept to himself," she told me again as I rebooted and zipped up my coat. "But if I remember anything, or see anything, I'll let you know."

I thanked her and headed out into a world that was white with snow and gray pretty much everywhere else. After turning around in Betty's driveway, I cruised the roads near Gerald's house, scouting the hilly landscape for signs of habitation. There weren't many homes out here to begin with, except for Betty's, and I didn't see a single place that looked occupied—something that was easy to tell because the driveways hadn't been plowed.

Not that I'd expected to learn much, but to learn essentially nothing was disappointing. Still, maybe Betty would remember something. Her memory was number-oriented, so it was possible that at some point something would jog her brain and she'd come up with a nugget of information that would explain everything.

I decided to hang on to that hope, because why not, and drove back to Chilson singing along to the one radio station I could get—classic rock from groups I often couldn't name, but whose lyrics I knew top to bottom thanks to the musical taste of my parents.

Humming "More Than a Feeling" by Boston, I parked my car in the library's employee lot and went in the side entrance, where Josh was lying in wait for me, his arms crossed, with a computer tablet dangling from one hand.

"Where have you been?" he demanded.

The door hadn't closed all the way. If I did a quick U-turn, I could hurry out and only Josh would know that I'd run away from my duties as the fill-in library director.

Click.

With my easy escape route closed off, there was little choice. I had to be a professional adult. I pasted on a smile. "Hey, Josh," I said, ignoring his implication that I was late, because I was more than an hour early for my scheduled start time. "What's up?"

"Then you haven't seen."

"Seen what?"

He thrust the table at me. "Look at this," he said, outrage making each consonant quiver. "Just look."

Since my eyes couldn't focus on something two inches from my nose, I gently took the object and started walking. "Let's go into my office. This sounds serious, so I want to take off my coat and boots before we dive into it, okay?"

"You have to do something about this," he insisted. "It can't wait."

Whatever this was, it was bad. Josh rarely got riled up, and when he did, it was more along the lines of a glower and a sarcastic insult. This was at least three levels up from that.

I tried to emanate calm and competence as I slid off my coat and toed off my boots, but since it was hard to look professional in stocking feet, I gave it up. Besides, I'd known

Josh for too long. He wasn't paying any attention to me, and he certainly wasn't going to be influenced by anything I did in the next ten seconds.

"Okay." I sat, pushed my feet into the shoes I kept under the desk, and refreshed the tablet's screen. "Let's see what this is and . . . oh . . . my . . ."

"I told you," Josh's voice was tight. "You have to do something." He stood over my shoulder and pointed. "Look at that!"

One glance was all I needed, but I gritted my teeth and kept looking at the library's new website. Rather, what I had to assume was the new site, because it had our logo at the top. Sort of. The forest green and lake blue had turned into blazing fluorescent pink and yellow, and the Arts and Crafts font that matched all the signage in the building was now Comic Sans. The home landing page, instead of a satisfying set of clickable blocks that sent you the places you wanted to go, was a gobbledygook string of random text and numbers with a photo of a dumpster fire smack in the middle.

It was horrifying.

"Tell me this isn't real." I pointed at the revoltingness. "I mean, it's not public, right?"

"Sort of. It hasn't replaced our old website, but it's out there. If anyone searched for the Chilson District Library website, this could come up." Josh started talking about search engine optimization, but I waved him down.

"Go away. I need to make a phone call."

"You're going to fix this, right?"

"Soon as you walk out the door," I said, and this time I must have communicated my calm and confidence properly, because he nodded and left, shutting the door behind him.

I picked up the landline and punched in the cell number that Graydon had emailed me. Erik Kotz, company owner, answered the phone.

"Minnie, I'm so glad you called. We've been trying to contact Graydon, but he isn't responding."

I vaguely mentioned non-emergency but critical family issues. "And you're going to tell me that you know what happened to our new website, and that you're going to fix it in a few hours."

"Oh, man, I wish I could. You've heard of ransomware, yeah?"

As had anyone who hadn't been living in a Wi-Fi-less cave for the last ten years. "I have."

"Our servers got hit," he said, sighing. "We think it's by the guy we fired the other day, but we can't prove it. Half our client sites have been hacked, yours being one of them. We're trying to get control."

My entire body clutched. "Trying?" I repeated.

"We will get control," he said. "We absolutely will. We just don't have the precise timeline yet."

Erik went on to reassure me that his entire team was working hard to restore services, that they were going to get the design back on track, saying all the things people say in crisis situations.

I told him to get me regular updates—daily at least—and hung up, thinking about timelines. If I was going to look into Gerald's death in a serious way, knowing when he died would be essential.

Timelines. Time.

Hmm.

* * *

Rafe had a night meeting, so when I left the library not long after the six PM closing time, I put my hands in my pockets, put my head down against the chill northwest wind that had popped up, and ventured through Chilson's dark residential streets.

The most expensive and exclusive places in town were out on the point, on a set of private roads that weren't gated but might as well have been. Back in the late 1800s, moneyed Chicago people took steamer boats north, complete with trunks, parasols, and servants. Most of those massive summer cottages were still summer cottages, and many were still owned by the original families.

Many other parts of Chilson were still primarily summer places, but with a twist. Corporations from all over the state and nation had snapped up practically every house that had been for sale the last few years and turned them into short-term rental units. It was great for the property owners, and maybe even area business owners, but there were two problems. The transient nature of the tenants was changing the feel of the community, and with so many houses turned into short-term rentals, long-term housing was becoming more and more difficult for the local workforce to find.

I trudged down the sidewalk, happy that Rafe and I had a wonderful place to live, sad that so many teachers, retail help, restaurant staff, law enforcement, and health care workers were having to drive forty-five minutes or more to their Chilson jobs. The city was working on a short-term rental ordinance that would limit their proliferation, but given the acrimonious planning commission meetings, I didn't think it would be approved anytime soon.

Since there was little I could do about any of that, I decided to enjoy my walk as best I could with a winter blast winding its way down my neck. I looked around, admiring the old houses, the leaf-bare maple trees, the dark clouds scudding across the night sky, and feeling a kinship with the occupants of the occasional car that drifted past, fellow travelers on a February evening, two of whom were Sebastian, my friend Leese's assistant, with Lloyd Goodwin, a library patron, in the passenger seat. I returned their waves, a bit puzzled at the pairing, but decided it was none of my business and kept walking.

Fifteen minutes later, I came to the large rambling house where I'd stayed with my aunt Frances for a few cozy winters before I began my life with Rafe. There were a few lights on, and it was easy to imagine the pine-paneled living room with its cushy couches and fieldstone fireplace, the kitchen with its expansive counters and round oak table scarred from decades of use, and the bathrooms with their claw-footed bathtubs.

Though Aunt Frances had, for years, rented out rooms to summer people boardinghouse-style, when she'd remarried she'd sold the house to our cousin Celeste. Not a fan of winter, Celeste was, at this moment, in her little camper in southern New Mexico. She'd also switched from summer vacationers to renting rooms to workers who couldn't find an affordable place to live. Right now, the old house was sheltering a couple of teachers and the district court administrator, and I was sure the place would be full up in summer with hospitality workers.

Across the street, I lifted the brass doorknocker of a white clapboard house, banged it three times, and went inside. "Hello?" I called. "Anyone home?"

"In here. Where else would I be?"

I unbooted, de-coated, slid into a pair of Minnie-sized slippers, and padded to the spacious kitchen. Aunt Frances, as tall and rangy as I was short and not, was standing at the island cooktop, stirring something in a large pot.

"You've started," I said. "How am I ever going to learn to cook properly if you start the lesson before I get here?"

She pished at me. "You'd be a fine cook if you could manage to focus on what you're doing for more than five minutes at one go."

"Hey, I can pay attention."

"Of course you can."

She reached out to pat me on the head, and I swatted her hand away. Only Rafe could do that and get away with it. And I did pay attention, every day. Just not to cooking. "Where's Otto?" I asked, looking around.

"Being a silent partner." She cast her gaze heavens-ward, and I laughed. Her newish husband had Paul Newman-esque good looks that matched her Katharine Hepburn-ness. He was a retired accountant and had started to chafe with boredom after a few months of nothing to do and nowhere to go. I'd dragooned him into doing financial planning classes at the library, and one of his attendees had been

Cody Sisk, a local bike shop owner. Fast forward a bit, and Otto had invested capital in the expansion that Cody had so badly needed.

"So it's just you and me." I put my elbows on the counter. "What's up for tonight's lesson? Beef Wellington? Coq au vin? No, hang on. Can we make those fancy omelets? You know, the ones you made over the holidays that Rafe likes so much."

My loving aunt snorted. "What is it now, the middle of February? And when is this birthday dinner you want to cook for him?"

"Less than two months," I muttered.

"Exactly. Make your goal reasonable, and you stand a much better chance of success."

"That seems kind of like cheating."

"Baby steps, my favorite niece. Baby steps." She held out the spoon with which she'd been stirring. "Here. We're making chicken alfredo, and I need to get something out of the back. This here"—she pointed at the pan—"is on its way to becoming white sauce. All you have to do is keep stirring. Think you can manage?"

"Of course I can." I snatched the spoon from her hand. "I'm not seven."

"Then start stirring. And keep stirring until I get back."

She opened the small door that led to their pantry and went through. The door closed behind her, and the sauce and I were alone together. I looked down at it; it looked up at me.

"Hope we get along," I murmured and started stirring. A few circles later, because stirring sauce wasn't holding my interest, my mind drifted away. To Rafe. To Eddie. To my parents. To my brother and his family. To the bookmobile. To the library. To Graydon. To the epically tragic website. To Gerald. To timing.

Timing.

I needed to know the medical examiner's time estimate for Gerald's death. It would be a range, of course, given all the circumstances, but anything would be helpful, even if to eliminate possibilities.

Timing was everything. With the right timing, anything was possible. I could make my next visit to Gerald's house time with the mail delivery and ask the mail carrier questions. And I could—

"Minnie!" my aunt called. "What are you doing?"

Startled, I looked down. At some point in the last few minutes, I'd stopped stirring. The sauce was bubbling and boiling and smoking something fierce.

And then the smoke alarm went off.

* * *

My friend Pam Fazio, owner of my favorite downtown retail store (if you didn't count Gennell Books & Goods), managed to keep a straight face as she listened to my story. Well, at least until she heard how my aunt had pushed me out her front door, promised to bill me if the pan was ruined and told me not to come back until the house hadn't smelled of smoke for a week.

"Nothing like family to keep you humble," Pam said through her laughter. "Everybody needs that, right?"

I eyed her sourly. "Then how does someone who moved hundreds of miles away from her family manage to stay humble?"

She grinned, her teeth flashing white, and pushed her straight black bobbed hair behind her ears. "I don't. Do you have any problem with that?"

Since she asked the question as she was handing me a mug of lovely-smelling decaf coffee and I didn't want to do anything to interrupt that, I shook my head.

Pam was a transplant from the middle of Ohio. She'd spent most of her career doing corporate graphic design, saved every penny she could, and moved north as soon as she judged her nest egg to be big enough to support herself for a couple of years while her store found its way in the world.

Since Pam's purchasing instincts were sounder than her coffee preferences—which were outstanding—her store's quirky mix of old and new, expensive and not, breakable and not, was a success right off the bat.

"Are you going to keep on with the cooking lessons?" She held out her own mug and we clinked edges. After I'd left my aunt's house, I'd headed home. Pam, who lived in a small bungalow on a side street, was out shoveling her driveway when I passed, and had invited me inside for coffee. As I'd never once refused a cup of coffee, even if it was decaf, I followed her in and sat happily at her kitchen table.

"More lessons?" I squinched my face. "Probably. Unless . . ." I perked up. "Unless you can think of the perfect birthday present for Rafe. You've known him for years, you have the best present ideas of anyone, and—"

And Pam was shaking her head. "I run a gift store, not a beer store."

"But . . ." My objection trailed off into nothing. "Never mind," I said, sighing. "I'll figure something out."

She gave me a thumbs up. "Don't look so glum. You have plenty of time, right?"

That timing thing again.

Huh.

* * *

Pam fed us a breakfast-for-dinner of scrambled eggs, bacon that she'd cooked weeks ago and frozen, toast, and more decaf. I halfway repaid the favor by washing the dishes, praising her coffee, and telling the white sauce story again, this time with sound effects.

Still laughing, she waved me off into the night, and I felt a glow of satisfaction as I headed home.

"Why satisfied?" I asked Eddie as I changed out of what I still called my school clothes and into the fleecy black-and-white plaid sweats my sister-in-law had given me for Christmas. "Because if I can't be a role model, I might as well be a cautionary tale, and if you're going to be a cautionary tale, why not be a funny one?"

Instead of continuing the improv act, Eddie, in the exact middle of the bed, yawned.

"Nice teeth," I said. "And what's with those weird ridges on the roof of your mouth? Why do you have those?"

My fuzzy friend blinked at me.

Either he didn't know, or he knew and wasn't going to share. I sort of remembered looking this up once before, but I couldn't remember the answer.

I sat on the edge of the bed and pulled my phone out of my pants pocket. A few finger taps later, I nodded and turned the screen around so Eddie could read it.

"Turns out that they have a name. Rugae, and no, I don't know how to pronounce that for sure. The all-knowing world wide web says they help you chew and swallow food, but they can't be super effective because I'm always cleaning bits of your food off the floor."

The cat in the room looked supremely uninterested in this mild critique of his behavior.

"Did you see this part?" I pointed at the screen. "Those ridges, those rugae, are tied into your sense of smell."

The low level of interest continued.

"Well, I thought it was interesting." I flopped backward onto the bed. "Sorry I wasn't doing my job of keeping you properly entertained."

Eddie opened one eye, closed it, and sighed.

"You're right. What I should be doing is some clever sleuthing. Let's see what I can find out about Gerald Arnhold on the socials."

I typed and tapped and searched every social media platform I'd ever come across and found a sum total of nothing.

"And by that," I said to an Eddie who was now flopped across my legs, "I mean zero. No references whatsoever. Sure, he was in his eighties, but he was a techy kind of guy. He had a pretty new computer in his home office, with two screens, so he must have been serious about something."

I let my phone drop to the bed. "I don't know," I said to the ceiling. "Maybe I'm wrong. Maybe it *was* an accident. They do happen. They can happen to anyone, even the most careful person. A split second of inattention and—ow!"

Eddie jumped off the bed, using my legs as a launching pad with his back claws extended for maximum effect.

"What was that all about?" I asked, rubbing my shins.

"Mrr!"

"Back at you," I called as he thumped down the stairs.

He was so weird.

I went back to contemplating the ceiling.

Timing. So much about life was about timing. With Graydon gone for two or three weeks, I'd be busy at the library. I didn't really have time to look into a death that was almost certainly just a sad accident.

I'd spend one day on it.

Well, two. At the most. Then I'd be done.

Chapter Four

At lunchtime on the fifth day after I'd decided that I'd look into Gerald's death for a total of two days, I was sitting at my office desk hunting around on the Internet, trying to find any information whatsoever about Gerald Arnhold.

I'd quickly revised my starter guess of one day, two at most, because that would have been a Thursday and a Friday, regular work days at the library, so those could hardly count as a full or even half day of researching. Plus Friday night Rafe and I had gone out to dinner with Ash and Chelsea, so there's no way that could count. And Saturday I was at the library, working the front desk, so that was also out as a day to count. On Sunday, I did spend some time looking for electronic signs of Gerald, but other than a notice on the Scovill Funeral Home's website, I'd found nothing, and I wasn't finding anything now.

As I ate my lunch, I read the short notice for the forty-eleventh time.

Gerald John Arnhold. Born in Petoskey, Michigan, in 1945 to Edward and Marcella Arnhold. Predeceased by his parents and brother Roger (Mary) of St. Louis, Missouri. Survived by a niece and nephew.

Nothing about how much he liked hot buttered popcorn. Nothing about how the edges of his mouth curled up when he was about to make one of his horrible puns. Nothing about his gift for doing math problems in his head. Nothing about the way he never said anything negative about anyone or anything, not even the weather. Nothing about how, when Julia and Eddie and I were getting ready to leave, he would always always always tell us to stay safe and sound.

It said nothing at all.

I pushed back from my desk, irritated with the notice and irritated with myself. What had I really expected to learn from the Internet? Gerald had been a very private person—I'd never even known he had a brother, let alone a niece and nephew—so why had I thought I'd learn anything of significance online? The whole thing had been a waste of time.

"So this is where you hide out?"

I looked up. "Hey, Jim. What can I do for you?"

Jim Kittle, a sixtyish library patron, was standing in the doorway, scanning my office with an expression that exuded criticism.

I tried not to take it personally. Jim was one of those unfortunate people who found fault in everything, including every single one of the guy-on-his-own-saves-the-world thrillers that were his sole reading choice, no matter how many times I suggested something else. However, when his gaze landed on the lighthouse drawing my youngest niece had sent me for Christmas that I'd pinned to my bulletin board and his expression shifted to a sneer, my chin went up.

"What can I do for you?" I asked again, this time with a bit of starch.

Jim either didn't notice or didn't care. He jerked a thumb in the direction of the front desk. "The girls up there told me that Cain's gone for two or three weeks."

Girls? Really?

I shifted my focus away from his salt-and-pepper hair, his aquiline nose, and his shiny black zip fleece to the wall to his left and tried to come up with a name for the paint color. Ivory? Ecru? Cream? Buff?

When I decided that beige would cover it, and having successfully used the calming technique I'd learned at my last librarian conference in one second flat, I looked back at Jim.

"That's right," I said, sitting back, raising one knee slightly and looping my hands around it, and deciding not to ask for a third time what I could do for him.

"So you're the one I need to talk to."

"If it's an urgent matter, yes. If not," I said, trying not to sound hopeful, "I'll ask Graydon to reach out as soon as he gets back."

If I were a betting person, which I wasn't except for the five-dollar bets that Rafe and I routinely exchanged—and I didn't count those because we used the same well-worn bill every time—I would have laid money that, whatever Jim wanted, it could easily wait. And I would double down and bet that he wouldn't want to wait because that was the kind of guy he was.

Jim wasn't a problem patron, exactly, but he did require a lot of attention. He owned his own company, a metal fabrication business, which was successful enough that Jim hired someone to run it for him, so all he had to do was show up every so often to check on things.

I'd heard from an employee or two that things ran better when he was gone, and if his behavior in the library was any indication of his behavior at his own facility, I believed them, wholly and completely.

"If something needs to be fixed," he said, sitting in my spare chair without an invitation, "it shouldn't wait."

I nodded and stuck an interested expression on my face. "You're absolutely right."

For the next twenty minutes, I was treated to a step-by-step account of things the library needed to do to get to the next level. I kept up the nodding and the interested expression until I was afraid it was going to freeze on my face for good. I took notes. I said I'd pass his ideas along to Graydon. I did not tell him that his ideas were financially impossible (e.g., gifting an e-reader to every second grader), illegal (e.g., publishing the titles of the books checked out by elected officials), or already underway (expanding the library's outreach efforts at summer events).

He was launching into a description of a library motorcycle he'd seen in Brazil when Kelsey Lyons, one of our part-time library clerks, knocked on the door frame.

"Um, Minnie?" The thirty-something mother of two glanced at the man who had earlier referred to her as a girl.

"Sorry to bother you, but we have a . . . kind of an emergency. Josh said it's a . . . a server thing."

I stood immediately. Kelsey, normally the picture of health, a circumstance I was happy to attribute to the immensely strong pots of coffee she brewed every chance she got, was looking pale. She was also clearly uncomfortable, her gaze darting this way and that, her weight shifting from one foot to the other. Something was up.

"Sorry, Jim," I said. "Duty calls. Tell you what. Why don't you send me an email with all your ideas, and I'll go over them with Graydon when he gets back."

Jim blustered a bit, but I handed him my business card, got us both out of my office, and shut the door behind me.

Kelsey and I parted ways with Jim at the main desk and made our way down the hall to where Josh and his servers lived, with Kelsey very quiet all the way there.

At the door, I punched in the access code, the door unlocked, and we went inside.

"Okay," I said. "What's the problem?"

Kelsey stood in front of me, hanging her head. "I am so sorry, Minnie. If you have to fire me, I get it. But it was an accident. I was looking at it on my phone and the kids were fighting, and . . . and I'm so sorry."

I looked from Kelsey to Josh, who was whacking at his keyboard with a ferocious intensity. "Will someone tell me what's going on?"

"Can't fix it," Josh muttered. "It's out there, and there's nothing we can do."

It was then that I noticed what was on one of his many computer screens—the ugliest website in the history of websites, our hijacked library website.

I didn't understand the problem. "And?" I asked. "We knew it was out there. We knew it was going to take Erik and his team some time to regain control. All we have to do is keep quiet and—"

"But that's just it." Kelsey was crossing her arms, holding herself tight. "Josh sent me the link this morning."

My stomach clenched in on itself and I suddenly regretted my lunch choice of New England clam chowder. Though the creamy goodness had hit the spot, its richness was now threatening the equilibrium of my insides. "Kelsey . . ."

"I'm so sorry," she said, "but I accidentally posted it on my Facebook page. I took it down as soon as I realized what happened, but it was up for a couple of hours. A bunch of my friends reposted. I asked them to delete it, and they did, only . . ." She sighed. "Other people picked it up. It's everywhere."

I turned to look at Josh's screen. The design looked, if possible, even worse than it had the first time I'd seen it.

This was bad.

Very bad.

My mouth opened. Closed. Reopened. Closed a second time. *Think, Minnie, think.*

"Okay," I said after an eternal five seconds. "This is what we're going to do. I'm going to contact Erik and see if there's any progress. Then I'll write a short post for you"—I pointed at Kelsey—"to put on your Facebook page. You then post it on the pages of all your friends who reposted the site. I'll write up something and put it on the library's home page. Send out a press release to the media and all our partners. And somewhere in there . . ." I took a deep breath and let it out. "I have to call everyone on the library board."

* * *

I started by calling Trent Ross, the library board chair. After I'd ripped that bandage off, I moved on to the vice chair and all the others, saving the newest board member for last.

In her mid-fifties, Carolyn Mathews had been administrator of the region's largest hospital for almost three years. Before that, she'd been a successful and popular doctor in Chilson. Her husband, latest in a long line of local attorney ancestors, was the new circuit court judge. Carolyn had more savoir faire in the tip of her pinky fingernail than I did in my entire body, but she was surprisingly happy to meet up with me every so often, mentor-like, and this time was no exception.

"Lunch," she said with no hesitation. "My treat. The roads are dry. Shall we meet at the Red House Café?"

I hadn't been there in ages, so after a quick online check to make sure they were open on a mid-February Monday, I was happy to agree.

We arrived in the parking lot at the same time, and she greeted me with a smile and a quick hug.

"Dear Minnie," she said, releasing me. "It's been too long since we've talked, and don't say we talk at the library board meetings, because that is not the same thing."

"Not even close." I held the door for her, and we went into what had originally been a one-room schoolhouse but had been added on to by various owners in the sixty years since.

Sunny, the current owner, had repainted the exterior a solid red with white trim and converted the schoolroom into restaurant seating. Wooden school chairs served as dining chairs, lunch buckets of all shapes and sizes were perched on a shallow shelf that circled the room, and a school bell hung from the ceiling above the front counter.

The room was mostly empty, and we sat ourselves near the front window. A smiling waitress handed us menus, told us that Sunny was currently in Florida for two weeks but that the assistant chef was doing just fine, and took our orders.

With that done, Carolyn put her elbows on the table and leaned forward over her laced fingers. "Let me take a good look at you."

I shifted uncomfortably. Being stared at always gave me the willies. I took a sip of my water and tried not to fidget.

After an eternity, she sat back. "Yes," she said, nodding. "Marriage agrees with you."

I laughed. "That was why you wanted to meet up for lunch? You could have just asked."

"Ah, but if you were unhappy, would you have been truthful?" She arched her eyebrows. "And I needed a reason to get out. This time of year I get office-bound."

"You could retire and become a part-time bookmobile clerk."

"I'll keep it in mind," she said, smiling. "Now. Tell me what our esteemed board president said about this website debacle."

It didn't take long. Trent, a retired downstate attorney, had recommend that, in addition to what I'd already planned and set in motion, I contact the library's attorney, just to let her know.

Carolyn nodded. "Excellent advice. It will blow over in a few days."

I wasn't so sure but hoped she was right.

"Now what's this I hear about poor Gerald Arnhold?"

I blinked. "Oh, I'm sorry. I didn't realize you knew him."

"Not particularly. He was more a contemporary of my parents." She tapped her fingers on the wooden table. "Younger than they were, but close. We lived across the street from his house in Chilson."

My ears perked. "He lived in town? I didn't know that. I thought he always lived out on that little lake."

She shook her head. "I grew up on Fourth Street. Whoever owns it now has done an amazing job of landscaping. Beautiful peonies, roses, hydrangeas."

"That house?" I walked by it regularly all summer long, stoking my first ever case of garden envy. "I had no idea you grew up there."

"Mr. Arnhold's house was directly across the street. He always had such lovely grass. Then one year when I was, oh maybe twenty, I came home from college and he'd up and moved. My parents didn't say a word about why, and at that age I was too preoccupied with myself to wonder."

Huh, I thought. *How very huh.*

* * *

That night, after a Rafe-cooked and relatively healthy dinner of grilled chicken fajitas with a side of more grilled chicken fajitas, we started a fire in the fireplace, put our feet up on the coffee table, pulled a cozy blanket over us, added an Eddie, and turned on the television.

Rafe thumbed the remote to a hockey game and looked at me. "You okay to watch the Wings?"

All teams and all sports interested me equally—as in not at all—but since it was good for me to expand my world, and to learn a little bit about the things my beloved cared about, I said, "Sure." But fifteen minutes into the Detroit Red Wings playing the Chicago Blackhawks, I surreptitiously reached out from under the blankie and oh-so-slowly pulled my tablet and my phone from the end table and onto my lap.

I needn't have worried. Rafe was glued to the screen and had, I was fairly certain, forgotten I existed.

It had been a few days since I'd heard from my best friend, so before I turned on the tablet, I texted Kristen.

Me: *Hey there. Are they quiet?*

I'd called her on Friday to tell her about Gerald, but she'd been distracted by the cries of one or both of her twins. Eloise and Lloyd (nicknamed Cooper because Kristen had been as big as a car when pregnant) were now going on eight months old, and Kristen often wasn't able to focus on what I was telling her. While I waited for her to respond, I sort of watched the hockey game, but mostly thought about Kristen, now technically a Gronkowski, but still a Jurek to me and to everyone who ate at her Chilson destination restaurant, the Three Seasons.

Kristen's husband carried the ironic nickname of Scruffy, which had been bestowed upon him as a child because no matter the environmental conditions, he always managed to look as if he'd stepped out of a stock photograph captioned "cleanest child alive." Kristen and Scruffy had met when the Scruff had been scouting locations for his father's nationally syndicated television cooking show, *Trock's Troubles*. The show featured Trock Farrand (not his real name), a kitchen disaster, and a solution, at different restaurants all over the country, and even the world. The Three Seasons was so named because it offered locally sourced food three seasons a year, then closed in mid-October when Kristen, not a lover of cold and snow, high-tailed it for Key West where she tended bar for a friend and spent a lot of time napping in a hammock, resting up for spring.

All that had changed, of course, when she'd married Scruffy Gronkowski, and even more since the twins were born last summer. I'd been concerned that the family was going to be spending more and more time in New York, where Trock's show was based, but she'd told me not long ago that she and the Scruff had decided that Chilson was where they were going to raise Eloise and Cooper.

I'd been giddy with relief, but since then they'd been bopping all over the country scouting locations of future episodes *Trock's Troubles*, and I was starting to think that her definition of the word *raising* was different than mine.

Kristen: *For now. Bet it's cold and gray and snowy there. Heh heh heh.*

Me: *Not that cold. It's almost 25 degrees. And we had a full day of blue sky just last week.*

Kristen: *Not selling it, Min.*

Me: *Speaking of selling, I'm trying to sell Rafe on writing a personal strategic plan. What does yours look like?*

Kristen: *A lot like my business plan. Wait, it is my business plan. No one writes a personal strategic plan.*

Me: *Lots of people do. I checked.*

Kristen: *On the Internet?*

Of course on the Internet. What else was I going to do, buttonhole people on the street and ask them personal questions?

Me: *Among other places.*

Kristen: *Well I'm no help and I gotta go. Kids are waking up from their nap.*

Me (frowning at the phone): *Nap? It's 8 pm.*

Kristen: *Time zones. Ever hear of them?*

Me (still frowning): *Where are you?*

Kristen: *Sunny, warm Hawaii. See ya.*

And she was gone.

I pictured my blond friend frolicking with her husband and babies in the gentle wash of the ocean, sighed, tossed my phone aside, and focused on the hockey game.

One goal and two power plays later, I unsuccessfully stifled a yawn and powered up my newest piece of electronics, a tablet that my dad had given me for Christmas. Though I hadn't been quite sure why I needed one, since it was from Dad I'd given it the old college try, and now I was using it regularly during the current kind of circumstance.

After staring at the blank screen for a moment, I made my way to the Tonedagana County website. The property records page, specifically.

Under property owner, I typed in Gerald Arnhold's name, and lo and behold, two properties came up. The one out on the little lake, and the one in Chilson that Carolyn had described. I scrolled down into the historical data that was available right there for free—property description, property tax amount, date of purchase, document number—and thought some more.

Gerald had bought the house in Chilson in 1983. He'd bought the little lake house in 1990.

"Huh," I said.

"I know, right?" Rafe bumped my shoulder. "Great save."

"Mmm."

1990. Had something happened in 1990 that had driven Gerald to become a recluse? 1990 wasn't even a real memory for me, so I typed "1990 world events" into the search engine.

Reunification of Germany. Launch of the Hubble Space Telescope. Margaret Thatcher resigned from her role as UK's prime minister. The first web server was created. *Home Alone*, *Ghost*, *The Hunt for Red October*, and *Pretty Woman* were in movie theaters. And a bunch of songs I didn't know were in the top ten.

"Don't see how any of that could have anything to do with Gerald," I muttered.

"Mrr!"

I glanced at my cat, who was now sitting up and staring straight at me.

"Blink," I told him. "Otherwise your eyeballs will dry up and fall out of your head."

"MRR!"

After that earsplitting comment, Eddie jumped down, disdain oozing from every cell in his furry self, and stalked off.

"Love you, too!" I called after him and received no reply.

Cats.

Chapter Five

At breakfast the next morning, I asked Rafe what Chilson had been like in 1990.

"You'd be better off asking someone who might remember," he said. "Like my parents. Or Frances. Anyway, what does it matter? How could something from that long ago have anything to do with Gerald's death?"

"No idea." I scooped up another bite of oatmeal, making sure I would end up with a final spoonful that had blueberries in it, because a blueberry-less last bite would be a poor start to a bookmobile day. "But you never know, right?"

"Fair point. What did The Blond have to say for herself last night?"

It had been the year I'd turned twelve, the first summer I'd been sent to stay with Aunt Frances, that I'd met first Kristen, and then Rafe, on Janay Lake's city beach. We'd been a trio for years, drifted apart during college, then reunited when I'd moved to Chilson permanently. Kristen had never loved the nickname Rafe had bestowed upon her, but when he'd suggested much worse ones, she'd given up.

I'd gone up to bed before the hockey game was over and had managed to fall asleep over an old copy of William Goldman's *Marathon Man*, so I hadn't told him about our text exchange.

"She's in Hawaii," I said.

"And?"

"And she's napping in hammocks, taking long walks on the beach, and enjoying the sunsets."

Rafe gave a snorty sort of noise. "More like she's bent on eating at all the restaurants on whatever island they're staying at and making notes about everything she, Scruff, and the kids eat."

That sounded accurate, except for one thing. "And the dishes eaten by everyone at neighboring tables." Going out to eat with Kristen was always interesting, usually entertaining, and sometime embarrassing, but it was never boring.

I then felt the need to confess what she'd told me and what I was still surprised at learning. "She has a business plan that she revises every year, but there's no Kristen Jurek Gronkowski personal strategic plan."

"Yeah?" Rafe glanced at the clock, which made me look, too.

"Not sure how it got so late," I said. "I'll take care of the dishes."

He got up, slid his feet into the boots waiting by the back door, grabbed his coat from its hook, and bestowed a kiss on my head. "Thanks, my little snickerdoodle. See you tonight."

As the door shut behind him, I looked at Eddie. "Snickerdoodle?" I repeated. "That cannot possibly stick."

For months, my favorite husband had been trying out different nicknames for me. I had no idea why he'd decided it was a task that needed doing, but he seemed intent on finding just the right one. Though the fact that most of the ones he'd tried had to do with food bothered me on occasion, I took comfort in the knowledge that at least he wasn't using beer names. Or the names of sports teams.

Eddie jumped on top of his carrier and glared at me. "Mrr!"

"Half an hour, bud." I slid off the stool and started the exhausting work of washing two bowls, two spoons, and two coffee mugs. "Lots of time." How he knew it was a bookmobile day, I wasn't sure, but he got it right almost every time.

Thirty minutes later, I was driving down the quiet morning streets of downtown Chilson with a cat-laden carrier buckled into the passenger seat.

"It's going to be a busy day," I told Eddie. "We're stopping at two schools, one adult foster care, one church, and two township halls."

"Mrr."

"Right." I nodded. "And that convenience store. The one where the cashier always comes out to give you treats. Silly me for forgetting."

"Mrr!"

"I wouldn't really have forgotten to stop, you know. It's more of a rest stop for us than a real bookmobile visit, that's why I didn't—"

"MRR!"

I winced at the sound level. "What's the matter? Wake up on the wrong side of the bed? Not sure what side that would be, though. Rafe is bigger than me, so there's less room for you, but his side is closer to the bedroom door, which has its advantages." I tipped my head to the left. "My side is . . . huh. You know what . . ."

It was well before anything downtown opened, but the lights of Chilson's toy store were beaming brightly. The street was empty of parked cars and traffic, so it was easy to park right outside the store.

"Be back before you know it," I said, but my cat had already curled up into an Eddie-shaped ball.

The store's cheery bells dinged as I walked inside and saw a jeaned and sweatered man about my age in a deep kissing hug with a trim blond woman who was wearing heeled boots, what might have been a cashmere overcoat, and a bright red beret.

Though I would have thought the bells would have alerted them, I was ignored until I said loudly, "Don't you two have somewhere better to do that?"

Bianca (Sims) Koyne pulled away from her husband and laughed. "Morning, Minnie. And yes, but it's fun to do it here."

Mitchell, turning to face me, slung an arm around his wife's shoulders and squeezed. "Plus she's leaving me for a week for some conference in Florida. Wanted to get in one last round of making out before she heads for the airport."

Most of Chilson continued to be amazed about the changes in Mitchell. Not so long ago, he'd been living in his sister's attic and cobbling together a living through summer landscaping work and winter snowplowing and ski resort work. Not only had he married the region's most successful real estate agent, but by all appearances he was making a success of the marriage.

I'd known for years that Mitchell's brain had a tremendous capacity—he'd spent a lot of time in the library reading room after a former library director banned him from borrowing books due to exorbitant overdue fees. It wasn't until Bianca that he'd bothered to apply himself. How he'd landed the job at the toy store, I wasn't quite sure, but he seemed to be making a success of that, too.

I looked at the toy store's busy ceiling, wondering if there was anything new. Mitchell's ceiling accessories had started with model airplanes and had expanded into papier-mâché birds, balloons, dinosaurs, and clouds. And now even more celestial objects. "Mars?" I asked, pointing.

He nodded. "Working on Venus. Should be done before Bee gets back."

An industrious Mitchell. Wonders never ceased. And another wonder was that something else Mitchell had become was a person who often had excellent gift ideas, which was why I was there. "Sounds cool. And I'll be out of your hair in a second. Just wanted to ask if you have any ideas for a birthday present for Rafe."

He rubbed his face. "Huh. Not off the top of my head, but I'll think about it. Give me a couple of days."

After thanking him and wishing Bianca safe travels, I headed for the door but stopped and turned back.

"Quick question for the real estate agent in the room," I said. "Did you know Gerald Arnhold?"

"I knew of him," she said, readjusting her beret, balancing it just so on her smooth hair. "Sad the way he died, out there all alone."

Shutting away the images, I asked, "Did you know he owned a house here in town? Over on Fourth Street?"

"Sure. Don Fedrow has been renting it out for him for . . . well, I suppose I don't know how long. Longer than I've been in the business, anyway."

Which meant at least twenty years. "Okay," I said. "Thanks."

"Why do you ask?" Bianca's face was quietly alert. "You and Rafe thinking about buying an investment property? I can ask Don, see if he's heard from the heirs about selling."

"No, no, nothing like that," I said, mentally kicking myself for asking a real estate agent a question that I could have found the answer to by other means. "I was just . . . um . . . curious."

And before Bianca, whose face stated clearly that she didn't believe me, could say anything else, I said a hurried good-bye and fled.

* * *

When I told the story to Rila, our other part-time bookmobile clerk, her reaction surprised me—she laughed so hard I was afraid she was going to go into spasms.

"Minnie," she said after wiping her eyes and patting her stomach to apparently make sure it was still in place, "you are a bundle of contradictions. You drive this behemoth of a vehicle without thinking twice, you right wrongs, you give speeches in front of hundreds at library conferences, you go down to Lansing to speak to the legislative committee for crying out loud, yet you're afraid of a real estate agent's sales pitch."

"Not afraid." I heard an echo of teenaged sulk in my words and felt the need to expand. "More like . . . uncomfortable."

"Just say no," Rila said before going off on another laughter jag.

I slid her an outwardly sour look, but on the inside I was beyond pleased to see her like that. She'd had a hard time of it the last few years, and especially the last few months. Rila, still shy of thirty years old, had been a soccer phenom through middle and high school. She'd been recruited by top colleges, twice led her team to a national championship, married, and had signed on to play professionally with a top European team. She was all set for a shining and lucrative career, but a bad knee injury had ended that life almost before it started.

Her now ex-husband had taken the change in their fortunes badly. Worse than badly, really, and he was currently in the county jail waiting for a trial date.

To see Rila laughing made my heart sing. She would be okay. Financially she was stretched, but her house was paid off thanks to the smart move she'd made with the locked-in signing bonus she'd been paid when turning pro. Though losing her ex-husband's income meant she'd had to find more work than the high school coaching she had been doing, bookmobile work was filling the gap and would tide her over while she finished up the classes she needed to get a teaching degree.

"Here we are," I said unnecessarily as I took a right-hand turn into Svenson Township Hall's parking lot. Svenson was one of the smaller townships in the county. The hall was open to the public all of two mornings a week, and that was only if Maureen Gertz, the township clerk, liked the look of the roads when she looked out her kitchen window that morning.

Today, all must have been fine on Maureen's road, because her car was in the gravel lot, right next to the front door. The hall itself was a small flat-roofed concrete block building that was cold in the winter and hot in the summer. But it served their needs, and who needed something fancy when, outside of elections, you're open barely eight hours a week?

We stopped and quickly ran through the opening-up checklist. Rila, her brown hair swinging around in a long curly ponytail, leaned down to open Eddie's carrier door. "You coming out?" she asked, peering inside.

I glanced over from my work of booting up the front computer. "He was super vocal on the way into the library. All that whining must have tired him out, and . . . oh, rats. I forgot."

"What's the matter?" Rila asked.

"Forgot to refill his water bottle." It was sitting in the small closet three feet away from me, and I'd completely blanked on taking it home last time. I was the worst cat mom in the whole wide world.

"Happy to share mine," Rila said. "He can't drink that much, right?"

"You'd like to think so, but sometimes . . ." I got up. "I'll get some from inside. If I'm not out in ten minutes, honk the horn, okay?"

Rila smiled and said she and Eddie would be fine, but I hadn't been worried about them; it was me I was concerned about. Maureen was many things. She was a wife, a mother, a grandmother with a lap that could accommodate multiple grandchildren at one time, a retired nurse, a highly talented quilter, and an experienced and knowledgeable township clerk. She was also a powerful personality and had what my aunt Frances called "a tremendous gift of gab."

"Minnie Hamilton Niswander," she boomed out as I crossed the threshold. "Just the person I wanted to talk to."

Oh, boy.

"And you're just the person I need." I held up the water bottle. "This is Eddie's. Can I fill it up?"

"Sure, sure." Maureen, sitting at a battered metal desk, gestured toward a small door. "Let me know if you can't fit the bottle under the tap."

It was a tight fit between the tall bottle and the old low faucet, but it worked. "Thanks," I said as I left the small restroom, threading the bottle top back on. "And Eddie thanks you."

"Anything for that little guy." Maureen nodded, which loosened a strand of her salt-and-pepper hair. She pushed it back behind her ear impatiently. "I'd come out and see him, but it's cold, so I don't want to."

"He'll understand." Or not. It could be hard to tell. "You said you wanted to talk to me?"

She leaned forward, her chair creaking. "Gerald Arnhold. I heard you found him. And I heard the sheriff's office is saying it was an accident."

I hadn't realized the news was out and about, but I also wasn't surprised. "That's what I heard, too."

Maureen pointed at me so hard I almost flinched. "What do *you* think?"

"Me?" I blinked.

"Don't pretend to be less than you are, Minerva Joy, and don't look surprised that I'm familiar with your full birth name. You knew Gerald. Do you think he could have fallen through the ice by accident?"

The room was so quiet that I could hear the ticking of the wall clock, large and round with a black rim and probably original to the building. At long last, I looked up from my contemplation of Eddie's water bottle. "No. I don't. But I also can't find any other explanation."

"You can't? Well, isn't *that* interesting." Maureen sat back, her scary pointer finger now tapping her desktop. Sort of. Her desk was piled high with paper piles of various heights, so she was actually tapping paper, making a soft crinkly noise with every beat.

I edged closer. "How? The only thing I've found remotely interesting is that he bought his little lake house in 1990 and has been renting his Chilson house ever since."

"Exactly," she said, folding her arms.

I clearly wasn't grasping something important, and my expression must have shown my confusion, because Maureen heaved a sigh. "All these years later, and still no one wants to talk about what happened."

"In Chilson?" I asked. "In 1990?"

She gave a hacking laugh. "The things kids don't know could fill a book the size of the *Oxford English Dictionary*. Yes, Chilson and yes, 1990. Go on, tell me you've never heard of the GAC."

Obediently, I said, "I've never heard of the GAC." And I had no idea what the initials could mean. General Air Conditioning? Gentle Aardvark Committee? Green Apple Cupcakes?

"It was the Great Airport Controversy," Maureen said.

If she'd given me a million years, I might have come up with that, but probably not even then. "Tell me."

"Back then," she said, stringing her words together in true storyteller fashion, "Chilson was a different place. Smaller. Quieter. Calmer. Which meant it was a struggle for many business owners. Some folks came up with the idea of expanding the airport, almost doubling the runway, pushing it to a full ten thousand feet to catch the commercial airline traffic."

I pictured the existing airport. On the outskirts of town, it was still small, quiet, and calm, so the expansion must not have happened. To double the runway, a lot of houses would have had to be demolished. Some businesses, too. And roads would have had to be reworked. "That idea," I said slowly, "must have upset a lot of people."

"Hoo boy, did it." Maureen was tapping the paper again. "Split the town, neighbor against neighbor, family against family. If you tried to stay on the fence, both sides took against you."

"Sounds awful," I said. "Why haven't I ever heard about this?"

Maureen shrugged. "It was a long time ago, and the expansion never happened. No money, for one thing. But I bet the main reason people don't talk about it is they don't want to bring it up again. What would be the point? Lots of people behaved very badly, and who wants to remember that?"

Made sense. One thing, however, wasn't making sense. "What does any of this have to do with Gerald?"

"Dear Minnie." Maureen smiled. "Gerald was the airport manager. In the middle of it all, he quit, bought that house, started doing accounting out of his home office, and hardly talked to anyone ever again."

My mouth opened and shut a few times before I could say, "I had no idea. But . . . still. Like you said, that airport thing was decades ago."

"The GAC."

Whatever. "How could anything from that long ago have anything to do with Gerald's death?"

"Don't know," Maureen said. "But it's a place to start looking, don't you think?"

Chapter Six

I thought about Gerald and the airport thing and the years between then and now for the rest of the day and was still thinking about it as I was carrying Eddie into my aunt's house for my next cooking lesson. I'd arranged with her a couple of days earlier to cook something I could bring home for dinner, so I'd told Rafe that I'd be home a little late, but with food.

"I'm here," I sang out as I de-booted and de-coated myself. "Anyone home?"

"Get back here," my aunt called. "You have things to learn and not much time to do it in."

"Hear that, Eddie? I'm going to learn things." I opened his door, but he didn't move from his meatloaf position in the back corner. I left him to his pose and went to the kitchen, where Aunt Frances was at the island chopping vegetables with a frighteningly large knife that I eyed warily. "You don't expect me to use that, do you?"

"Don't be silly. That one is yours." She tipped her head at a Minnie-sized blade. "Now get busy. We're making a stir fry, and that's a lot of chopping at the beginning but not much cooking at the end."

And if I remembered correctly, it was also a lot of dishwashing at the very end, but I wasn't going to worry about that now.

Hesitantly, I took up the knife and started slicing the green onions my beloved relative slid in front of me.

"On the diagonal," she said. "About an inch long, no, a real inch, not your made-up version. That's better. Not perfect, but it'll do. Here." She swept my cut-up bits to the side. "Next are carrots, I've peeled them for you. These really need to be all the same size."

I wasn't sure I was up to that. "What happens if they aren't?"

"The world ends," she said dolefully. "Oh, for crying out loud. Nothing happens except unevenly cooked carrots. Remind me again how you got to be this old and know so little about cooking? Especially when your best friend is a well-known chef?"

"You seriously think Kristen would let me touch a thing in her kitchen?" I rolled a carrot toward me and started slicing. "We stopped at the Svenson Township Hall today."

"And how is Maureen? Still working on township consolidations? That's not going to make her any friends."

"She didn't say. But she did tell me about what was happening in Chilson in 1990." I looked over and saw no reaction from my aunt. "About the airport."

"The GAC," she said matter-of-factly. "If you cut those carrots smaller, they'll cook faster."

"Maureen said Gerald Arnhold was airport manager at the time."

My aunt's knife slowed, then sped back up. "Yes. Now, if you're done with those carrots, we'll work on mushrooms, broccoli, cauliflower, and the chicken."

"Mushrooms?" I squinched my face.

"Just a few. Adds an earthy tone."

Why food needed to taste like dirt I wasn't sure, but I wasn't about to argue with someone holding a massive knife.

After a thousand years, the slicing and dicing was done and the rice water was boiling. Aunt Frances put a shockingly large pan on the cooktop, added the avocado oil, butter, and herb mixture she'd had me prepare, and turned on the heat.

"Chicken first. Then carrots, then everything but the mushrooms. A minute before everything is done, add those."

I stared at her, disbelieving. "How am I supposed to know when it's a minute before everything is done?"

"Doesn't have to be an exact minute." My loving aunt rolled her eyes. "This isn't baking. It's cooking."

In theory, I knew there was a difference. In practice, not so much.

"But—"

"Quit being such a worrywart. I'll be right here."

And she was, right up until her phone rang. She looked at the counter where it lay, face up. "Otto," she said, reaching. "He's on his way back from a meeting in Traverse."

I nodded in understanding. Winter driving always included an element of anxiety, because you never knew where it might be snowy or icy.

"You okay?" she asked the phone.

Though I couldn't hear what Otto said, I saw her shoulders relax. "Stir fry," she responded. "Chicken. Hope you didn't have that for lunch."

She moved over to the breakfast nook and slid into the booth, chatting amicably like the happily married woman she was.

Idly, I wondered if the conversations Rafe and I had sounded like that to eavesdroppers. Then again, since we were millennials, we didn't talk on the phone much, because texting had been possible for years. Then I thought about texting, and its ephemeral nature. My mom still had the cards and letters my dad had sent her before they married. The only thing Rafe had sent me was . . . actually I couldn't remember him ever sending me anything, and vice versa. Did it matter? Or would we regret it someday? Maybe we should—

"Minnie!"

My aunt's shriek woke me out of my reverie. I looked down. Just as I registered the hot smoke that was billowing out of the pan, the smoke alarm went off.

Again.

After the kitchen was clear of smoke and the pan was scoured of black, I apologized for the disaster.

"My fault," Aunt Frances said. "I left you unsupervised. But I think it's time to think about oven-cooked foods." She pursed her lips, thinking. "Or maybe recipes that don't require heat at all."

I tried not to be dejected. "Looks like I'm picking up Fat Boys sub sandwiches for dinner," I said.

Aunt Frances patted my shoulder. "Probably what he was expecting, anyway."

I took some comfort in that, because it was almost certainly true. But what kind of wife was I if I couldn't cook anything more complicated than cold cereal?

* * *

Rafe had seemed happy enough with the meat-heavy sub I brought home for his dinner, and since my lessons with Aunt Frances were a secret, I couldn't tell him about my repeated failures, but my cooking deficits were starting to eat at me, chewing away at the edges of my self-esteem.

I woke up the next morning with remnants of wispy dreams wandering around in my head. I'd been serving charred food to the library board members on a frozen lake. Mitchell's ceiling airplanes had come to life and flown around the toy store. Rafe and Eddie laughing at me for misspelling Niswander. My brother shaking his head when the flashlight wouldn't work after I'd put new batteries in it, and it was because I'd put them in the wrong way.

"Six," I muttered, flinging back the covers and dropping my feet to the floor. "I was six years old. Who knows about positive and negative when they're six? I was just trying to help."

Rafe, who had a breakfast meeting scheduled with the school superintendent, was already gone, so it was me and Eddie making coffee and oatmeal, just like the old times on my adorable little houseboat.

"See?" I spread my hands, palms up, at the mug and bowl. "I can cook. I'm not completely useless in the kitchen."

My cat, who was lying on a windowsill that was a titch too narrow for him, was apparently too busy to respond. As it was still mostly dark out—and even if the sun had been all the way over the horizon, the day was giving every indication of being another dull gray one—there wasn't much he could see other than his own reflection, but maybe that was enough for him.

Whatever.

An hour later, I was brewing the library's first pot of coffee and deciding that I definitely deserved extra cream in my mug since I'd just spent at least thirty minutes hauling heavy book crates into my car for delivery to the Lake View Medical Care Facility.

I was stirring away when a slim, gray-haired woman walked into the break room. "Morning, Donna."

"And to you," she said, smiling cheerfully.

Donna Beene was in her early seventies and was someone I wanted to be when I grew up. Sort of. Her job at the library was part time, and she kept at it primarily to fund her travel expenses. Donna traveled all over the country, and occasionally internationally, which was the part I liked. The part I wasn't so sure I had the capacity to emulate was that she traveled for the sake of running marathons and long-distance snowshoeing races, something I hadn't even known existed until I'd met her.

"How are things going?" she asked. "Any word from our fearless leader?"

"Got a text yesterday. They made it to Missouri, but his dad came down with bronchitis, so the actual moving in part is being delayed."

Donna poured herself a mug of coffee. "Being sick and not being in your own bedroom can't be any fun."

"They're staying with a cousin, so at least they're not in a hotel." I paused, then said, "Yesterday I heard about the airport expansion fuss from back in 1990. Do you remember much about it?"

Donna's gaze skidded away. "The GAC. It was a long time ago. And speaking of time, I need to get going. The garden club is using the small meeting room today, and I told them I'd bring in every gardening book we had."

She hurried off and I stared after her, frowning. The garden club didn't meet until three in the afternoon. Why did she need to get the books out so early? But Donna was one of those if-you're-not-ten-minutes-early-you're-late people, so this was probably another manifestation of that character quirk.

Shrugging, I went to my office, took care of some emails, took care of a few things on my to-do list, then put on boots and my coat and headed outside. I brushed a fresh inch of snow off my windshield, roof, and back window, and drove up the hill to Lake View.

The medical care facility did, in fact, have a view of Janay Lake, at least from the rooms in the front. The back rooms looked onto gardens that were lovely in the summer but were bare and white this time of year. Then again, basically everything outside was bare and white, so there was that.

I unfolded the nifty handcart that Gareth, the library's maintenance magician, had found for me, loaded the book crates onto it, and pulled it through the light snow and into the lobby.

The front desk was empty, but I knew the drill and wrote my name, cell number, and the current time on the top sign in/out sheet of a thick stack, some complete, some blank. *To keep track*, I'd been told a few months ago. *Just in case there's an emergency and we have to clear the building.*

I pulled my cart over to a set of bookshelves next to a cozy gas fireplace, pulled over a chair, opened my tablet, and started the comparison of what was left on the shelves to what I'd dropped off a few weeks ago. When that was done, I did some judicious replacements, then stood.

The clock on the tablet was telling me I had time, so I wheeled the cart up against the wall and out of the way and went to find my favorite nursing home resident.

Max Compton, whose eighty-eighth birthday celebration I'd attended last month, was not in his room. This wasn't a huge surprise, because if there was something going on in the building, Max was sure to be there. I finally tracked him down in the community lounge, where he was ostensibly helping the activities director set up for a crafts project, though it looked to me like he was distracting her with a story about what Bernice in room 117 and Robert in room 239 had been doing last night.

"If it isn't my favorite bookmobile librarian!" Max reached out for my hand and gave the back of it a smacking air kiss. "Ms. Minnie, you are a delight for the senses. I regret the day that rascal Rafe Niswander stole you away from me."

"You had your chance," I said. "And I couldn't wait forever. Your age, you know."

He slumped in his wheelchair. "Age discrimination. I wouldn't have thought it of you."

"We'll always have John Sandford," I said, pulling up a chair.

Max brightened. "Has the man released another book?"

"Not for months."

He got a wheedling look in his eye. "Any chance of getting an advance reader copy? My age, as you say. Any day could be my last and I don't want to go without having read all of his books."

"Max, you're going to outlive everybody in this building, and that includes me. But I want to ask you about something."

He rolled himself forward an inch. "If it's about why the Dolores in room 124 and the Dolores in room 141 aren't talking," he said in a loud whisper, "then I have the scoop. Did you know that—"

"I want to know what you remember about the 1990 airport expansion."

"The GAC." Max leaned back. "Nothing to tell." His voice was oddly flat. "It didn't happen. The airport is the same now as it was then. And now, my dear Minnie . . ." Without looking at me, he nodded and rolled away.

My mouth hung open as I watched him go. No one wanted to talk to me about the airport thing, not my aunt, not Donna, and not even the always loquacious Max.

It was time to dig deeper.

* * *

I returned to the library in a thoughtful mood. At lunchtime, I snarfed down my lunch of a small turkey sandwich with a small dish of cottage cheese (protein!), told Donna I was headed out for a few errands, and walked over to the city hall.

My friend Cathy, the Chilson city clerk, greeted me with her typical smile, but it faded when I asked about the 1990 airport expansion.

"I was still in high school," she said quietly after looking left and right. "And it's not like I was paying that much attention to city politics. But it got noisy."

"What do you mean, noisy?"

"Everybody had an opinion. And you were forced to pick a side."

I nodded but didn't quite believe her. "Sounds difficult. I was wondering, could I take a look at the city council minutes from back then?"

"Sure." Cathy stood and led me down the hall. She stopped in front of a heavy door and, with both hands, pulled it open. "This is the vault. It's fireproof, and all our permanent records are stored here."

She showed me where the council's minutes were shelved and left me to it.

I pulled the heavy book titled *Council Minutes: July 1989 to October 2005*, put it on the one flat surface in the room, a small table, pulled up the shell chair, and started reading.

Forty-five minutes later, I sat back and thought about what I'd learned. Two things, really. One, that the Chilson City Council didn't control the airport, the Airport Authority did. Two, that fact hadn't stopped the good citizens of Chilson from showing up at council meetings and speaking their mind about the expansion. For months, the public comment periods—one at the beginning of each meeting and one at the end—had gone on and on. For hours.

I felt a massive pang of sympathy for the city staff who'd had to sit through all that negativity, shut the book, and put it back on the shelf. I closed the vault door and went to talk to Cathy, but she was on the phone, so I waved, mouthed "Thank you!" and went back to the library.

At some point in the afternoon, my slow brain came up with the blindingly obvious idea of reading local newspaper articles from 1990. Embarrassing for a librarian, but better late than never. Though I knew the historical society maintained the oldest issues of the *Chilson Gazette*, their building was closed in winter. I could probably call someone and get access, but it would take time. Then again, basically underneath me was a storage room that housed more recent decades.

Since I knew I wouldn't be able to focus on my work until I figured this out, I went downstairs to the storage room. "1990, 1990, 1990," I murmured as I ran my finger down the index pinned to the bulletin board. "Hah. Cool." That year was still in paper, not microfilmed onto rolls of horizontally moving film that were guaranteed to give me motion sickness.

I wheeled the rolling rack around to expose the shelves that I needed and walked down the newly created aisle, passing through the seventies and eighties and arriving at 1990 just before I ran into the back wall.

"Okay, then." With great care and caution, I took a rack of brittle newspapers from 1990 to the front of the room and laid them on the large table. I reached for the Minnie-sized gloves that I always left on the table and started reading.

Time must have passed, but I wasn't aware of the minutes ticking by. I was deep in a time long past and had to focus on what I was looking for, and be strong enough to avoid reading grocery store advertisements for a pound of hamburger for under a dollar fifty and a dozen eggs at less than a dollar. I also quickly learned to avoid reading the letters to the editor. Pro or con, the letters were filled with invective and what I devoutly hoped were misrepresentations and half-truths. Instead, I stuck to the front pages. Facts, that was what I was looking for, not the, as Cathy had said, noisy opinions of everybody in town.

But, really, it was all fairly predictable. An expansion was proposed. Some people thought it would be just what the town needed. Others thought it would ruin everything that was good in Chilson, and the handful of people who said it would change things, but probably not that much, were overwhelmed by all the other voices.

Interestingly, Gerald's name did not come up that often; it was the Airport Authority that was pushing for the expansion, not Gerald. Still, he was at all the meetings and was occasionally quoted. I tried to see the solitary and kind Gerald that I knew in the middle of such a maelstrom but couldn't imagine it.

I was thinking about that, turning the pages, when the headlines changed.

"Co-Ed Activist Killed," it stated in bold black type. "Airport to Blame?"

I started at the page. Murder? Was this the real reason no one wanted to talk to me about the airport? And could this be the real reason Gerald had been killed?

Chapter Seven

On the bookmobile the next day, I told Julia what I'd learned in the newspaper archives.

"Her name was Cheryl Webb, and she was only twenty years old. She was a Chilson High School graduate, and she was taking accounting classes at the community college in Petoskey. The paper printed her high school senior picture. She had blond hair that was full and floofy, if you know what I mean, and a big smile. She was pretty. Really pretty."

Julia finished using the tiny scissors of my Swiss Army not-a-knife and handed it to me. "So sad. I remember my mom telling me that a young woman was murdered, but I was in New York and not thinking about anything except getting my first big role."

I took the not-a-knife and slid it into my pants pocket, where I kept it pretty much all the time now. It had turned out to be remarkably handy around the bookmobile, library, and even at home, and I wasn't sure how I'd lived without it all those years. It had been an excellent present, which made me all the more determined to find something equivalent for Rafe's birthday.

"I read all the papers I could, but I couldn't find anything saying that anyone was ever arrested for her murder." I'd even scanned the papers one year, five years, and ten years later, but there was nothing.

"No other details?" Julia asked. "Surely there was something."

What I had read was that Cheryl Webb had been strangled, and that her body had been found in front of a large "No New Airport" sign. I hadn't wanted to tell Julia those bits because it would give her nightmares, but I could tell she wasn't going to give up until I told her everything, so I did.

She shivered. "Why did you tell me that? It's all I'm going to dream about tonight."

I looked over and shared a commiserating glance with Eddie.

Julia gave a final over-the-top shudder. "What have people been telling you about the airport project? What's the acronym?"

"GAC. The Great Airport Controversy. One of the city council members called it that during one of their meetings and it stuck. And people aren't telling me anything. I asked Aunt Frances, Donna, and Max, and they all changed the subject. Like right away."

"Max?" Julia did the one-eyebrow thing. "That's beyond odd."

It was seriously strange, and even stranger that all three of them had done the same thing. "I don't know if it's because of the controversy itself, or if it's because of

Cheryl's murder, or if it's because no one was ever arrested for her murder."

"Any one of those would be difficult to deal with," Julia said. "All three together must have been brutal."

She was right, and I thought about that the rest of the way to our first stop, a store and restaurant combination run by a farming family. After we parked and finished the setup tasks, I sat at my desk, pulled out my phone, and sent Detective Ash Wolverson a text.

Me: *Are you familiar with the Cheryl Webb murder?*

There was no response for an eternal minute, then the three dots appeared.

Ash: *Yes*

Me (after rolling my eyes): *Was anyone ever arrested for it?*

Ash: *No*

I gave in to an impulse to be petty, texted him a single *K*, and slid the phone back into my pocket.

Cheryl's murder remained unsolved. Gerald was dead. Both Gerald and Cheryl had been involved with the GAC. If Gerald's death wasn't an accident, and I had the backing of Maureen Gertz on my instinct that it wasn't, a connection between the two seemed . . . well, maybe not likely, but certainly possible.

I considered telling Ash about Gerald's former job as airport manager, but if Ash knew the details of Cheryl's murder, then he knew about Gerald, and if I mentioned Gerald's history to Ash just to make sure, he'd get irritated that I'd think he wouldn't already have known and then I'd get irritated that he was being irritated, and that was a cycle I didn't want to start.

"You know what we have to do," Julia said, hands on hips.

"No, but why do I have the feeling that you're going to tell me and that I'm not going to like it?"

"We have to ask everyone who steps inside this bookmobile what they remember about the what-do-you-call-it, the GAC. This is a friendly and safe place. People talk here, you know they do."

"And what happens on the bookmobile stays on the bookmobile," I said, quoting our unofficial motto. "It can't hurt, so sure. Let's try it."

But trying didn't help. No matter how gently we brought up the topic, every single person we talked to backed away from conversation about the GAC, sometimes figuratively, sometimes literally. It wasn't until the last stop of the day, with the last person to leave the bookmobile, that we got a response.

The always chatty Mrs. Dugan was hesitant at first, but when I said, in a tired voice that wasn't an act, that no one was willing to tell me anything about an important event in Chilson's history, not even library patrons, she gave me an odd look, then shook her head, her firm white curls staying in place.

"It was such a shame. So many people behaved very poorly, and who wants to remember that? And that poor girl." Mrs. Dugan sighed. "She got caught up in it. Wanted to make a difference, was what I heard she was all about. Just goes to show."

Julia and I exchanged a glance. "Goes to show what?" I asked.

"Why, that passion can be dangerous. That poor Cheryl got recruited by the pro-airport people. Looking back, it seems almost like a cult. Lloyd was their ringleader, and I can well believe he's not talking to you about it, given the circumstances."

"Lloyd?" I echoed. "You mean Lloyd Goodwin?"

She frowned. "Of course Lloyd Goodwin. Didn't you know? He supported the airport expansion from day one. He rounded up dozens, hundreds of volunteers to show up at meetings, to go door to door, to write letters to the editors, all that busywork." She waved a hand. "Cheryl joined the group; she must have been the youngest, but I heard she was also the most energetic. And that ended up as a problem."

"How?" Julia asked.

"She lied. She was telling people about the wonderful things that would happen if the airport expanded, things she had no business saying. Lloyd told her she had to leave the group, and she didn't like that. Not one little bit." Mrs. Dugan pulled on her gloves and picked up her book bag. "The poor girl," she said again, this time softly. "Such a shame."

I stared at the door after she'd left.

Lloyd Goodwin? My favorite patron, not that I had one? Cheerful, kindly Mr. Goodwin who never said a bad word about anyone or anything, not even when I'd forgotten to renew the subscription to his favorite magazine?

Eddie bumped his head against my shin.

I bent down, picked him up, and put my head against the back of his neck, hoping to feel the comfort of his purr, because I was suddenly grasping why people didn't like to talk about the GAC.

It had been ugly.

* * *

The next morning, since I'd completely blanked on stopping to buy milk on the way home, Rafe and I had breakfast at the Round Table.

As we slid into our favorite booth, I said, "Sorry again about the milk. I guess I was still trying to figure out how I felt about learning what Mr. Goodwin did back then."

Rafe turned our mugs over and slid them to the outside edge of the table. "If that's the worst mistake you make this week, you're doing good."

"That doesn't seem realistic, but thanks for thinking it's possible."

"You know," he said, "there's now a new question. How did Mrs. Dugan know so much about Lloyd Goodwin?"

"Aline Dugan?" Sabrina filled our mugs from the carafe she held. She'd always been Mrs. Dugan to me, but I was pretty sure Aline was her first name, so I nodded.

"Aline's husband and Lloyd Goodwin were best friends. The families did things together for years, up until that thing." She sniffed. "Hope you two want your usual. I already put the order in."

"That thing?" I asked. "You think she was talking about the GAC?"

Rafe shrugged. "Ask her."

So when she brought our food, I did.

"Horrible time." She crossed her arms, hugging herself. "People were nasty to each other, nasty down to the bone.

And after that Cheryl was killed, everyone just stopped talking about it."

The way she'd said Cheryl's name . . . "Did you know her?" I asked.

Sabrina gave the room a swift glance. "She waited tables here. Summers during school, then almost up until, well, you know what happened."

I tried to catch Sabrina's gaze, but she was already turning away. "What was Cheryl like?"

She stopped but didn't turn around. Over her shoulder she said, "Cheryl was an average waitress to most people. But if you were a good-looking man, young, old, or in-between, she was excellent."

"Well." Rafe picked up his fork. "Tell us what you really think, Sabrina."

Nodding, I put my napkin across my lap, but my mind was whirring with the effort of doing mental math. How old had Gerald been in 1990? Mid-forties? And Cheryl had been twenty. But where had Gerald been on the good-looking scale? Had he qualified for Cheryl's attention? Had he wanted to?

Definitely something to figure out. Unfortunately, I had no idea how to go about doing so.

* * *

Soon after we finished eating, Rafe slid out of the booth. "Time for me to go, my little peppermint patty." He leaned down to give me a kiss on my upturned face. "See you tonight."

"Your turn to cook?" At least I hoped it was, because if it was my turn, we'd be eating peanut butter and jelly sandwiches.

He winked, and my heart went a little mushy. "Culinary delights coming your way at six PM."

Smiling, I wrapped my hands around my coffee mug and watched through the diner's large plate glass window as he got into his truck, backed out of the parking space, and turned onto the street, heading up the hill to the middle school.

A tiny part of me—the wacko neurotic part that I would only admit to under duress—was terrified that I'd never see him again. Something horrible would happen and I'd be left alone the rest of my life, drifting around that big house wraith-like, sad and wan, fading away over the years to near invisibility, and then, finally, vanishing.

"Stop it," I murmured to myself. He was going to work, that was all. People the world over did it every day. I was going to do it myself in a few minutes, as soon as I finished my coffee and paid the bill. And maybe today would be the day that he called his car guy about getting a new muffler.

"You awake in there?" Sabrina topped off my mug. "The boys in the back have been trying to get your attention for the past five minutes."

"I . . . what?" Blinking, I turned around. The *boys* she'd referenced were indeed beckoning, although the term, if taken literally, was more than a stretch as the group's youth had been in the era when Elvis Presley was considered controversial.

Sabrina was right; the elderly men were all looking at me, and the one closest to me pushed out an empty chair. I looked around. There was no one else in the room—even Sabrina had vanished—so I got up, mug in hand, and walked over.

"You're Fran Pixley's niece," said the man who'd pushed out the chair.

I'd never once heard Aunt Frances called Fran, and her last name was Bingham now, but whatever. I nodded and sipped my coffee, unsure where this conversation was going. The morning men at the back table had a reputation—they were the rulers of Chilson. Though not the actual decision-makers, their opinions influenced the decisionmakers and pretty much everyone else.

I tended to keep my distance from the group for many reasons. I wasn't from Chilson. I was young. I was female. I'd married a local favorite. And worst of all, I'd changed things when I'd launched the bookmobile.

"You found Gerald Arnhold," the man to my left said.

Again I nodded.

"Heard about the GAC, have you?" the man on the far side of the table asked. "About Cheryl Webb?"

More nodding on my part.

The five men exchanged a collective glance. "There are things you should know," the first man said.

"Earl," another one said. "You sure about this?"

Ignoring the caution, Earl gave me a long look. His eye were bright blue, the color the sky had been that day on the little lake. "No one was ever arrested for Cheryl Webb's murder." He half smiled. "I see you knew that, but did you know that Gerry Arnhold was a suspect?"

My coffee mug froze halfway to my mouth. "No." The word came out as a croak, so I cleared my throat and tried again. "No, I didn't know that."

"Nothing came of it," the man to my left said, almost defensively. "It was a one-day wonder. And saying he was a suspect isn't right. They brought him in for an interview. That's all."

"Interview?" A man with a tonsure of white hair scoffed. "That was an interrogation."

Earl held out a knobby hand, quelling the nascent argument. "There's one other thing."

If it was remotely close to the impact of the first thing, I was pretty sure I didn't want to know. "Okay."

"It's about your Uncle Everett."

I blinked. That was unexpected. "I don't remember him." At all. Everything I knew about him was secondhand from photos and family stories.

Earl nodded. "Sure, sure. But if you're digging into the GAC, you should know that Everett was against the expansion."

"Oh. Okay. Well, thanks for the information, but—"

The man at the back banged his mug on the table. "He threatened us, Earl. That's a big step past being against something."

Four of them started talking at the same time, arguing about events of thirty-five years ago. Earl put his fingers in his mouth, gave a short, sharp, piercing whistle, and the men fell silent. "Thank you," he said calmly. "Sorry about that, Minnie."

He went on to say that if I had any questions to let them know and they'd do their best to get me answers. I thanked him and the rest of the table, paid my bill, and escaped. But on my walk up to the library, all I could think about was my Uncle Everett, a single question circling around and around: What else hadn't I been told about him?

Chapter Eight

By noon, I'd come to two conclusions.

One. I should have overcome my angst about the Round Table years ago. Earl, for instance, had not only been a successful business owner of an auto parts store with multiple locations, he'd also been Chilson's mayor for almost a decade, starting just after the GAC. And Donna told me that the man in the back had sold insurance to almost every Chilson resident for fifty years. The group was a treasure trove for local lore, and I was downright embarrassed that I hadn't tried, in any real way, to tap their knowledge before now.

Two. Predicting what might become a community hot topic was impossible.

I knew this because even though our hijacked and horrible website had been live for less than two days, its presence was still making itself felt.

Glumly, I read the latest posts on the library's social media pages, many of which were accompanied by screenshots of the blinding mess that had been available to the public for forty-three hours.

"Who's in charge at the library? Somebody should be fired!"

"THIS IS AWFUL!!!"

"Who approved this, some committee?!?"

All this despite the explanatory press release, despite the explanatory message on the official webpage, and despite multiple explanatory social media posts.

I sighed and typed the same response I'd typed to all the others. That there was a temporary situation out of our control, and that the date of the launch of the library's new website would be announced soon.

"Did you see?" Josh barreled into my office, waving a newspaper.

My gaze skidded left and right, trying to see what he was holding, but I gave it up quickly because motion sickness is a thing. "See what?"

He slapped down a copy of the *Chilson Gazette*. "Letters to the editor," he said, a little too loudly. "What is it with people? Why is this such a big deal to anyone?"

I was getting a very bad feeling about this. With great trepidation, I picked up the single-section paper and opened it to the middle, past the current events but before the sports pages and the classifieds.

Out loud, I read the titles of the letters. "'How Could This Happen?' 'Our Beloved Library Is Going Downhill,' and 'Deep Fake or Deep Conspiracy?'" I started to scan the letters themselves but wasn't seeing anything worse than what we'd already had posted on social media.

"Thought you knew the editor." Josh was still talking way louder than normal. "Why didn't she give you a heads up?"

"Camille's out of town," I murmured. On a cruise of the Greek islands. Or was it the Dalmatian Coast? Either way, somewhere warm and sunny. "A friend of hers from downstate is putting out a couple of editions, so . . ." My voice trailed off. "No. You have got to be kidding."

"What?" Josh tried to look over the top of the paper. "What's the matter?"

"This." I jabbed my index finger at the second letter to the editor, the one complaining that the library wasn't what it used to be, and that the website was getting worse and worse every year. "See who wrote it? Mort Neely!"

"Don't know him. Am I supposed to?"

"He and his wife are bookmobile people." Though come to think of it, I hadn't seen them in weeks. To serve more people, we'd rearranged some of the routes in January, and I wasn't sure I'd seen the Neelys since then. "But . . . they're nice people," I said.

"Sure about that?" Josh growled.

Well, no. Not now. But maybe I'd brought it on myself for not working harder to make sure everyone was okay with the route changes. Maybe this was the beginning of the end for the bookmobile's popularity. Maybe this was the start of a downhill slide that would end with the failure of the library's outreach program and me getting fired.

I took a deep breath and tried to be more like Aunt Frances, who never worried about anything.

"Did you see this?" Holly barged into my office, waving another copy of the *Gazette*.

"Yes," Josh and I said simultaneously. I wondered why my millennial coworkers were reading hard copies of something that was available online but decided not to ask.

"Did you see what that skunk Mort Neely wrote?" she demanded. "What a putz. The way he was ragging on us, you'd think he was from downstate."

I looked up from Mort's letter. It didn't come across as any nicer the second time I read it. "He is. He and his wife moved up here after they retired, about three years ago."

"He worked in Southfield for some fancy accounting firm," Holly said, "but he and his wife, Lisa, graduated from Dooley High School the same year as my mom." She riffled through the paper to the pertinent page and made a face at it. "What a rat." She wadded the paper into a fat ball and gave it an arcing toss toward my wastebasket. "My mom and Lisa stayed friends, before they moved downstate and after they came back."

I picked the newspaper ball off the floor, sort of flattened it, and dropped it into my box of recycling. "Why did they move downstate? Normal reasons?" For a better job, for city nightlife, for a change, for education of self or children, for better access to health care, to get away from the town where you'd grown up; all were reasons I'd heard in the past and would surely hear again.

"Guess so." Holly shrugged. "From what Mom said, I'm not sure Lisa wanted to move, but Mort took a new job down there, so off they went."

"When was this?" I asked.

"Mid-1990s?"

"After the Great Airport Controversy, then."

"Not sure. If you want, I can ask." When I nodded, she whipped out her cell phone. "Hey, Mom," she said, moving aside so Josh could get around her. "Minnie has a question about the Neelys. Did they move downstate after that thing with the airport? Putting you on speaker." She tapped the phone and held it flat.

"Hi, Mrs. Lewis," I said.

"Hello, Minnie, honey."

"Sorry to put you on the spot about the GAC. I'm learning that lots of people don't like to talk about it, so it's fine if you don't want to."

"Aww, you're so sweet. But it's okay. The GAC wasn't a thing I got involved with. Too busy raising kids." She laughed. "But Mort, he was heavily involved from the get-go."

"Which side?" I asked.

"Oh, in favor. Heavily. So much so that he volunteered to talk to people one on one, knocking on doors, if you can believe it. Not something people do much anymore, and . . ."

Holly and I exchanged a glance. "Mom?" she asked. "You still there?"

"What? Oh. Yes, yes, I am. It's just that . . . well, the airport people went in pairs to talk to people, for safety's sake, and they tried to put one woman and one man together, to make themselves more approachable, if you see what I mean. There weren't many people who were willing to do the door knocking, as you can imagine, so the few people who did ended up spending a lot of time together."

I looked at Holly, who was frowning at the phone. "And?" she asked. "You're holding out. Tell us."

Her mom gusted out a sigh. "And Mort and Cheryl Webb were paired up. Now don't quote me on this, but I think they were knocking on doors together the day she was killed."

* * *

I was beginning to be sorry that the Wright brothers had ever invented the airplane. Sure, if it hadn't been them, it would have been someone else, but still. Or if the flight at Kitty Hawk had been a year later, it would be the butterfly in the forest thing, that a small event can have a huge impact down the line, that maybe in 1990 the good people of Chilson would have been kinder to each other about the airport expansion, and Cheryl would never have been killed.

But they hadn't been kind, and Cheryl was dead. And given that everybody I talked to was easily able to summon up deep emotions about the GAC so many years later, it seemed more and more likely to me that Gerald's death was murder.

Why, though? And what could have triggered a murder at this late date? Why now, instead of back then?

I tossed the questions around in my head on my chilly walk up to the library, as I made coffee, as I drank coffee, as I started my morning's work, and came to a very obvious conclusion: I needed more information about what had happened back in 1990.

"So very obvious," I murmured, pushing myself back from my desk. Then I sat there, staring at my desk. At the untidiness I always generated during the workday. At the precarious piles of books. The piles of magazines and trade journals. The piles of paper. I was thinking about the relationship between the untidiness of desks and the minds that sat at them, when I heaved a huge sigh.

Avoidance behavior. That's what I was doing, and I could feel my mother's disapproval hovering over me like a dark cloud.

"Fine," I muttered and stood. Continued to stand. Stood so long that my knees started to ache. Finally, after my imaginary dark cloud showed signs of becoming a thunderstorm, I headed into the hallway and down to the reading room, where the odds were very good that I'd find Lloyd Goodwin sitting in one of two wing chairs next to the gas fireplace, turning the pages of the *Wall Street Journal*.

Mr. Goodwin, with his ready smile and his dapper cane. Mr. Goodwin, with his penchant for telling tales about the early days of Chilson that may or may not have been true but which always kept his audience riveted. Mr. Goodwin, who, back on the day Eddie had followed me home, had noticed my feline shadow and implied that I now owned a cat. And who Mrs. Dugan said had been a vocal and active supporter of the airport expansion.

I stepped off the hallway's tile floor and onto the reading room's carpet. Inside was a twenty-something I didn't recognize who was perusing the library's selection of nontraditional items to borrow, e.g., a ukelele, a microscope, a blood pressure reader, and a scary-looking kitchen stand mixer.

And there, in the wing chair closest to the fire, was Mr. Goodwin. He looked to be two-thirds of the way through the paper, so I spent a few minutes straightening the magazine racks while I waited for him to finish. When I heard the rustle of newspaper folding, I walked over and sat on the large ottoman that sat between the wing chairs.

"Well, good morning, Minnie." He smiled at me. "Lovely day to be inside in the library, isn't it?" Reflexively, we both turned and looked through the tall multipaned windows to the white outside. A strong west wind had come up and was blowing intermittent curls of fresh snow from left to right.

Mr. Goodwin, who I could never manage to call Lloyd no matter how many times he asked me to, gave a violent shiver that I assumed was contrived, and turned back. "Is this a social call, or does the library need my help on some vitally important matter?"

I realized that my hands were gripping each other so tightly that my knuckles were aching. "In a way, it's both."

"Oh?" He tipped his head to one side. "How, pray tell?"

"It's . . . well . . . what I'm . . ."

"Dear Minnie." His smile was gentle. "Spit it out."

The words came tumbling out. "It's about the airport expansion," I said all in a rush. "Julia and I are the ones who realized what happened to Gerald Arnhold, I've heard that you were pushing for the expansion, and I just found out about Cheryl Webb, and everyone I talk to about the GAC goes all weird about it, so I thought I'd ask you."

He nodded gravely. "And you're wondering how kindly Mr. Goodwin could ever have been a firebrand. How it is that the people of Chilson could have turned against each other, creating such a deep divide that the scars are visible more than thirty years later. How the death of a good man could bring up all this angst. And," he said, sighing, "how it is that a young woman was murdered."

"Yes," I said.

Mr. Goodwin gave a one-sided smile. "Succinctness. Lovely." He pulled in a long breath, then let it out. "But I'm sad to say that I don't have any answers. Well, except for why I got involved. You're not old enough to remember, but we were going through a recession at the time, and times were hard. I thought—still think—that an airport expansion would grow Chilson's economy, spur growth, bring in good jobs."

"But other people disagreed."

"So many." He shook his head. "We couldn't understand their point of view, they couldn't understand ours. It was a chasm that grew wider and wider. Friends became enemies and stayed that way."

Something in the way he'd said that last sentence . . . "Did you lose a friend?" I asked quietly.

He stared at me without blinking. "Ah. You don't know."

"Know what?" I asked cautiously.

"Everett Pixley and I had been close friends for years. But I was pro-airport expansion and he was against it. After one particularly raucous meeting of the airport board, we never spoke again."

Another Uncle Everett story I hadn't heard. I really needed to talk to my Aunt Frances about her first husband. After a pause, I asked, "I heard that Mort Neely and Cheryl Webb were paired for knocking on doors, and that they were together the day she was killed."

"So long ago, yet it could be yesterday." Slowly, he shook his head. "I'd asked Cheryl to detach herself from our group the day before she was killed. She was a bright girl, but . . .

well, let's just say that she didn't let truth get in the way of a good story. She shouldn't have gone out with Mort, but that doesn't mean she didn't. And I shouldn't . . ." He looked at his hands. "And I shouldn't have involved her in the first place," he said so quietly that I almost couldn't hear him. "She was too young. Far, far too young."

We sat in silence for a moment, then Mr. Goodwin leaned down to pick his cane off the floor. "Minnie," he said, "I don't believe that I feel the need to read the *Free Press* today, or to attend the Encore meeting. If you would be so kind, please give them my regrets."

He walked out of the room, limping slightly, and there was only one thought in my head—that not attending the senior book club was far from his only regret.

* * *

Via a long string of text messages, I arranged to meet Aunt Frances at Corner Coffee on Saturday morning on the pretext of wanting to try the new pecan pie muffins that library patrons had been raving about, but when I encouraged her to sit at the corner table—prized in summer because of the big windows that if you leaned to the left had a lovely view of Janay Lake, but typically avoided in winter because of the cold that seeped in through the acres of glass—she gave me a look.

"Something's up," she said flatly as she slowly sat in the chair I pushed toward her.

I nodded and slid a large cup of coffee across the table to her. "Many things. Balloons. Elevators. Ladders. The temperature, even. Did you know it's supposed to get above freezing today? Not until late afternoon, and for only an hour, but still."

My beloved aunt ignored my attempt at conversational diversion. "What's up?" she asked. "If it's marital issues, I don't want details, but it's surely Rafe's fault, and I will send Cousin Celeste after him when she gets back."

I grinned into my steaming cup. Celeste was the sole member of the family whose height was on par with mine.

"If," my aunt went on, "this has to do with the library website . . ." She took in my vehement headshake. "Okay, then," she said. "I'm fresh out of guesses. You're going to have to tell me."

Now that the moment was in front of me, I wasn't sure how to get started. Then again, if all else fails, start at the very beginning. I broke a small piece from the family-sized muffin that sat between us and said, "There's so much family history I don't know. Including how you and Uncle Everett met."

My aunt's gaze narrowed. "That's your question?" When I shrugged, she made a rude noise in the back of her throat, then ate her own muffin bit. "Not much to tell, really," she said, but her voice had taken on a soft tone. "Downstate college girl spends a summer Up North, staying at the cottage of a family friend and waiting tables. Meets a local boy, and stays forever." She was smiling, a soft version I wasn't sure I'd ever seen before.

"Your parents didn't mind you moving away?" My grandparents had died before I was born, and what I knew of them came from photos and the memories of their offspring, my aunt and my dad.

"They didn't love it, but what were they going to do? Physically drag me back to Dearborn?"

She was still smiling. I didn't want to see it vanish, but if I didn't raise the subject now, when would I? "Um, I'm hearing that Uncle Everett was on the against side during the GAC."

My aunt's face went blank. More than blank, if such a thing were possible. "It was a long time ago," she said. "Lots of water under the bridge."

I blinked. Aunt Frances was not an aphorism kind of person. I pulled off another muffin piece. "Why was he so against it?"

She looked away from me, out the windows that were starting to fog up from interior heat and moisture. "Ev thought it would change Chilson too much. He said an airport that big would put us on the national map. People from all over would visit here, buy second homes here, or move here permanently; people who wouldn't understand Chilson. It would change us forever."

Well. I looked out the window, too, seeing the changes that had taken place in the years I'd lived here. There were more restaurants and boutique retail stores with items that locals couldn't afford. More second-floor storage spaces renovated into seasonal apartments. And just out of view, more and more condominiums being built, with the vast majority of the units sure to be short-term rentals. The changes Uncle Everett had been so concerned about were here; they'd just been delayed by thirty-odd years.

"It became the most important thing in his life," Aunt Frances was saying. "Saving Chilson, he called it, as if we were under attack, and to his mind we were. He talked the ear off anyone who would listen, and even people who didn't want to listen." She sighed. "He talked to the city council. To township boards. To state legislators. To congressmen and US senators. He even went downstate to Lansing, to speak to the aeronautics board, or whatever it is that approves those things at the state level. He spent so much time and energy fighting. So much time."

She fell silent and I felt . . . hollow, almost. There was so much history just under the surface of people, even people you'd known your entire life. What else didn't I know?

My aunt rubbed her forehead. "Correlation is not causation, but I will always connect his heart attack with the GAC."

I reached out for her hand, and we sat there for a few moments, both of us looking out the window at the white winter world, connecting through the touch of our skin, being together, feeling close.

But half an hour later, when our emotions had leveled off and we parted at the front door, I walked home, head down, with my thoughts in a dark place.

Because if Uncle Everett had been so vested in fighting the airport expansion, that certainly seemed like he had a motive to kill a young woman who'd been willing to lie to people about the glorious benefits of an airport expansion.

Chapter Nine

The rest of Saturday and most of Sunday, I spent a lot of time reminding myself that there was no way my uncle, the man for whom Aunt Frances had left home and hearth, had killed a young woman because they were polar opposites on the airport expansion. No way whatsoever.

"And besides," I told Eddie as I stood next to the bed, sorting the warm socks that were the last thing in the laundry basket, "even if the police had suspected him back then, they must have cleared him, because he was never arrested."

Eddie, who'd been slowly extending one paw toward a pile of folded T-shirts, stopped and looked up at me.

"Okay, sure." I paired two of Rafe's black socks. This was easier than it sounded, because for the last ten years of his life he'd made it a point to buy the same kind of sock from the same manufacturer. It was a brilliant tactic, and I was trying to do the same thing with my socks. Though it wasn't so easy with women's clothing, which changed faster than the seasons, I was doing my best. "Yes, I know. Sometimes the police know who committed the crime and they don't have enough evidence to arrest, charge, and convict. But this is a small town. You'd think that someone would have seen something."

However, no one had. Or at least no one had come forward. So now what should I do? What came next?

"No idea," I muttered to the final pair of socks. I looked over at Eddie, hoping for assistance, inspiration, or at least comic relief, but he'd flopped over onto his side and was snoring lightly.

"Thanks for your help," I said, but I said it quietly so as to not disturb any part of his twenty-two daily hours of sleep. After putting my clothes away, putting Rafe's on top of his dresser, and patting Eddie on the head, I wandered downstairs to find the love of my life and tracked him down in the kitchen, where he was making a batch of chili. It wasn't something I cared for, so he made a big pot of it every so often, then divvied it up into lunch-sized packets and popped them in the freezer.

As I came in, he looked up from his stirring of a stockpot with sides so high I would have needed a ladder to see into it. "What's happening, my sweet meringue pie?"

"Redundant." I hopped onto my stool and put my elbows on the island's counter and my chin in my hands. "Meringue is sweet by definition. And nothing. Absolutely nothing is happening."

"Huh. Sounds serious. A diagnosis is needed." Rafe's stirring slowed, and he gave me a long, serious look. "Could be cabin fever. Or plain old winter doldrums. Or seasonal affective disorder, even though we got a couple hours of sunshine the other day."

"None of the above." Talking with my chin in my hands wasn't easy, but I couldn't be bothered to move. "I just don't know what to do next about Gerald. Everything keeps pulling me back to that airport thing, but I have no idea if it's actually connected to Gerald's death or not. It was a massive deal, but it was so long ago." I shook my head, also not easy to do with your chin in your hands. "And now there's Cheryl Webb's death. It's all so . . . sad. And I don't know what to do."

I gazed idly at the counter and tried to define what I was feeling and came up with torpor, lassitude, languor, lethargy, lots of L words—

"You may not, but I do." Rafe clicked the cooktop's burner to off. "Boot up and suit up, my little duckling. We're going for a ride."

"But . . ." I used my index finger to point at the chili pot. "You're cooking."

He covered the pot with a lid the size of a cymbal. "Done. Needs to cool before I can bag it."

"Where are we going?" I looked down at my winter Sunday afternoon attire of slippers, saggy leggings, and an oversize fleece sweatshirt spotted with at least three colors of paint. "I should change."

"Don't need to. Not unless you think my mom will criticize what you're wearing."

I jumped down, ran upstairs, and came back down wearing newish leggings and the oversized bright pink fleece sweatshirt his mom had given me for Christmas last year. In short order we were sitting in the kitchen of the classic bungalow where he'd been raised, drinking hot chocolate topped with whipped cream and chocolate sprinkles.

"This is wonderful." I licked the foam off my lips. "Thank you. It's just what I needed."

My mother-in-law gave her infectious laugh. "Rafe said you needed a pick-me-up. Hot chocolate has always been my answer for that."

Lois was someone else I wanted to be when I became a real adult. She took very few things personally, managed to find humor in almost everything, and had the kindest heart of anyone I'd ever met. I sometimes joked with Rafe that I'd married him for his parents, and though that wasn't at all true, having fantastic in-laws was a wonderful bonus.

"Where's Dad?" Rafe asked.

Lois added another shake of sprinkles to her hot chocolate. "Over at Al's, helping him finish a three-season porch that Al promised his wife would get done before Thanksgiving."

I smiled. Rafe was definitely following in his father's footsteps. Helping friends with home improvement projects was how he spent half his weekends. Though I hadn't yet grasped that the trend would continue for the rest of our lives, I suppose it wasn't surprising.

"So what's been going on with you two?" Lois asked. "And, Minnie, I heard that you were the one to find poor Gerald Arnhold. If you don't want talk about it, I understand."

"Oh. Um, thanks." My hands soaked in the mug's warmth. "There's not much to say. Other than that, until the other day, I'd never known anything about the GAC, or Cheryl Webb's death."

Lois's lips pursed, making thin vertical lines around her mouth. "Cheryl. This many years later, and she's still . . ." My mother-in-law shook her head.

I looked at Rafe. He shrugged, and I turned back to Lois. "Still what?" I asked softly.

After a long, considering pause, she nodded to herself and looked at me straight on. "Don't like to speak ill of the dead, but that young woman was a menace."

I set down my mug. "A . . . menace?"

"Not in a violent way, but in the I'm-so-pretty-I-can-get-whatever-I-want kind of way. Do you know what I'm talking about? She was stunningly pretty, there was no doubt of that, anyone who had eyes could see it, and she played it up to her advantage with every breath."

This had been what Sabrina had said, the other morning at the Round Table. "Did she, um . . ." I held out one hand, palm up.

"Sleep around?" Lois gave a short laugh. "Who knows? Lots of talk, though. She got flirty with any man who came close to matching her for looks. Single men, engaged men, married men, young men, old men. They were all fair game for her."

Never once had I heard Lois sound so bitter. I wondered if Rick had been one of Cheryl's targets and quickly pushed the thought out of my head. Rick and Lois were the happiest couple I'd ever met. There was no possible way that Rafe's dad could have even considered being unfaithful.

"But it was just talk?" I asked. "No one ever knew for sure?"

Lois sighed and nodded. "Not for sure. One thing is certain, though. Cheryl didn't have any real friends, none that showed up to her funeral, anyway. What does that say about a person?"

I didn't know.

But I was suddenly sure that I needed to learn a lot more about Cheryl Webb.

* * *

Monday morning I was at my desk, reading the emails that Graydon had forwarded and asked me to deal with. He'd called on Sunday night, telling me that his dad's health was improving.

"Getting better," he'd said, "but 'better' is relative, because he hasn't improved enough to go home. He's being transferred to a long-term rehab facility, and they're not sure how long it will be. Might bc a couple of days, might be a couple of weeks."

I'd heard the fatigue in his voice. "What can I do?"

Which was when he'd told me about the emails he was going to forward. A contract for a summer paving project. Details about a major upcoming software upgrade. Information about changes to the insurance that covered the building. All things I'd need to talk to Gareth or Josh about, make lots of notes about, and follow up on.

I'd just printed the paving contract and was going at it with a red pen and highlighter—how on earth did the contractor think the first week of June was the best time to close the library's parking lot?—when there was a sharp knock on my door frame. Surprised, I looked up and saw a man in his mid-sixties. Thin face, smooth hair cut to a professional length. Slacks, a buttoned shirt, and a sport coat were visible under the tasteful plaid scarf and camel-colored overcoat. Trent Ross.

"Good morning, Minnie," he said.

"Um." No other words came out, because my brain had shut down. There was no way that having the chair of the library board at my office door an hour before the building technically opened was a good sign. "Um," I said again. "Morning."

"Do you have a few minutes? And"—he looked around my small office with its one extra chair, which was currently piled high with books—"perhaps a conference room? Bruce and Carolyn are right behind me."

"Of course," I said, because there was no other possible answer. "Does anyone want coffee?"

A few minutes later, the four of us were upstairs in the small conference room. Since none of the others had wanted coffee, I left my own mug downstairs, but that left me with nothing to do with my hands except fiddle with the pen and paper that precedent had told me would be wise to bring along, even if no one else at the table had any writing implements. Maybe even especially if no one else had any.

Trent tapped the table, calling the impromptu meeting to order. "I know you're trying, Minnie, but this website thing is out of control."

"And that's an understatement," Bruce said. "You wouldn't believe the emails and phone calls I got over the weekend. So many."

Bruce was also on the city council, and he had a tendency to exaggerate. But if I asked how many he'd had—and my guess was maybe half a dozen total—he'd take it as a character attack, and our cordial relationship would be gone forever. And at the end of the day, the number didn't matter. He felt it was a lot, so it was.

I nodded, though I wasn't sure what I was nodding about. "Erik, the owner of the website design company, is scheduled to call me in an hour. We believe that as soon as the new site is up and running everyone will forget about the hijacked one." At least I hoped so.

"When will that be?" Bruce demanded. "We need to tell people something."

"As soon as I get off the phone with Erik, I'll notify the full board, write a media release, and push the information out."

"You'll include the newspaper?" Trent asked.

I nodded. "Always. And thanks to Rila, our new bookmobile clerk, we have contacts with the TV network, so there's a chance we could get exposure there, too." Rila's contacts were sports-oriented and unlikely to care much about the library, but you never knew.

Bruce heaved a massive sigh. "Too little too late. This has been a disaster. I said all along that there's nothing wrong with the old website. You should have left well enough alone."

My insides clenched tight against his accusatory tone. I thought back to all the design meetings, meetings in which he'd done more than his fair share of criticizing the existing site, and kept my mouth firmly shut.

"The redesign was a board decision," Trent said mildly. "And Minnie is right, this will blow over."

"Not soon enough," Bruce grumbled.

"I'm sure we can all agree on that," Carolyn said. "Why don't we let Minnie get back to work? She has a press release to write, yes?"

Still grumbling, Bruce left the room without looking at me. Trent gave me a nod and went after him. Their voices, echoing in the hard spaces of the hallway, were loud enough for me to hear without actual eavesdropping, and happily had to do with skiing in Park City and not about firing Minnie Niswander for being the worst acting library director in the history of acting library directors.

"Don't look so worried," Carolyn said.

I tried to wipe the fear from my face but was absolutely sure I hadn't done a good job. "Kind of hard not to."

"This little meeting was all Bruce, you know." Her smile was kind. "Trent called last night and asked me to come along, just in case our Bruce got carried away. It was a close thing there, wasn't it?" She looked thoughtful. "My only real question is, where did he learn math? I hope it wasn't the Chilson schools, because that's where my offspring were educated."

"Math?" I asked, bewildered.

"That's right. Because when he and I were walking in, not fifteen minutes ago, he said he'd had one phone call and two emails about the website. If he defines that as 'many,' I shudder to think what he would consider six. Or even seven."

And, just like that, my anxiety vanished. It was probably a life lesson, abolishing worry with levity, and when I had time I'd try to remember to think about it.

"It's odd, being in this room again." Carolyn was looking around: at the oak window trim, the wooden floor covered under the table with an area rug purchased from a local loom artisan, the smooth plaster walls, the schoolhouse pendant light fixtures that hung from the ceiling. "Fourth grade. Mrs. Ryan's desk was there." She nodded at the front of the room. "And though things shrink as you grow up, I would have sworn this room was bigger."

I laughed. "You are correct. During the renovation, some of the old schoolroom walls were resized to fit what the library needed." We got similar comments from patrons on a regular basis. "It bothers some people; others don't seem to care."

"People and change," she said, shaking her head. "It's the fear, you know. Of the unknown. Known is safe, because we're alive and breathing and doing okay. With the unknown we don't know precisely what's going to happen, so it feels safer to stick to the known. Very atavistic of us, but humankind got this far, so it must work to some extent."

Part of my brain was getting tugged into a philosophical direction about how far humans had come and how much further we might go, but the other part was circling around Carolyn's comment about this being her fourth-grade classroom. And how old Carolyn was.

As casually as I could, I asked, "Were you in the same grade as Cheryl Webb?"

Carolyn's calm face went still. "I haven't heard that name in a long time," she said slowly. "I suppose this has to do with Mr. Arnhold's death."

I sort of nodded, sort of didn't. "I spent all my summers up here from age twelve through college, have been a full-time resident about six years, and I heard about the 1990 airport expansion and Cheryl's death less than a week ago."

"It's not surprising," Carolyn said. "That was an ugly time in the town's history. Revisiting it would be unpleasant."

"A young woman was murdered." I felt my jaw clench. Took a deep breath to release it. I wasn't angry at Carolyn.

I was angry at whoever killed Cheryl. At whoever might have killed Gerald. "And no one was ever arrested for it. Her killer is still walking around, living their life, breathing the air."

Carolyn studied me. "The injustice rankles, doesn't it? I can see it in the set of your shoulders."

I desperately wanted to get the rankle rubbed out of my shoulders but was pretty sure Rafe's neck rubs wouldn't do the trick. "Did you know Cheryl?" I asked.

"The pretty Ms. Webb." Carolyn leaned back. "Yes. We were indeed in the same graduating class, but we weren't friends. Or enemies, for that matter. I was busy with books, she was busy with boys. Not exactly kindred spirits."

I smiled at the *Anne of Green Gables* quote. "What was she like?"

Carolyn stood and walked toward one of the windows. "Her desk was here, and she spent most of her time watching whatever was going on out there. She always seemed to be somewhere else."

It was an interesting viewpoint, one that I doubted anyone else could have told me. I thanked her, and we walked downstairs companionably, chatting about the newest book from Isabel Allende.

As we stood in the lobby, finishing our conversation, Mort and Lisa Neely walked in. Mort's nasty letter to the editor came rushing back into my head, but I stuck a professional smile on my face. "Good morning, Lisa. Mort."

Lisa smiled back. "Morning, Minnie. Hello, Carolyn."

Mort gave us a brief nod and basically blew past as if we weren't even there.

I watched them go into the main stacks. Lisa had told me that Mort refused to wear the hearing aids he needed, which might explain why he hadn't heard my polite greeting, but it didn't explain his frosty non-greeting. "I didn't realize you knew Lisa."

Carolyn buttoned her wool coat. "And her husband. They're important donors to the hospital foundation."

That made sense. What didn't make sense was Carolyn's guarded tone. I walked with her out of the lobby, through the first set of double doors, and into the vestibule entrance. "I take it they're not your favorite donors?" I asked quietly.

She pulled on leather gloves. "Lisa is wonderful. Mort? Let's just say I'm not surprised his first wife divorced him." She gave me a quick hug and went out into the cold.

I wrapped my arms around my chilly self, thinking.

So Lisa was Mort's second wife. Interesting. And it might be even more interesting if I knew when he and his first wife divorced.

* * *

"And do you know what I found out?" I asked.

There was no audible response to my question. Which wasn't a huge surprise because Rafe was in the basement, tinkering with a recalcitrant vacuum cleaner, and Eddie wasn't big on straight-up answers. If he did anything at all, it would mostly likely be the feline equivalent of an eye roll, with the accompanying grunt that could only mean "Whatever."

I was in the dining room rearranging books. When Rafe and I had set up house together, I hadn't put as much thought as I should have into what went where, and just that evening, walking through from the kitchen to the living room, I'd decided that our personal science fiction and fantasy section should be upper shelves, not the lower ones where they currently resided.

"Because," I said to the cat I'd last seen squirreling his way behind our teeny tiny section of math, statistics, and math-adjacent books, "sci-fi and fantasy almost always have flying things in them, spaceships or dragons or whatever, so it makes sense to put them on high shelves."

I heard a muffled "Mrr."

"Good to know that you agree. Back to what I found out. Donna didn't know when Mort and his first wife divorced, and neither did Aunt Frances, not for sure. I checked to see what I could find online, and the court records for divorces only go back about ten years. I called Sophia—you remember her, she's the district court administrator and magistrate, and she's renting my old room in the boardinghouse—and she said I needed to talk to the court's Family Division. So I went over there at lunch. They looked it up and told me that the divorce between Mort and his first wife was final in 1992."

"Mrr!"

"Right? Interesting." Looking at the heap of books on the dining table, I spent a few moments debating whether or not to separate fantasy from sci-fi. In the end, I decided to leave them together, mostly because categorizing Frank Herbert's *Dune* was too hard.

"But also interesting is what I've been learning about Uncle Everett." This time I heard nothing from the peanut gallery. "He was a key player for the against side, which, in the end, prevailed. I really don't want to think he had anything to do with Cheryl's death, and surely the sheriff's office looked at all that back then, but . . . could he have done it?"

I thought of the man I'd never met. The question, though, wasn't *could* he have done it, because pretty much anyone could kill, if they were driven to it. The question was *did* he?

But I had no clue. How could I? I hadn't known him. And I didn't understand anything about the Great Airport Controversy, not from an emotional point of view, so guessing at motivations and trying to reconstruct what had happened from current time was more than pointless.

"It's unproductive," I said, looking down at a copy of Stephen King's *The Waste Lands*, the third book in the *Dark Tower* series.

"Mrr."

I looked over and saw Eddie's yellow eyes rising above the top of *The Woman Who Smashed Codes*.

"Yes," I told him, "I know you've perfected the art of wasting time, and I applaud you for that, but it's different for cats. Many of us humans feel the need to be productive. It's a primal urge."

"Mrr!"

"It's okay," I said soothingly. "Tell you what. If you want, you can be productive tomorrow on the bookmobile."

His head disappeared and I went back to shelving and thinking out loud. To a cat. "So. If I'm going to be productive, almost always a good goal, I need to focus more on Gerald's role in the GAC and not Cheryl."

This meant I didn't need to dig any deeper into Uncle Everett. At that conclusion, I felt a profound sense of relief, which I immediately questioned. Had I decided against looking into Cheryl's death so I could leave the memories of Uncle Everett alone?

I looked at the question from every angle I could, then shook my head. I didn't know, not for sure. All I could do was my best, and at this point my best would be to help find Gerald's killer. It had been two weeks since his death, and I didn't feel any closer to answers now than when I'd started.

"What do you think?" I asked Eddie, who had just emerged from his cozy book space.

As he stalked past me, he flicked his tail in my general direction. "Mrr," he said.

Chapter Ten

Julia clapped her mittened hands together. "Brava!"

I shrugged. "Thanks, but it was no big deal." Because it really wasn't. All I'd done was watch the road, notice the massive chunk of snow that had fallen off the vehicle in front of us, and drive around it.

"Take every bow you can," Julia chided in a French accent. "Have I taught you nothing?"

"You've taught me a lot," I said. "The name of all the shows you were in when you won Tony Awards. Which restaurants in New York are—"

"Theater District only, daah-ling."

"Which New York Theater District restaurants are next level. What dress I should wear when I go to a Broadway show. More importantly, what shoes I should wear when going to that show. And most important of all, never ever buy a theater seat behind a pillar."

She put one hand to her parka-ed chest and gave a contented sigh. "Lovely that my knowledge is being passed on to a new generation."

"Before I go"—not that I had any plans to go anywhere anytime soon, but it was good to be prepared—"I'll need the answer to one question."

"Ask away," she said grandly.

"You said 'brava.' What's the difference between 'brava' and 'bravo'?"

She readjusted her knit hat. "Depends on how Italian you want to be," she said in her normal voice. "Brava is the feminine singular, bravo is the masculine singular. Brave and bravi for the respective plural forms."

Interesting, but there was no way I was going to remember any of that. I nodded. "Okay. Thanks."

"You're not going to remember any of that, are you?"

"Doubtful." I squinted at the road, weighing my penchant to learn new things against my regrettable tendency to forget things. "But I'm pretty sure I'll remember that there are female, male, plural, and singular versions."

"A win!" Julia clasped her hands together—not an easy thing to do while wearing mittens—and held them up, victory-style. "Ta-dah! Cheers to me!"

"Mrr!"

"Thank you, Monsieur Edward." Julia tapped her boot toes on Eddie's carrier. "It is delightful to have your support."

I was fairly sure Eddie's comment had been more along the lines of "Are we there yet?" but I didn't disabuse Julia of her anthropomorphism, because who was I to talk?

A few minutes later, we came to a stop outside the front door of a long and rambling single-story building that had begun its life as a normal-sized home. A few years ago, after

Wanda Panovich's parents passed away, she and her husband Ken had moved back north from their downstate jobs of nurse and paramedic and renovated the house where she'd grown up into an adult foster care facility. Honey Hollow, it was called, and we'd only recently started making stops there.

Julia unbuckled her seat belt and glanced at the entrance. "No welcoming committee?"

I looked at the empty front door. Every time before this, Wanda had greeted us at the front door, chatting about this and that and helping us carry materials inside. "Looks as if we're on our own today," I said, hoping that everything was okay, because it just as easily might not be. Caring for the elderly brought with it a guarantee of loss, and I was very glad there were people willing to endure the grief in exchange for the reward of caring.

Julia opened the back door, lowered the lift, and took out the handy dandy garden cart we used to haul the book crates in and out. After we loaded the cart, I grabbed Eddie's carrier, Julia grabbed the cart's handle, and we traipsed through the slushy parking lot to the door, where there was still no Wanda.

Odd, but I decided not to worry. Honey Hollow had twelve residents, after all, so she was undoubtedly busy. And we knew where to go and what to do. There was no need for her to meet us.

Shaking off a tickle of unease, I carried Mr. Ed through the empty lobby and into the dining room. We were halfway through our unpacking when Wanda hurried in. "Minnie! Julia! Eddie! I am so sorry I wasn't up front to greet you!"

"Hope it's okay that we just got started." I nodded at the spread of books.

"Oh, it's absolutely fine."

And just like that, she stopped talking.

I exchanged a look with Julia. "Are you okay?" I asked. Because normally Wanda bubbled with energy, chatting nonstop, often bouncing on the toes of her pink running shoes. Even the medical scrubs she habitually wore seemed subdued today; just a deep maroon top and bottom. No cheery print, no bright colors.

"We don't know." Her voice was vague, but as I watched her with growing concern, she snapped awake. "Sorry," she said. "Alicia had a stroke yesterday. She's in the hospital, and we don't know what's going to happen. Ken's with her, waiting for the family to get here from North Carolina, I think, so I'm getting regular updates, but . . . we don't know."

I stood still, my arms laden with large-print books. Alicia Gwaltny, shorter than my efficient five feet. Alicia with the thick glasses with lime-green frames. Alicia, frail and ninety if she was a day. Alicia, who had volumes of Tonedagana County history in her head, and whom I'd wanted to talk to that day about Gerald, the GAC, and Cheryl.

"Oh, honey." Julia wrapped her arms around Wanda. "We're so sorry. That wonderful woman. But if anyone can come back from a stroke at her age, it's Alicia."

"Exactly," I said. "She has goals, and no stroke is going to stop her from achieving them." Alicia regularly proclaimed that she wasn't ready to go until she turned one hundred and got a kiss on the cheek from Ryan Reynolds.

"She's a wonder, that's for sure." Wanda half smiled, then her gaze lasered in on me. "Minnie. You're here."

I blinked. "I am."

Wanda blew out a breath and looked at the ceiling. "The other day, Alicia said something about you, that she needed to talk to you. Now what was it?" She crossed her arms, her fingers tapping. "Not anything about books or the bookmobile."

"Mrr!"

"No, sorry, it wasn't about you either, Eddie. It was about something that happened a week or two ago. She wanted to make sure to tell you . . ."

I stayed quiet, not wanting to disturb her memory search. Julia had no such compunctions. "Was it about Gerald Arnhold?" she asked.

"That's it!" Wanda snapped her fingers. "Gerald Arnhold. Alicia said he'd worked at the Chilson Airport years ago. She was the janitor for the airport, so she knew Gerald. She said he was the nicest persnickety grump she'd ever met. And that if he'd drowned accidentally, she'd eat her hat."

* * *

"The nicest what?" Rafe asked.

"Nicest persnickety grump she'd met in her life."

He frowned, but since he was also twirling spaghetti onto his fork, I wasn't sure if the frown was directed at Alicia's comment or at the pasta.

"Isn't that what they call a tautology?" he asked.

I didn't think so, but though I was fairly sure I knew what a tautology was, I wasn't one hundred percent, and we'd banned the use of cell phones at the dining table. I nodded at the shelf of reference books. "Dictionaries are over there, if you want to check."

To my utter shock, he abandoned his food and fetched the dictionary his grandparents had given him as a high school graduation present. He flipped through the thin pages. "Nope," he said after a moment. "A tautology is saying the same thing twice. Like saying when Eddie woke us up 'it was five AM in the morning.' Or that us agreeing to go to Hoppe's Brewing for supper on Friday night will be 'totally unanimous.'"

"Saying 'ATM machine,'" I said. "Or 'UPC code.'"

Rafe shut the book and returned his attention to his fork. "So saying 'nicest persnickety grump' isn't a tautology. But it's something. What's the difference between a contradiction in terms and an oxymoron?"

This one I knew. "Contradiction in terms is a general thing. Oxymoron is a specific kind of contradiction in terms, something used intentionally as a literary device. Like . . ." I rooted around in my brain for an example.

"Jumbo shrimp?"

"Like Juliet saying 'parting is such sweet sorrow.' See the difference?"

My beloved did not. He also didn't appear to care much about the topic, so I moved on. "I don't suppose you've given any more thought to a personal strategic plan?"

A faint groan emanated from his side of the table, at an elevation that made it impossible for the groan to have come from the floor-lounging Eddie.

"So you're still thinking about this," Rafe said.

"Of course I am. I brought it up because I think it's a good idea."

"Yeah, but . . ."

Though I waited, he didn't say anything more. "But what?" I asked, going for a tone of curiosity, not testiness. It almost worked.

"But I get enough of that kind of stuff at work. I don't need to do it here, too."

I sort of saw his point, sort of didn't. I was fine with doing things at home that reflected work tasks. However, Rafe and I were two different people, so I didn't say anything.

"And mostly," Rafe said, clearly not hearing my internal monologue, "what would be on it? Live in a cool house in Chilson near the water? Done." He made an air check mark. "Have jobs we really like?" Another air check. "Build a gazebo in the back yard? Be active in the community? Have a great set of friends?" Three fast checks. "We're good, Min. What else do we need?"

"Goals," I said emphatically. "If we don't have goals, we'll get into a rut. We'll stagnate. We'll turn into That Couple."

He frowned. "What couple?"

"The one who never ventures out of their comfort zone. The one who goes to the same restaurant at the same time every Thursday every week of their lives. The couple who goes to the same place on vacation every year. The couple who always buys the same kind of vehicle, who always plants the same annual flowers, who has the same people over for a Fourth of July cookout every year."

Rafe added more parmesan cheese to his plate. "Doesn't sound all bad."

"It's not bad," I said. "I just . . . don't want to be like that."

"Then don't." He shrugged. "Not sure why you need a fancy plan."

"Mrr."

Rafe grinned. "Eddie agrees. Vote of two to one, majority says no plan." He stood, picked up our plates, kissed the top of my head, and went to the kitchen.

When he was out of the room, I leaned over and gave my furry friend a hard glare. "Doesn't count. You're not registered to vote."

Eddie gazed up at me, yawned, stretched, stood, and sauntered off to join Rafe.

I slumped in my chair and heaved an Eddie-quality sigh. Maybe Rafe was right. Maybe we didn't need a plan. Maybe I just needed to be self-aware. To think big picture on a regular basis. To review where we'd been and where we were going. To make sure we were still where we wanted to be.

"But," I muttered to myself, "all that would be easier if we had a plan."

* * *

I fell asleep thinking about the plan I didn't have and woke up thinking about the one I sort of had, the one that had to do with convincing at least one detective at the sheriff's office that Gerald had been murdered.

"It's not much of a plan," I told Eddie as I hung my wet towel on the rack, "but it's better than nothing."

The cat in the room, who was flopped up against the side of the bathtub, didn't reply. Didn't look at me. Didn't even twitch his ears.

"Are you still mad about me shoving you off the bed at three in the morning? I already told you umpteen times, it was an accident."

Again no response. I peered at him closely to make sure he was breathing. Yep, my furry friend's little kitty sides were going up and down, up and down, just like normal.

"Here's an idea," I said. "To make up for it, how about a double helping of treats this morning?"

The long tail gave one slow thump, then went still.

"Fine. Be that way. But if you keep this up, the neighbor's cat will get your treats."

His head jerked up and I could almost see the thought bubble over the top of his head: "Treats? I thought you said cleats, and I don't need any." He jumped to his feet and tried to get a running start on the bath mat, which curled underneath him like a wave. When his feet hit the actual tile floor, his speed went from zero to zoom instantaneously.

"You are so weird," I called after him, but since he was already mostly down the stairs, he probably didn't hear what I said.

The kitchen held a lovely scent of coffee, but no Rafe. I silently blessed him for brewing a pot before he left for his early meeting and made a mental note to tell him that night that he was the best husband I'd ever had.

"Mrr." Eddie was sitting in classic cat statue pose next to the cabinet that held his treats.

Right. I'd already forgotten. Worst cat mom in the whole world.

I got out the treat can and shook out what may or may not have been a double helping, and by the time I'd taken my prepped bowl of oatmeal out of the fridge and turned to put it in the microwave, that particular square foot of floor was empty.

"You're welcome," I said loudly.

There was a short pause, then: "Mrr!"

So I was smiling as I ate my oatmeal, smiling when I was walking up the hill to downtown Chilson, and must still have been smiling when I walked into the sheriff's office, because Chelsea slid the glass window open, took one look at me, and asked, "What's so funny?"

"Eddie," I said.

She laughed. "Accurate and amusing in one word. You get a gold star for the day."

"How about a quick conversation with a detective or two?"

"Not sure that's much of a prize, but I can check. Hang on."

A couple of minutes later, I was sitting in the interview room, waiting for Detective Hal Inwood to grace me with his presence. Ash was, unfortunately for me, out doing detective-y things, so it was either Hal or no one.

But, really, they had things to do. I shouldn't expect that either one of them was going to be in the office when I wanted to talk to them. I could have scheduled an appointment. Texted. Emailed. Called, even.

Sighing, I murmured, "I should have had a better plan."

"Wise words." Hal sat heavily in the chair opposite me. "What can I do for you this morning, Ms. Niswander?"

I peered at him, noting the bleary eyes, the red nose, and the air of fatigue "You okay?"

"Just a head cold," he said. "Taking me a while to get rid of it."

I slid my chair backward. "Oh. Well, I hope you feel better soon." I also hoped that he didn't sneeze all over me, and that he hadn't recently touched anything that I had. "I just wanted to let you know what I've found out in the last few days."

"Please. Do tell."

It was sarcasm with a veil so thin it might as well have been nonexistent, but I smiled brightly. "Thanks, Hal. I will." I took a deep breath and launched into one very long run-on sentence with no punctuation, taking no breaths that might give him a chance of stopping my information flow unless he summoned the energy to interrupt me—though given his already sagging shoulders, that didn't seem likely.

"The unsolved 1990 murder of Cheryl Webb happened during the Great Airport Controversy and since she was an active participant in the pro side she had to know Gerald Arnhold and even more than thirty-five years later the GAC still stirs up nothing but ill-feeling if you can even get someone to talk about it which means someone could still be angry enough about it to kill again so how could you not be looking at Gerald's death as a murder because anyone who knew him knew that he would never be so careless as to drown while ice fishing."

Hal took a handkerchief out of a pants pocket, blew his nose, and put the white square back into his pocket. "Mr. Arnhold was interviewed. He was not charged with anything. Ms. Webb's murder remained unsolved. We review it once a year, which we did soon after Mr. Arnhold's death. There was no connection between the two deaths."

"Just because no connection was found," I said, trying to sound reasonable, "doesn't mean one doesn't exist."

The gusting sigh from across the table was almost visible. "Ms. Niswander, an elderly man fell through the ice. Sad, but it happens every year. Now, unless there's something else?" He stood and held out a long arm, indicating that I should scurry away and leave him to his misery.

I gave him an unfocused nod and headed out, trying to project calm and professionalism, and not imitate the foot-stomping two-year-old that was welling up inside of me.

After skating a wave at the on-the-phone Chelsea, I banged through the outside doors and into the gloomy dark grayness of late winter, muttering to myself about many things, none of them productive. I was irritated and frustrated and needed a mood change.

Luckily, I knew just how to fix myself.

Chapter Eleven

Pam Fazio eyed me over the top of her steaming coffee mug. "My guess is you didn't sound as reasonable as you thought you did. How exactly did you say it?"

I cleared my throat, imagined myself back in the interview room, and quoted myself. "Just because no connection was found doesn't mean one doesn't exist."

"Try again," she said, sounding way more amused than she should have been.

"No."

"Come on, please? Look. I'm Hal Inwood." She grabbed a tissue from the box she kept on her checkout counter, fake-blew her nose in it, and shoved it into the pocket of her sweater.

I laughed, which was probably what she'd intended since she had seen me do the grump walk in through her door, and was what I'd been hoping for. "Do you ever wonder what Tabitha and Hal talk about at the dinner table?"

"That way lies madness," she said. "They could talk about their favorite dental floss, they could be talking about dark matter, they could be talking about the Detroit Red Wings, they could be talking about the latest issue of *Positive News*. Do you really want to find out and ruin the fun we can have speculating?"

After squinching up my face, which I was convinced made thinking easier, I said, "Absolutely not," and was rewarded with Pam's happy peal of laughter.

It occurred to me, for basically the first time, that I knew essentially nothing about Pam's partnership status. She lived alone, that I did know, but other than that, I didn't know anything, and until that moment I hadn't realized I didn't know. She was such a self-contained person that seeing her emotionally attached to someone else would have been . . . weird.

"Now what's the matter?" she asked. "You look funny."

If she'd wanted me to know about her personal life, she would have told me, and I understood and respected that. "All good," I said. "What about you? How's the winter going, store-wise?"

She looked away from her examination of my face—hooray!—and gazed at the interior of her store. Her brow furrowed, and the longer she gazed, the deeper the furrows became.

I turned around so I could see what was making my friend unhappy.

Pam's store, Older Than Dirt, was an eclectic mix of items. There were things that were old and new, expensive and not, colorful and pastel, heavy and light, big and small. To me, in addition to the unique ways that she displayed items, what was tremendous was the amazing variety of objects that one could buy.

I closed my eyes and played the memory game.

Over toward the front windows were old dressers, drawers open, filled and topped with quirky and kitschy kitchen towels, gloriously colorful placemats, vintage dishes, and a collection of chef's hats. Against the back wall was a circa 1980s entertainment center turned into a display case for that era's books, vinyl records, cassette tapes, and even a few eight-tracks. In the corner was a rack made from old skis that held bathrobes so plush I wanted to sink into one right then and there. At the back of the store was a heap of suitcases in various sizes, ages, and materials: fabric, cardboard, leather, and canvas. On the floor below the suitcases were children's pull toys, old and new, all lined up in a row like cars starting a road rally. And right in front of me was a three-foot-high cheetah that must have come from an old carousel.

"It's getting stale," she said.

My eyes flew open and I looked, startled, at my coffee.

"Not that, silly." Pam held out her hand, palm up, indicating the amazing variety of goods for sale. "That."

I blinked. "You're kidding, right?"

"Stale," she repeated. "Same old, same old. Maybe a few things rotate out, but overall? It's the same stuff, over and over again."

I couldn't think of anything in front of me that had been there last fall, even the entertainment center, but her standards could be vastly different than mine. "Won't container day fix that?"

Pam went on buying trips on a regular basis, sometimes in Michigan, sometimes in other states, sometimes in

Canada, sometimes in Mexico, sometimes overseas. On the big trips, the fruits of her labors were packed into a semi-truck container and shipped to Chilson. The day the container arrived was like Christmas. It was so much fun to see what she'd bought that staff, friends, and neighbors volunteered to unpack the glories, and the pizza she fed us was more than enough pay.

"Eh." She shrugged. "Wasn't that great a trip this year."

I couldn't remember where she'd gone, but as it was obviously not a good memory, I decided not to ask.

"Maybe I need some new displays," she said.

"But these are great!"

"Eh." She shrugged again. Then she saw my stricken face and laughed. "Dearest Minnie, don't look like that. I'm just having a day. I'll be fine. You go on up to your library and take care of all the things. I'm fine."

I didn't like to leave her here by herself in this mood. "I can stay for a while."

"Git." She made shooing motions. "My eager beaver assistant will be here in five minutes, so I need to start acting like I've been doing something."

"If you're sure . . ."

She said she was, so I slugged the rest of my coffee and stood. "You know, there's someone you could ask for ideas about the store. Mitchell."

An expression of shock crossed her face, which was quickly followed by horror, which was immediately wiped off and replaced by a tactful smile. "Thank you, Ms. Niswander. I'll take your suggestion into consideration and let you know."

For some reason, the roots of which were sure to say something horrible about my deepest character traits, that made me laugh. Which made Pam laugh.

Which made everything all right again.

* * *

I spent the morning doing what I needed to do to take care of our website woes, then at lunchtime fast-walked over to my aunt's house for another cooking lesson.

Half an hour later, we were peering at a sticky brown residue at the bottom of a saucepan that, not long before, had been about to be a nice wintertime lunch of clam chowder.

"I've never seen anything like this," Aunt Frances said. "You have a tremendous gift."

"For what, destroying anything I touch?" Morosely, I prodded the mess with the tip of a spoon. "Not sure that's much of a benefit to anyone."

"If you can't be the role model, be the cautionary tale."

I shifted from standing on my tippy toes to flat feet. "Trock could make a show out of me."

My beloved aunt snorted, then got a frighteningly thoughtful expression on her face. "You know, that's not a bad idea. You could—"

Me? On a television show? One that would do nothing but showcase my limitations and mistakes? No one would watch that, at least not more than once. I wasn't that interesting or that funny. And dealing with all the baggage that came with television work?

I shuddered. "Not a chance." I took the pot, scooped the icky glop into the wastebasket, and put the pot into the sink. I ran hot soapy water into it, then turned around to see that Aunt Frances was making us a backup lunch of grilled cheese, the plates to her left already prepped with side salads and small bowls of chocolate pudding.

The speed of it made my Spidey sense tingle. I dried my hands and asked suspiciously, "Did you have that prepped and ready to go because you assumed that I'd ruin the chowder?"

"You know what assuming does," she said casually, but her smirk was a dead giveaway.

"If it weren't for mean aunts, I wouldn't have any aunts at all," I muttered, but since my mean aunt was making me lunch and doing her best to teach me to cook, I didn't say it very loud.

I took care of the hard part of our lunch—filling two water glasses and adding ice without splashing water on anything at all—and we sat in the breakfast nook to eat.

"Best ever," I said after eating a bite.

"Flattery will get you nowhere, but thank you."

"Just trying to make sure you don't hate me after ruining another of your pots."

She glared at me. "You've ruined nothing. Our pots and pans are unruinable. They cost the earth, but in the long run, it's worth it. But now that we've established, beyond a shadow of a doubt, that you can't be trusted to cook anything because your brain keeps chasing whatever shiny thing pops into it, we need to rethink next steps."

My cell phone was on the table, face up in case the library needed me. "More restaurant takeout apps on my favorites list?"

"No," Aunt Frances said, in her best don't-argue-with-me tone. Even though she'd never been a mother, her years as a woodworking teacher had given her adjacent skills. "You're not giving up. We're not giving up. I will find something you can cook and cook well enough to serve to guests."

It was a lovely goal, but I wasn't sure it was achievable. Stick to your strengths, and my cooking strength began and ended with making coffee. But my aunt looked determined, and disappointing Aunt Frances was not anything I'd ever wanted to do.

"Thanks," I said, trying to sound sincere. "If anyone can teach me, it's you."

"Glad you recognize my abilities." Ignoring her salad, she scooped up a spoonful of pudding. "But I also have liabilities."

"Oh?" I cleaned the buttery residue from my fingers and picked up my salad fork. "Anything you're going to share with your niece?"

"I don't like to talk about the past," she said bluntly. "Especially the uncomfortable parts."

"Ah," I said. I'd known that for a long time, actually, but it was interesting that she was saying so. "Any particular reason you're telling me this now?"

She looked at her pudding cup, which was empty, though she didn't put it down. Instead, she held on to it so tightly that her knuckles whitened. "The GAC," she said quietly. "I hated all the fighting. Hated it then, hate it now. But there are things you should know."

I kept quiet, not wanting to interrupt her thoughts.

"The sheriff's office questioned Everett about Cheryl Webb's murder. More than once. And there's something else." Her words were stretched tight with tension. "Rick. Your father-in-law. They questioned him, too."

The world went still. Upright, open, transparent Rick? That couldn't be right.

"And they questioned him more than once, too," she went on miserably. "The gossip was awful, people speculating about affairs between Rick and Cheryl, Everett and Cheryl. Lois and I couldn't go anywhere without hearing the whispers. That's how we got to be such good friends—for a few months, everyone else was just too busy to do anything with either one of us." Her voice ached with the remembered pain.

I pushed away my freak-out thoughts about Rick, reached across the table, and took the pudding cup from her shaking hands. "It'll be okay," I said. "It *is* okay."

After a moment, she looked at me, tipping her head to one side. "You know, you're a good person to have around. Helpful, even."

I sat up straight. "Can I quote you?"

She smiled. "To anyone but Hal Inwood."

* * *

My aunt's exception made sense. Even though Hal had known Aunt Frances for years, and knew that she was as truthful as a bathroom scale, he would never take the testimony of a close relative as anything but biased.

As I walked back to the library along the quiet residential streets, I tried to evaluate my own biases. One of my professors in graduate school had emphasized the need for leaders to "Know thyself." She'd told us that over and over again, and the idea had always made me squirm with discomfort. It seemed like bragging to be hyperaware of the things I was good at and depressing to think too much about the many things that weren't my strong suit, and the zillion things that I couldn't do at all.

Years later, I was finally starting to understand her point. If you didn't know what you did well, how could you identify what you didn't do well? And if you didn't know the difference . . . well, that wasn't going to be good. Not for whoever you worked for, not for the people you worked with, and not for yourself.

I was pretty sure that one of the things I was good at doing was believing the best of people, assuming goodwill until proved differently. But if you took that inclination up a level, did I believe the best of people when I shouldn't? Especially if it was about people I liked? Did I need to be more suspicious of . . . everyone?

"Don't want to," I muttered to my feet. Today I was actually paying attention to where I was walking, because yesterday's above-freezing temperatures combined with last night's below-freezing temps and today hovering right at thirty-two degrees made for patchy ice designed for catching the unwary.

But if I was going to figure out what had happened to Gerald, I had to look at every possibility. And that list of possibilities now included my father-in-law.

I pictured Rick. He was who Rafe was destined to look like in another thirty years if he didn't eat too much pizza. Rick worked for a regional power company, starting as a lineman before Rafe was born, was soon promoted to crew foreman, then went up the ladder to where he was today, a vice president who made a lot of outreach presentations to local units of government. He and my mother-in-law, Lois, had never moved from the house where Rafe had grown up, and I doubted they ever would, not unless something horrific happened to their health, and I was happy to believe that would be true forever.

Rick was a good human being. Their next-door neighbors were in their late eighties, and he shoveled their driveway and took care of their trash. He tipped wait staff generously. He picked litter up off the sidewalk. How could someone like that be involved in murder?

"Doesn't matter," I told my boot uppers, who didn't seem to be listening. "I have to look at everyone."

And that included Mr. Goodwin as well.

I was so intent on my thoughts, and so intent on crossing the icy street without falling down, that I didn't hear the SUV until it was almost on top of me.

The vehicle's engine noise shocked me to red alert status. Without thinking, without planning, I hurtled myself forward, too fast for fear, all energy going into getting to safety. No time to worry, no time to do anything except move.

Whoosh!

The road-salt-covered SUV zoomed by, bare inches from the soles of my running feet.

Panting, I turned and watched it go past, wondering why on earth the driver hadn't seen me. Texting, even though it was against the law? Fiddling with the radio? Talking on the phone?

I got my breath back and thought about reporting the incident. But I could already hear the questions and my lame responses. Had I seen the license plate? Of course I hadn't. Had I noticed the make, model, and age of the vehicle? Of course not. I could barely remember what *I* drove.

Sighing, I made yet another vow to be more situationally aware. Today. And if not today, tomorrow for sure.

Thinking about talking to the police made me think about lawyers and courts, and I remembered something. Quickly, before the thought left my head, I pulled out my cell phone and called my attorney friend Leese Lacombe.

"Minnie!" her big voice boomed out.

"Leese!"

She laughed. "You're funny. And I was just thinking about you. Haven't seen you since you got back from the land of red double-decker buses. How was the trip?"

I gave her a quick overview of our fantastic honeymoon in London, then said, "I have an ulterior motive for calling."

"Never doubted it," she said promptly. "Whatever you want, not a problem."

I crossed my eyes in her general direction. Leese continued to think she owed me for helping to find her father's killer, and I continued to tell her to stop that. "Did I see

Sebastian driving Lloyd Goodwin around the other day? If so, when did your attorney services start including taxi rides?"

"Lacombe Law is a full-service firm. I thought you knew," she said, chuckling. "Yes, we're helping Mr. Goodwin with transportation, but it's a temporary thing. His beloved Buick died the middle of last month. We helped him order a new one, but it won't get here for a couple of weeks. Instead of him paying all that money to rent a car, Sebastian said he'd drive him wherever he needed. Of course, Bass said that before he knew about all those trips to Traverse City." She laughed again.

"Traverse?" I asked. "Hope it's not anything medical."

"No, no. Mr. Goodwin's been taking a Monday class at some music store down there since last summer. To learn how to play the banjo."

I passed on the intriguing image of Mr. Goodwin playing in a bluegrass band and focused on the important thing. "Monday. In the afternoon?"

"Nope. Morning. They leave at oh dark thirty to get there at eight forty-five. A ninety-minute lesson, then back to Chilson. Mr. Goodwin always buys Bass lunch on the way back. The other day I think it was Sam's Grace in Petoskey."

* * *

When I got home that night, I gave Eddie the news as I was changing into my lovely comfy leggings and oversized fleece sweatshirt. "Mr. Goodwin was gone all morning," I said. "He couldn't have killed Gerald."

Eddie, who sitting directly in my path of travel, yawned.

I stepped over him for the third time so I could get to my slippers. "Well, *you* may have known he was innocent, and I certainly wanted him to be, but I had to be sure. Due diligence. No stone unturned. The truth will out."

My feline friend yawned again and curled up, shrimp-like. I patted him on the head and headed downstairs.

Being sure that Mr. Goodwin had nothing to do with Gerald's death made my breathing easier. Or it did until I remembered that another of the people pulled in for questioning about Cheryl Webb's murder was my father-in-law.

Chapter Twelve

The next day was a bookmobile day, so after breakfast, I loaded Eddie into the car and started the drive up to the library. But as we went past the toy store, I saw that the lights were on. "Just a quick stop," I said. "You'll hardly notice I was gone."

Though I knew this to be true since I could hear his little kitty snores, I also wanted to salve my conscience if he woke up and was scared to be all by himself. Not that he understood human speech. Of course he didn't. Still, I felt I had to say something just in case something oozed into his sleepy brain.

The bells on the door clinked as I went inside, and Mitchell looked away from the front counter's computer. "Morning, Minnie. What's up?"

"Bianca back from her conference?"

"Today." He beamed. "Can't wait. We haven't been apart this long since we got married. I tell you, it's no fun being all by myself anymore, now that I'm used to being part of a pair."

I thought about that. Some couples spent a lot of time apart and didn't seem the worse for wear. A college friend of mine and his wife had lived on opposite sides of the country for three years and managed to make it work, but I also knew people who would drive twelve hours in one day—six hours down and six hours back—to downstate meetings so they didn't have to sleep apart. Though Rafe and I hadn't yet had to face that particular issue, I was pretty sure we would land more toward the second category than the first.

"Any chance you've had time to think about a birthday present for Rafe?"

He grinned, pulled a spiral bound notebook from under the counter and flourished it. "This here is my book of gift ideas. Some of these are generic—six-year-old who likes video games, eleven-year-old into volcanoes, like that. But back here"—he flipped to the back pages, then turned them one by one—"are the specific pages, and now there's one with Rafe's name at the top."

I leaned on the counter. "Lay it on me."

"Hockey bingo." At my look of query, he explained. "It's a bingo game, but instead of someone calling out letters, the squares are things that happen on the ice. Backhand goal. Ten minute major. Like that."

"Hmm." It sounded fun, but there were minuses, the primary one being that Rafe would pay even more attention to hockey. "What else?"

"A tabletop pinball game that you build yourself. That one's pricey, but it's really cool." When I hesitated, he nodded and went back to the list. His other ideas included glasses with maps of Chilson etched into them, a weighted relaxation robe, and a fancy charging station for his electronics. All decent ideas, but none of them seemed worthy of being the first birthday present of our marriage.

"Thanks," I said. "These are great ideas. I appreciate your time, I really do."

Mitchell must have caught my half-heartedness. "I'll keep thinking," he said, shutting the notebook. "If I come up with something else, I'll let you know. Gifts can be tough," he said, rubbing his face and making a raspy noise on his day-old stubble.

"Lots of things are tough." I smiled, then sighed. "Like a personal strategic plan."

"That's what got me here." Mitchell looked around the bright, cheerful store. "When I started seeing Bianca, I knew I needed to do something different. Figured this was the perfect place for me, so I made a plan to get here. And I'm talking to the owner about buying it, when the time comes."

Classic slacker Mitchell had become a man with a plan. The world was upside down. I thanked him again for his gift ideas and started to leave. But then, suddenly remembering who had a passel of grandchildren and so were likely to be frequent visitors to the toy store, I stopped. "Do you know Lisa and Mort Neely?"

"Sure." Mitchell nodded. "They come in here a lot. One of their granddaughters is a big fan of those dinosaur models. Plus Mort's a friend of my dad's."

Six degrees of separation had nothing on small towns. "I found out the other day that Lisa is Mort's second wife. Did you know that?"

"Well, yeah." He shrugged. "Everybody does."

Maybe everybody who'd lived in Chilson all their life. "Do you know who his first wife was?"

And it turned out that he did.

* * *

"Can you believe it?" I asked Julia as she buckled herself into the bookmobile's passenger seat. "Sondra Luth was Mort Neely's first wife."

My strawberry blond coworker went still. "Is that Sondra Larsen?"

I nodded, because I'd taken a look on Sondra's Facebook page, which was titled "Sondra Larsen Luth." Nothing about being a Neely, because why list the last name of a guy you'd divorced decades ago?

"She's been on the library board forever," I said. "Her name's on the plaque in the lobby as being on the board when they started the capital campaign to raise funds for the renovation." Local donations had paid for almost half the cost, and the millage had carried it past the finish line.

"I graduated high school with her," Julia said, then tapped the top of cat carrier with her toes. "The girl could sing. Three octaves of silky warmth."

I glanced over as I started the engine. "Sounds like a quote."

"What the newspaper said after the first night of the school musical our senior year. They staged *Brigadoon* that year, just for Sondra."

It was no secret that Julia couldn't carry a tune in a bucket, even if Barbra Streisand handed the bucket to her personally. Though she usually didn't seem to care about that lack, I'd heard regret in her voice. "Yet you were the one who ended up winning Tony Awards," I said.

"That is true." Julia grinned. "And now I get to ride the bookmobile and she has to sit through boring board meetings. I got the better end of the deal, didn't I, Sir Edward?"

"Mrr" was the sleepy response.

It was that kind of day. Low, dense cloud cover carrying with it a threat of snow that could turn to freezing rain at any minute. It was days like this that drove people to purchase standby tickets to the closest location with a weather forecast of more than a half hour of sunshine.

I didn't know if it was the weather or the contagiousness of Eddie's snores, but almost everybody on the bookmobile that day seemed half asleep, even the eternally chipper and sprightly Mr. Zonne.

"My apologies," he said, yawning for the third time as I checked out the books he was borrowing; *The Art Thief* by Michael Finkel, *Wintering* by Katherine May, and *The Lincoln Highway* by Amor Towles. "'Tis not the fault of your company, dear ladies and gentleman cat. 'Tis the winter doldrums."

"Sir, oh, sir, is there any cure?" Julia clasped her hands and opened her eyes wide, and I could easily see the starry-eyed ingenue she'd once been.

The octogenarian laughed. "Time is the only true cure, but good company and good stories are excellent antidotes. And the story I'd like to hear from Ms. Minnie is the Tale of the Library Website."

"Ongoing," I said, smiling through the mental pain, and as I told him the dreary saga, I got an idea for how I could talk to Sondra Luth about her first husband.

The rest of the morning and half the afternoon, I took the opportunity of any quiet bookmobile time and called library board members, telling them about the additional security measures Josh and Erik had put in place, about the revised timeline for the new website, and about the positive feedback we were getting from the multiple press releases and social media posts. I had to leave one voicemail but got through to all the others.

"It's an unfortunate episode," I told Sondra, the last board member I called. "But because of it, our online presence will be more secure than it has ever been."

"Always a silver lining," she said. "To tell you the truth, though, I wasn't all that bothered by the negativity. Some people are just like that."

And just like that, she'd given me the perfect opening. "One of the really negative people was Mort Neely. I, um, I just found out that you used to be . . . um . . ."

"Married to him?" She made a rude noise in the back of her throat. "Worst three years of my life. Don't know what I was thinking. Young and stupid, I guess. On the plus side," she said, more cheerfully, "being married to someone who lied and cheated made it far easier for me to appreciate a good man."

Lied and cheated? I took a breath for bravery. "He cheated on you?"

"For sure one time," she said, "but probably more. I mean, if he could do it once, what's to keep him from doing it over and over?"

Before I could ask another probing personal question, she kept going.

"It was so long ago," she said musingly. "My husband and I ran into Lisa and Mort last summer, and I felt nothing. The best revenge of all, really. The anger I had the day I found out about him and his girlfriend, well, just consumed me. I remember it clear as anything—May of 1992, the Saturday before Memorial Weekend—but it's like it happened to someone else. We were divorced by the end of the year, and I met Danny the next spring, so all's well that ends well!"

I thanked her for her time and told her to call me if she had any questions about the library website, or anything else.

When I thumbed off the phone, Julia was in the back, talking to a young mother who had one toddler by the hand and a sleeping baby in her arms.

I looked at Eddie, who was sitting in his current favorite spot, the interior of the cabinet into which the front computer tablet nestled when we were on the road.

"She divorced him because he cheated on her," I said. "Two years after Cheryl's death."

"Mrr."

"Right. Lots of questions. Was 1992 the first time he had an affair? Did he have one with Cheryl? Could that have led to her murder?"

"Mrr!"

I frantically patted the air with my hands. "Shh! Don't wake the baby!"

"Mrr," he said softly.

"Thanks, bud," I said as I scratched the back of his head, because sometimes it really did seem as if he understood what I was saying.

* * *

I spent that night cleaning bathrooms while catching up with one of my of favorite podcasts, *Everything Everywhere Daily*. I liked it partly because of the amazing variety of topics—history, science, people from all walks of life, and math that I mostly understood—but also because they rarely lasted longer than fifteen minutes. Just long enough to whet my appetite to learn more about something that tweaked my interest, but not long enough to get bored if the math was too much for me.

It was during an episode titled "The Lost Legion," about the Roman Ninth Spanish Legion, that I started to see similarities between the events of two thousand years ago in what is now Yorkshire and what happened in Chilson in 1990.

"Not super similar similarities," I said to Eddie, who was following me around and visually criticizing everything I did, "but there are some things. It was a long time ago, and no one knows for sure what happened."

Eddie looked at me as if I wasn't there.

"If I'm that uninteresting, why are you following me around?"

"Mrr," he said, and stalked off, his tail as straight as a flagpole.

I ignored his ignoring of me, went back to my comparison, and revised. Whoever killed Cheryl knew exactly what happened. Not that I was trying to figure that out, but there was still a strong possibility that Cheryl's and Gerald's deaths were connected. I needed to learn more about the 1990 murder investigation, but how? No one at the sheriff's office was going to give me any details, so—

Something in my brain went *click*, and I knew exactly what I needed to do.

Doing it, however, might be a bit of a trick, so I spent the night in a sleep so fitful that in the morning I apologized to both Rafe and Eddie.

"Huh," the love of my life said. "Didn't notice."

"Mrr," my furry pal said, in the same tone that Rafe had used.

While it was nice to know I hadn't bothered either of them, it was a bit curious that I could toss and turn all night and not have any impact on the males in my life. But I decided not to think about that too much and gave Rafe a hearty kiss on his way out the door.

As soon as his truck backed out of the driveway, I pulled out my cell phone and texted Ash.

Me: *Any idea what Don Devereaux is doing these days?*

Ash (after a brief pause): *Playing golf.*

Me (after looking out at the white landscape): *Today?*

Ash: *Spring, summer, and fall. If today is Friday, he's having breakfast at the diner in Dooley. Why?*

Me: *Thanks. See ya!*

Don Devereaux was retired from being a detective with the Tonedagana Sheriff's Office. If I was right about two things—his age and that he'd been working for the sheriff's office since he started in law enforcement—he would have been a deputy in 1990.

I thought it through.

Was it worth driving over to Dooley? What if he didn't remember me? What if he did but didn't want to talk to me?

What if he was willing to talk to me but didn't remember anything about the 1990 investigation? What if he remembered but didn't want to talk to me about it?

"Stop it," I said out loud. The worst that could happen was a dollop of Minnie embarrassment, and that wouldn't hurt me. Not long term, anyway. And if I could learn something—anything—it would be embarrassment well earned.

So half an hour later, when I opened the door to the Dooley Diner to the *tink* of silverware and the chattering of many voices, I was ready for everyone in the restaurant to turn and stare at the interloper. Or for everyone to ignore me. What I got was a bright smile from the twentysomething man with a tidy beard and round glasses who greeted me.

"Good morning," he said, smiling. "Have you been here before?"

"Um." I looked around at the bright white walls, the brightly patterned carpet, the framed tiled mosaics on the walls. "I thought I had, but . . ."

He laughed. "New owners last year. They're also the chefs, and they're on premises now."

"Oh. Um, I was mostly hoping for a cup of coffee."

"Not a problem. Would you like a table, or a seat at the bar?" He gestured at a long expanse of glass and chrome.

Though the bar was so sleek it was intimidating, it also had high stools and would have the best vantage point to view the room's other occupants, of which there were more than I'd anticipated on a March morning. I'd just finished hitching myself up onto a stool when I heard a drawling voice say, "Well, well, well. If it isn't Miss Minnie Hamilton. What are you doing out here?"

I spun around to look at Don Devereaux, but the man in front of me bore only a passing resemblance to the man I'd last seen a few years ago, when he'd been sixty-ish, almost as wide around as he was tall, and tired to the bone. The man in front of me had shed dozens of pounds and looked positively healthy. The biggest change, though, was that he looked relaxed. Carefree, even.

"Looking for you," I said. "And I got married. It's Minnie Niswander, now."

His bushy eyebrows went up, and he sat down next to me. "That Rafe finally tied you down, eh? Figured that might happen. What can I do for you?" He signaled to the bearded guy for a cup of coffee. "If it's about Woody, I can't help you. He's never going to change."

I laughed. Far as I knew, Don was the only person who'd ever called Hal Inwood by that nickname. "Gave that up a long time ago," I said. "But I'm not sure Tabitha has."

"Fact." He nodded, adding more sugar to his coffee than his dentist would have liked. "So what's up?"

"Did you hear that Gerald Arnhold died?"

"Yeah. Sad. He was a good guy. Rotten that he got caught up in that airport mess all those years ago."

"That's what I wanted to talk to you about."

More eyebrow action. "The GAC?"

"Cheryl Webb."

His comfortable demeanor vanished. He leaned slightly away from me and stared at his coffee. "Minnie, I really don't—"

"All I want to know," I said as persuasively as I could, "are the names of the people who were questioned more than once about Cheryl's murder. See, I think there's a connection between her death and Gerald's, and if I can get just a little information about what happened back then, I can look and see if there are any dots to connect."

He slid me a look. "It's an active investigation. You should be asking Woody. Or Ash Wolverson."

I wasn't about to tell him that I had, and that they wouldn't tell me a thing. "I already know that Everett Pixley and Rick Niswander were brought in more than once. What I don't know is whether or not there were others."

Don gave a *humph* sort of noise. "Oh, there were more."

And, after a long minute, he told me their names.

Chapter Thirteen

I drove to the library, trying not to freak out about the names Don Devereaux had given me, and totally failing, because it was a basically a list of the people in Chilson I cared about.

"Gerald Arnhold, Rick, and Uncle Everett," I said. Since I'd already known about them, they hadn't been a surprise, but I had been surprised at my visceral reaction to hearing my father-in-law cited as a person of interest. I blew out a breath and moved on to the next name Don had given me.

"Lloyd Goodwin." Also not a surprise. His involvement with the supporters of the airport expansion and his parting of the ways with Cheryl had to have made him a prime suspect.

"Mort Neely." Still another that wasn't a surprise. Just because he was a philanderer didn't mean he was a murderer, but the knowledge that he'd cheated on Sondra didn't endear him to me. And if you did one bad thing, did that make it easier to do more bad things? My mind wanted to play with that idea, but I forced it to move on to the first of the four surprising names.

"Max Compton." I was having a hard time believing that Max and Cheryl, both employees of the Road Commission back in the day, could have had an argument that escalated into Max committing murder. Of course, I'd also had a hard time picturing him lining up for public comment at meeting after meeting, or knocking on doors to talk to people about the benefits of a bigger airport. Though time did tend to mellow people, I'd always considered Max's personality traits as set in stone; that he was the same person now that he'd been when he was five years old.

I said the next name with a sigh. "Duffy Ulrich." Duffy was high energy, full of ideas, perpetually positive, and the best Friends of the Library president I'd ever worked with, and I was having a very hard time picturing her sitting in the sheriff's office interview room.

"Jim Kittle." Now there was a name that made sense. Jim could be difficult. Every book we recommended was either too long, too short, had dialogue that was too flat, had dialogue that didn't make sense, had too many descriptions, or had too few descriptions. Sometimes it had all of those.

Then there were the last two names. "Sabrina." It was well known that the Round Table's forever waitress had a temper. If she had a temper now, at age sixty, what had it been like thirty-some years ago? I didn't want to think of her as a killer—she brought me extra cream for my coffee without me having to ask—but the possibility had to be considered.

And finally, "Linda Kopecky." Linda Driscoll, before she'd married. Linda was another library board member, which was sort of weird, but sort of not. Chilson was a small town, and that kind of weirdness was something I'd become accustomed to.

I pulled in a deep breath. A deep, calming breath. It helped a teensy bit, so I took a few more.

"Okay," I murmured. Because there were all sorts of people I loved and cared about who *weren't* on the list. Eddie's vet. Cade and Barb McCade. Aunt Frances. The people at the marina where I'd moored my little houseboat. Cookie Tom. The library staff. There were way more people *not* on the list than were on it, and I needed to keep that in mind.

What I didn't have in mind was how some of Don's list connected with Cheryl Webb. I also wasn't sure how to find out, and maybe it didn't matter, because it was Gerald's death I was trying to figure out. Still, it didn't hurt to try.

And since Linda was the board member I'd had to leave a voicemail message for the previous day, she was the perfect place to start.

"Minnie! It was nice of you to leave me a message yesterday," she said in her high-pitched voice when I called her from my office, "but you didn't need to. People will forget about this by next week, if they haven't already."

Linda was a designer for one of the bigger landscaping firms in the region. She never had a bad word for anyone, and thanks to her deep dislike of exercise, she had the muscle tone of a soft pillow. The idea of her killing someone was absurd. And—I did some quick math in my head—she couldn't have been more than fifteen years old when Cheryl died.

"I have a question," I said. "If you have a minute."

"Fire away."

"The last week or two, I've been learning about the Great Airport Controversy. I'd never heard anyone talk about it before." The silence at the other end of the phone tweaked my internal radar. I waited, heard nothing, then went on. "And I heard that a young woman working with the airport expansion group was murdered. Do you remember that?"

More silence.

"Linda? Are you still there?"

A heavy sigh blew into and through the phone. "Yup. Still here. It was such a long time ago. Everyone has tried so hard to forget it, but it doesn't go away, does it? It just lies there, buried, waiting for us in our dreams."

It was a creepy image. "You were pretty young, weren't you?"

"Just turned fifteen," she said. "I was working with Cheryl that summer. At the old fudge shop downtown."

"What was she like?" I asked quietly.

"Honestly? I thought she was . . . well, she was a queen bee, if you know what I mean, and she wanted everyone to know it. She was pretty and smart enough, but so sure of herself it was obnoxious."

Well, that was interesting. But Linda wasn't done.

"She was a hard worker, though, I'll give her that. She was working every part-time job she could to make enough money to get out of Chilson and into the real world."

Like Julia, I thought. But Julia didn't give out a single queen bee vibe.

"The week before she was killed," Linda said musingly, "she picked a fight with me. I don't remember what it was about, just that I went home in tears." She gave a brittle laugh. "Cheryl fights with me, and I have to talk to the police about it after she gets killed. I was terrified. Couldn't sleep for a week, afraid that they were going to arrest me for . . . well, I didn't know what, but that doesn't matter when you're scared."

I agreed, then, not wanting to leave her with such a bad memory, shifted the conversation to the library's strategic plan, and what she thought we should do to help meet the outreach goals.

When we disconnected, I thought about the conversation.

Everything I'd learned about Cheryl led me to believe that she hadn't been a particularly nice person. She'd been a manipulator. Selfish. Driven.

But did that have anything to do with her death? With Gerald's death?

I had absolutely no idea.

* * *

"What's that?" Rafe peered at the pile of papers I'd stacked on the corner of his dresser.

It was a small pile. Not big at all. Less than twenty-five pages. Maybe less than twenty. Okay, not less than twenty, but not much more than that.

"Samples," I said.

"Of what?"

If he read the title of the top paper, he'd know, because it said in bold 16-point Calibri font what it was. This likely meant that he already knew what the papers were and was working on some avoidance behavior because he'd already told me he didn't want to do this. Though it wasn't fair of me to keep pressing, I also thought this was important.

"Personal strategic plans. They're simple," I said quickly. "Most are only a page or two." Except for the one I really liked, which was five pages, but I'd put it at the back.

"Minnie . . ." His voice disappeared as he pulled on his favorite Friday-night-out-in-winter pullover, a smooth dark-green fleece that zipped at the neck and had the letters of his alma mater on the left side: MSU. His voice came back as his head reappeared. "I don't see the point of doing this."

"Just take a look," I said. "Please. After that, if you want nothing to do with it, I'll toss the papers into the recycling and never mention it again."

He eyed me, then turned to Eddie. "'Never mention it again,' she said. You heard it, pal, right?"

"Mrr."

The men in my life were ganging up on me. Nice. I pulled out my one big gun. "Mitchell Koyne has a strategic plan."

I'd guessed that Rafe would be one of three things when he heard about Mitchell: impressed, moved by peer pressure, or completely disbelieving. What I didn't expect, but in retrospect should have, was what he actually did.

He laughed.

Hard enough to trigger stomach cramps.

When the spasms stopped, he managed to wheeze out a few words. "Proof . . . that miracles are . . . a real thing."

"Unkind," I murmured, but I knew what he meant. You never really expected people to change. Mitchell had. Then again, had he? Maybe the manager and hopeful owner of the toy store had been inside all along. Maybe all he'd needed was someone to believe in him, and Bianca had triggered his emergence from the cocoon.

As Rafe and I walked, hand in hand, to the restaurant where we were meeting Aunt Frances and Otto, I posed the question, "Can people really change? Or is it more an evolution of possibilities?"

My beloved slid me a wary glance. "Is this a pointed question or more a philosophical one?"

We walked in the door of Hoppe's Brewing and I said, "Started as pointed when you were laughing about poor Mitchell, but then it became more a general philosophical thought."

My aunt and Otto were seated at the end of the long bar, and at my last words, Otto's expression went instantly from affable courtesy to intent curiosity.

"You have a philosophical question?" he asked, rubbing his hands. "Pose away, Minnie. I haven't had a good conundrum in ages."

"Give him a puzzle, Minnie," Aunt Frances said fondly. "It's only the first week of March, and he's already getting cabin fever. He needs a distraction."

A twentysomething led us to Rafe's favorite table—the only one that was equidistant from the dart board, the pool table, bar, and the restrooms—and I said, "It's not much of a question. And I'm not sure it can even be answered."

"Perfect," my aunt said almost gleefully. "Something like that will keep his brain busy for weeks."

Otto held out a chair for Aunt Frances and kissed the top of her head as she sat down. "Kind of you to be concerned about my mental well-being."

"In my best interest," she said, nodding. "Ask away, Minnie."

Though by this time I'd already lost interest in the question. "It's nothing new," I said. "Just that when people change, is it a true change, or is it just a development of something that was there all along and came to the surface because of circumstances?"

"Example?" Otto asked.

Lucky for me, our waiter showed up at that point to run through the specials and to take any drink orders. By the time she left, I'd come up with a way to tell the story without naming names. "Say you're born with a fair amount of brains, but you're raised in an environment that mistrusts education and doesn't value any kind of learning. Though you have lots of potential, you don't do anything with it until something happens in your life that kind of wakes you up."

My aunt squinted at me. "Are you talking about Mitchell Koyne?"

"Who else?" Rafe accepted a foamy pint from our waiter.

I ignored them and focused on Otto. "Is that a person changing, or is it potential realized?"

"Hmm." He considered the question for a long moment. "I think," he said thoughtfully, "that they're the same thing.

There can be no change without potential, and no potential without the capacity to change." He laughed when he noted my face. "And you're not happy with that answer."

I unsquished my face. "Guess not." I weighed what he'd said against the deep wisdom I'd been hoping to hear, and said slowly, "But I think you're right."

By this time, our food had been ordered, and Otto and Rafe were conferring on their choices for a second beverage.

"What was that about?" Aunt Frances asked. "Not like you to go all existential."

I shook my head. "Nothing, really."

"Must be about something," she said.

"Well . . ."

My aunt smiled. "You can trust your Aunt Frances, you know. She won't tell a soul, even if it's something that's deeply embarrassing to you."

"Not embarrassing, just . . ."

"Liven up my evening, favorite niece."

"It's the GAC," I blurted out. "And I know you don't want to talk about it, but I just have this feeling that Gerald's death is connected to it, and maybe to Cheryl Webb's murder."

"Oh." My aunt's face closed up. "That."

"It's just . . . there were all those suspects. Or, if not suspects, so many people that the sheriff's office talked to more than once, which had to make them feel like suspects, even if they weren't."

My aunt firmed her lips and made a grunting sort of sound, one that indicated acceptance, if not agreement.

I took that as a sign to continue. "What seems weird is they had nothing in common, except for being questioned. Take their ages."

Then I hesitated, not wanting to say their names out loud. Don hadn't told me to keep this information to myself, but I didn't want to bandy these names about a very public place. I'd done some mild Internet stalking during lunch and found that, back then, in addition to Linda Kopecky, née Driscoll, being fifteen years old, Jim Kittle had been twenty-two. Sabrina had been twenty-three, Duffy was twenty-seven, my father-in-law twenty-eight. Uncle Everett had been thirty, Mort Neely thirty-two, Mr. Goodwin forty-two, and Max had been fifty-one.

"Their ages," I said finally, "ranged from fifteen to fifty-one. And so many different occupations and income levels. It seems odd that they were so varied. Other than being asked about Cheryl's death, did they have anything in common?"

Aunt Frances looked at me, but I got the distinct impression she didn't see me at all. "I didn't know then," she said in a tight voice, "and I don't know now."

I started to ask another question but let it die unasked. My aunt didn't want to talk about this, and I loved her enough to let it go.

At least for now.

Chapter Fourteen

In spite of the fact that we'd had a restaurant dinner the night before, Rafe and I decided to go to the Round Table for Saturday breakfast.

"You have to work at the library most of the day," he said by way of justification. "And I promised Bob that I'd help him replace a sink and a toilet, which is a three-trips-to-the-hardware-store kind of job, so I'll probably be gone most of the day, too."

I bought into his theory straight away. "We don't want to overextend ourselves. Cooking breakfast at home might push us—well, you—to the edge, and risking that sounds like a horrible idea."

"Good thing we married each other." He grinned, which made my heart go a little mushy.

"See you soon," I called to Eddie as I shut the back door. Though I might have imagined a sulky "Mrr" in response, I was fairly sure I hadn't. There was precedent. Lots of it.

As Rafe and I slid into our preferred booth, I looked around and said, "This is exactly what I'm talking about."

Since we'd barely said a word on the short ride to the restaurant other than commenting about the thickness of the cloud cover, it shouldn't have been surprising that my husband—and I was still getting used to saying that word—gave me a puzzled look. "What did I miss?" he asked.

"Nothing." I turned our coffee mugs over so Carol, the diner's other forever waitress, could fill them. Not long ago, Sabrina had made it clear to Cookie, owner and chef, that she was too old to work on the weekends, and that every other Friday off would go a long way toward employee retention.

Cookie was overly aware that Sabrina's marriage to Bill D'Arcy made any employment for her an option, not a need. Bill was one of those people who spent his days glued to a computer screen making pots of money in mysterious ways. He spent many of those days in the back corner booth of the Round Table, and the only fly in their marriage ointment was his macular degeneration. Happily, the rate of deterioration had slowed to a practical stop, but their lives centered around Bill's treatments in Traverse City, and sometimes all the way down in Grand Rapids.

"It's just . . ." I waved vaguely at the room, which I was pretty sure hadn't changed in any significant way since 1973. "We've been married for less than six months, and we're already in a rut. Friday night dinner at Hoppe's. Saturday morning breakfast at the Round Table. We're doing the same things over and over again."

"You went to Dooley yesterday," he reminded me. "That was different."

It had been, but not all that much. Was this the way my life was going to be? Nothing but a series of restaurant conversations? Sure, Don had given me some names, and I'd gained a deeper understanding of how much Aunt Frances did not want to talk about the events of 1990, but restaurants weren't the only places to learn things.

"I need to get out more," I said.

Rafe nodded. "Yeah, it's that time of year. Things will be better in a month."

We turned to look through the window and saw that, since we'd sat down, it had started to snow in big fat flakes, the kind that took accumulation seriously. Here in the Up North, early March was not anything close to spring. The few days above freezing had started the thawing process, but this snow and cold would resolidify everything.

"A month," he repeated, then amended it. "Six weeks, tops."

Carol returned and, unlike Sabrina, she listened to our order and wrote it down verbatim. While we ate, Rafe and I discussed our plans for the rest of our weekend, and as soon as his plate was empty, Rafe tidily put his silverware on his plate. "I'll settle up at the counter." He stood and pulled on his coat. "Gotta get started on that first trip to the hardware store. See you later, gator." He kissed the top of my head and was gone.

With my fork, I chased the last few strands of hash browns around my plate but gave it up as a lost cause. They were cold now, anyway.

I stacked our plates and silverware, pushed them to the aisle edge of the table, and reached for my coffee mug, head down and thinking about food and cooking and methods of learning, when someone sat heavily in the spot Rafe had just vacated.

Startled, I looked up. "Oh," I said, recognizing one of the elderly men from the big back table. Had it only been last week that I'd talked to them? "Morning, Earl."

"Ms. Niswander." He nodded at the approaching Carol. "Bring my mug over, will you, kiddo? Thanks." We sat in a comfortable silence as the caffeine was delivered.

After a couple of rejuvenating sips, he looked at me with his bright blue eyes. "I hear you've been talking to Donnie Devereaux."

My insides gave a sharp clutch, as if I'd been hauled into the principal's office. Then I remembered that I was a legal adult. A married legal adult. One with a real job, real responsibilities, and a real cat. Well, sort of real.

I gave him a steady look. "That's right."

"He tell you about Sabrina?"

"Only that the sheriff's office interviewed her."

"Huh." Earl brought his mug halfway to his mouth, stopped, put it down, added two packs of sugar, and picked it up again. "Cheryl worked here that summer. 1990."

My mouth opened. Shut. Sabrina had told me that, but I'd forgotten. Completely.

Earl took a sip of his coffee. "Yup. Sabrina started here right after high school, so even then she had seniority. Cheryl didn't like that one bit. Took a mile if she was given an inch, if you know what I mean."

He stopped. I nodded my understanding, and he continued.

"So you can imagine those two working together. Cats and dogs got nothing on them. One Saturday—lunch it was, middle of July—they had a shouting match right there."

He pointed at the floor ten feet away. "Cheryl pulled off her apron and flung it at Sabrina, saying Sabrina couldn't fire her because she quit."

"What did Sabrina do?" I asked, oddly fascinated at this peek into the past.

Earl chuckled. "Picked up the apron, tossed it in the trash, and started covering all of their tables. Did a fine job of it, but you could tell she was steaming mad. Red-faced and brittle, you see?"

I did see. And I could see the shade of yesterday's volatile Sabrina echoing in today's more mellow version. But there were two big pulsing questions.

Had that very public argument led to Cheryl's murder? And did that have anything to do with Gerald's death?

* * *

Earl had a lot more to say—about the 1990 Tonedagana County Board of Commissioners' decision to renovate the historic courthouse, about how 1990 was when the Road Commission finally paved Buchanan Street, about the 1990 seasons of the Detroit Lions, Tigers, and Red Wings, about the water quality of Janay Lake that year—but none of it felt connected to the airport, Cheryl, or Gerald.

When he started talking about the 1990 college football season, I edged in a thank-you for his information and his time, said I had to get to the library, and slid away, trying to flee while trying to not look like I was fleeing. Though Earl was a deep well of information, there were things I didn't need to know.

Thanks to Earl's penchant for talking, and my reluctance to cut him short, I arrived at the library late. Well, late for me, which meant that I wouldn't be the first one in and wouldn't be the first one into the kitchen.

I shed my coat and mittens in my office, did a quick check of my email, and when I breezed back into the kitchen, mug in hand, the heavenly scent of coffee was wafting its merry way around the room. Kelsey Lyons, one of our part-time clerks, was doing the precarious act of pouring coffee from the pot into her mug while the coffee from above was still dripping. It was an act of great skill and courage, and while I had succeeded more than once, I didn't feel that the gain was worth the inherent fear factor, which surely took years off my life.

"Hey, Minnie." Kelsey put the pot back down with a clunk. I was sure it was heavier when she brewed the coffee, because she added double the grounds that anyone else did.

"Morning." I added half a cup of tap water to my mug and put it in the microwave. "So I just got an email from Erik, the website designer. They got control of their servers again, so they don't have to pay the ransom. He's uploading our new website as we speak." I'd already emailed the library board, Graydon, and Josh the happy news, and I could feel my worldview needle shifting a bit toward the happy side.

"It should never have happened."

She sounded almost . . . snippy. Surprising, because I would have voted the always calm Kelsey as the library staffer least likely to get upset about anything. "Sorry?" The microwave beeped; I removed my boiling-hot water and filled my mug with Kelsey coffee.

"I know it's on me that the hijacked site was spread all over," she said, "and I'm so sorry about that, I really am, but that website design company shouldn't have let it be hijacked in the first place. That Erik should be fired, and are we looking at suing them? Dereliction of duty, or something?"

Josh, who I suddenly remembered was working today because he was taking a day off next week for Mia to have the first baby ultrasound, had entered the room partway through Kelsey's monologue and now barged into the conversation.

"Don't be stupid," he said.

"Josh," I murmured.

"Well, it is stupid. There's no system on earth that is one hundred percent safe, because the worst attacks come from inside. Who can protect against that? No one."

The two started bickering back and forth, and I made the time-out signal with my hands. "Erik has the site back, and our new website will be up in a couple of days. That's good news. Why do we need to dwell on the bad?"

Kelsey and Josh glared at me. In unison.

"Because," Josh said in his annoyingly patient voice, "people need to understand how this stuff works."

"Because we have to keep it from happening again," Kelsey said in a "duh" tone of voice.

"Points taken." I nodded. "I'll makes notes, put them in a file titled 'New Website,' and with any luck I'll remember to pull them out the next time we do a website revamp."

"Good idea," Kelsey said. "That should help."

Though Josh rolled his eyes, he didn't say anything.

I toasted them with my mug and headed back to my office, patting myself on the back for defusing the situation in a calm and professional manner. But when I was halfway down the hall, I heard their voices rise again.

"So much for Minnie's management skills," I said, sighing, and left them to their own devices.

* * *

One benefit of working on Saturday was the comparative lack of distractions, and the morning zoomed past as I prepared the agenda packet for the next board meeting.

It was a task I'd often helped Graydon with, but this was the first time I'd done it all by myself. I read and reread the memos, checked and double-checked the attachments, and emailed it to the board with only the faintest whisper of fear that I'd done something horribly wrong.

"It'll be fine," I said to myself, and repeated those three little words over and over as I ate my lunch of leftover macaroni and cheese from last night's dinner.

And then, since my morning had been so productive—yay, Minnie!—I was free to spend all afternoon doing one of my favorite things: staffing the reference desk. I loved the variety of questions that people brought me, and I loved learning from those questions, and most of all I loved helping people find answers.

Late winter Saturdays were a prime time for questions from many types of library patrons: kids working on school projects, senior citizens planning their next vacation, but mostly people of all ages looking for a distraction from their cabin fever.

I fielded questions about what website had the best gardening tips, what you might have to deal with if you traveled to Machu Picchu, what book to read to a seven-year-old that might get them hooked on reading forever, and the perennial favorite of how to start a business.

But come late afternoon, there was a distinct lull in the action. The only patrons in the entire main room were a high school boy and an elderly woman. The teenager was working on what he'd earnestly told me was his first novel and did I think I might have time to read it when he was done and give him some advice? The snow-haired woman was sitting deep into one of the upholstered chairs on the outside of the room and, given the odd breathing noises that were emanating from the region, I suspected that she was sound asleep and snoring.

It was that kind of day, and I felt my own eyes starting to droop. The third time I jerked myself out of doing head bobs, I pushed myself back from the reference desk, stood, and aimed myself toward the kitchen to get another watered-down cup of Kelsey coffee.

Halfway there, as I crossed the lobby, the front doors opened and Colleen Henika came in. Colleen was about sixty and a good friend of Pam Fazio's. She worked as a dental hygienist, was a recent widow, and had recently handed over management of her deceased husband's downtown destination of a candy store to a young couple with the eventual intention of letting them buy the store. Her black hair had more gray than when I'd last seen her, but the aura of heavy grief that she'd carried for so many months after her husband's death was gone.

"You're looking good," I said, nodding hello.

"Really?" She smiled. "And here I thought the grandkids were taking years off my life."

"If anything, I'd say the opposite."

She laughed and started to move on, but I stopped her. "Do you have a minute?" Yesterday's chat with Don, last night's dinner, and today's organization and reference desking had been tumbling together in my head and had just coalesced into a plan that was so banal it almost wasn't a plan at all.

"Of course. Here?" She looked around the lobby, with its echoing tile floor.

I led her to my office, eased the door almost shut, and leaned against my desk. "Did you know Gerald Arnhold?" I asked, gesturing to my spare chair.

She sat, pursing her lips. "Name's familiar. No, wait. Is he the one who died a couple of weeks ago? Some fishing accident."

"And he was the airport manager during the 1990 airport expansion." This was what I needed to do; talk to everyone I could think of who was an adult in Chilson at the time of the GAC. I'd done some of that already, but I needed to focus on learning more about the people on Don's list. In a clever but kindly manner, naturally.

"Oof. That was a long time ago." She smiled wryly, then a curious look came across her face. "Minnie, don't tell me you're the one who found that poor man."

"More or less." I gave a one-sided shrug. "Gerald's a housebound stop for the bookmobile. Julia Beaton and I noticed something was wrong and called nine-one-one."

Colleen smiled again, but this one had a distinctly sad cast. "You have a knack for finding trouble, don't you?" Since I didn't know what to say to that, I didn't say anything, and

Colleen continued. "But I can see why you're curious about the GAC. And you must have heard about Cheryl Webb by now? Yes, of course you have."

I'd done some research, dipping into Chilson High School yearbooks. The library hadn't had a full set, but after I'd noticed that the *Chilson Gazette* had duplicates up the wazoo, it had been easy to convince Camille, the *Gazette*'s owner and editor, to permanently lend us some of their extras. In my perusal of the 1980s editions, I'd found that Colleen had graduated three years ahead of Cheryl.

"I hadn't heard until recently," I said. "Did you know her?"

"Knew her name, but that's about it. She was three classes behind me. Half a lifetime in high school terms."

Understandable, even in a small school. I started to stand and thank her for her time, when she went on. "I didn't know Cheryl, but I did know Jim Kittle."

I frowned. "Um . . ."

"Ancient history, here, but Jim and Cheryl had been dating heavy her senior year. She was, what, two years younger than him? Anyway, when she realized he wasn't going to do anything past community college, wasn't going to become a fancy lawyer or doctor and drop her into the life she wanted so much, she broke up with him."

"When?" I asked.

So quietly I could barely hear her, Colleen said, "Just a couple of weeks before she was killed."

Chapter Fifteen

I wasn't sure which surprised me more, Colleen's revelation about the 1990 relationship between Jim Kittle and Cheryl Webb, or that the quintessentially nice Colleen had been snarky about Cheryl. Which made me wonder if Colleen had been interested in Jim herself and been cut out by Cheryl, the apparent siren.

After returning to the reference desk, I kept a slightly stalky eye on Colleen's movement in the library. Maybe I'd been wrong on my character assessment of her. Maybe she wasn't a kind and generous person. Maybe on the inside she was as mean and nasty as the rest of us.

But she stopped to help a young woman who had even more vertical efficiency than me get a book from a high shelf, and then she told an elderly and tottery man that he'd be doing her a favor if he took her arm and helped her across the sidewalk to the parking lot, because it looked icy out there, and you just never knew.

"Nope," I murmured.

Colleen was nice down to the bone, and her marriage with Whippy had been a happy one. That snark about Cheryl must have been residual from high school. Maybe once upon a time she'd had a thing for Jim Kittle, but I couldn't see how that connected with Cheryl's murder, let alone Gerald's.

Jim Kittle, though. Now *that* was interesting. Cheryl dumping him two weeks before she was killed? Surely that was a motive for murder. And the sheriff's office undoubtedly knew about the end of their relationship, so that was probably why he'd been hauled in for questioning. And maybe he was who they'd pegged for the murder, but they didn't have enough evidence to charge him.

Hmm.

I slid Jim Kittle to the top of my *Find Connection With Gerald* list and thought about next steps.

That didn't get me anywhere but running around in thought circles, so I leaned back in my chair, stared at the coffered ceiling, and fidgeted with a pen, my surefire trick to get my brain moving in a different direction.

"Good afternoon, Minnie."

I sat up so fast that I almost overbalanced in my chair. "Hi, Sondra," I said as brightly as I could while simultaneously being red-faced in front of a library board member. "Um, I was just . . . thinking."

She laughed. "That was obvious. I could see the wheels turning inside your head."

"Hamster wheel," I said, sighing. "And it was squeaking. Loudly."

I expected her to laugh again, tell me to have a good weekend, and move toward the shelves of poetry that I knew was her passion. Instead, she took hold of a chair at a nearby table, dragged it close, and sat next to me.

"First off," she said in an inside-the-library voice, "I wanted to thank you for your handling of the library website fiasco. Everything you did should have been done by Graydon—not that I'm blaming him for anything because family comes first and he's doing what's right—and you came up trumps."

"Oh." I blinked. "Thank you. That means a lot." And it did. I'd felt unsure throughout the whole episode, and knowing that at least one board member thought I'd done something right warmed my heart.

"Second off," she said, "it occurred to me why you were asking questions about my first husband."

"It . . . did?"

"You're trying to figure out what happened to Gerald Arnhold, aren't you?"

My eyes widened, then my brain belatedly kicked in, and I remembered that when Gerald had died, Graydon had still been here, and that he'd informed the board members what had happened.

Sondra hadn't stopped talking, and I tuned back in.

"—forever ago, but maybe you're right, and the GAC has something to do with Gerald's death. You think it's murder, don't you?"

"Well . . ."

She nodded. "Anyone who knew him knows there's no way that man could fall through the ice. He had backup plans for backup plans, and the notion that he would have been careless enough to die by drowning is beyond preposterous."

"The sheriff's office says—"

She waved away the opinion of trained law enforcement. "They didn't know Gerald. He and my dad bowled together every Thursday night for thirty years, and every Sunday dinner after church, my dad would have another story about, well, let's just say Gerald's highly developed need to pay acute attention to details."

I grinned. "Sounds accurate."

She hitched forward. "I'm happy to help in any way I can. Despite the involvement of my ex-husband, I wasn't involved in the GAC, but I knew a lot of the players. Ask away."

So I did.

* * *

At closing, after I locked the library's doors, I helped Kelsey close up at the main desk, checked my email one more time, and sent Rafe a text that I'd be home in less than an hour. Then I pulled on boots, coat, and gloves and headed outside, where I stopped short.

"Huh," I said out loud, because at some point during the day when I hadn't been paying attention, five inches of snow had fallen. I debated walking home to get my car, but Lake View Medical Care Facility was less than a ten-minute walk away, so time-wise, it would be a wash. Besides, I could use the exercise.

So I shouldered the backup backpack I kept in my office and headed up the hill, the intrepid librarian trudging through the snow in search of information. By the time I walked into the nursing home, however, I was overheated from the effort of walking half a mile through the slushy stuff, heartily regretting my decision to commit to that much exertion, and wondering if Rafe would mind picking me up in his truck.

I sent him a quick text.

Me: *Stopping at Lake View for a few minutes. You okay to pick me up in half an hour?*

Rafe (after a brief pause): *Sure. What do you want on your pizza?*

I interpreted the food-oriented non sequitur to mean that he'd had a long day helping Bob with his plumbing and didn't feel like cooking. Fine with me, so I told him sausage and onions and added a kissy face emoji.

The front desk was empty, so I scrawled my info on the sign-in sheet and went in search of Max, and this time I knew how to make him talk about things he didn't want to talk about.

I smiled a bit grimly and started the hunt. It was the end of dinner hour, and residents were trickling out of the dining room. Ambulatory senior citizens and those using walkers, wheelchairs, canes, and crutches were all making their way steadily to their rooms. Some were alone, many had assistance from aides. I smiled at each of them—none of whom were Max—and thought about the collective knowledge in the building.

These people had seen so much, learned so much, experienced so much. I was little more than a third of their age and I was feeling something akin to awe at the life wisdom in front of me.

"Yo, ho, ho," a chortling voice behind me said.

And then there was Max.

Before I turned around to face him, I made a promise to myself. "Focus," I murmured. "Steer the conversation. Do not succumb to his charms. Do not go with him down whatever rabbit hole topic is in his head. Focus, focus, focus."

"What's that you're saying?"

I jumped. In the last two seconds, Max had wheeled to my side and was peering up at me. His white hair was messier than usual, and I fought the urge to fix it for him.

"Just hardening my heart," I said. "We need to talk."

"My favorite thing." He rubbed his knobby arthritic hands together. "The big news is what happened at dinner tonight. Dwight and Chester—"

"Tell me later," I said firmly. Or better yet, not at all. "Right now, we need to go somewhere quiet."

Max drooped. "Away from all the action?"

"Yes," I said, and we headed for one of the small rooms off the main lobby. These parlor-type spaces had upholstered wing chairs, a love seat, paintings by local artists, and a gas fireplace, all of which provided a sense of warmth and a feeling akin to a family den.

The entire way there, Max kept up a running commentary about the events of the day, and I did my best not to listen to him. When we entered, I shut the door behind us and sat in the closest chair. Unfortunately, it was a low one, so I found myself looking up at Max, but moving to a higher elevation would have been awkward, so I squared my shoulders and interrupted his description of a visiting toddler and her escapades with Lake View's resident dog.

"I want to talk about 1990."

He shook his head, and another lock of white hair fell across his forehead and in front of his eyes. "No, you don't. No one does."

"I agree that no one wants to, but I need to know what happened."

He peered at me. "Why?"

"Gerald Arnhold."

"Aahhh." Max sat back. "You're connecting Gerry's death with the GAC."

"I think it's a serious possibility."

"And no one else does."

"The sheriff's office is saying it was an accident."

Max snorted. "Then they didn't know Gerry."

Hah! I had him. I kept my face from smiling. "Then you'll tell me why they interviewed you about Cheryl Webb's murder. I know that she worked at the Road Commission, and that you two didn't get along."

Another Max snort. "Worked? That's an exaggeration. We hired that girl for part-time janitorial work, and every time she was asked to actually clean, she acted as if it was beneath her. Cared more about her fingernails than doing her job."

All of that tracked with what I'd learned about Cheryl. "Okay," I said. "But why did the police talk to you?"

"Oh." He half grinned. "Because I volunteered to fire her. I was all ready to use some story about budget cuts. She saw through it straight away, she was no dummy, and . . . well, let's just say it didn't go well. Voices were raised. Things were thrown. At me, not her, just to be clear. Doors were slammed. But the minute she was gone, the office mood lightened. Tells you something, eh?"

Then he pulled in a long breath and let it out in a long, sad sigh. "Horrible what happened to her, though. No one deserves that."

We sat in silence for a few moments, both of us watching the gas fire's flickering dance.

When his face looked a little less sad, I said, "Thank you, Max. And I'm sorry for bringing up bad memories. To make up for it, I have a present. It just came in, so you'll be the first one to read it." I dug into my backpack and handed him an advance reader copy of the latest thriller by John Sandford.

* * *

"You should have seen his face," I said, smiling at the memory. "He looked happier than a kid on the first day of summer. Happier than a teenager getting an unrestricted driver's license."

"Mrr."

"Sorry." I patted my cat's head. We were in the study, where I was meant to be organizing the finances of Minnie and Rafe Niswander, but where I was instead talking to Eddie about my day. "Those aren't analogies you'd understand, are they? Apologies. How about, um, happier than an Eddie with a brand new roll of toilet paper to shred?"

My furry friend, who would go for months without paying any attention to paper products, had reverted to old habits with a vengeance. When Rafe had retrieved me from Lake View, he'd had an odd expression on his face. I'd asked him what was up and, he'd shaken his head and said, "You'll see."

What I'd seen when I'd walked in the back door was tiny clumps of toilet paper scattered all over the floor, and in the corner, the remnants of the cardboard core.

I'd almost asked my beloved husband why he hadn't cleaned it up, but I'd have done the same thing. Some things have to be seen to be believed.

I patted Eddie's head again. "At least toilet paper is relatively cheap." After all, he could have taken it into his little kitty head to destroy something far more expensive. Or historic. The early 1900s woodwork that was all over the house, say.

"Anyway," I said, "it was good to get Max back up to normal happiness levels. And to hear what happened between him and Cheryl."

Now that I knew some details, it made sense that a shouting match ending in slammed doors had piqued the interest of law enforcement, particularly when said argument happened a short time before Cheryl's death.

What had also been super interesting was that Max also thought Gerald's drowning couldn't possibly be accidental. I'd toyed with the idea of telling Detectives Hal and Ash, but decided that more opinions, on top of the ones I'd already given them, wouldn't do any good.

"Not that there's any connection between Max and Gerald's death," I said as I patted my lap, inviting Eddie to jump up. "Max has been in a wheelchair for years and hasn't had access to a car for even longer." Not that I wouldn't put it past him to figure out a way, if he was determined enough.

It was also possible that Max had run into Cheryl outside of the office, after he'd fired her from her janitorial job at the Road Commission. Maybe she'd confronted him, and maybe his temper had flared, and maybe he'd—

I gave a small *oof* as Eddie accepted my lap invitation.

"But the sheriff's office must have looked at all that," I said, snuggling my fuzzy friend close. "And where could something like that have happened without someone seeing? Chilson doesn't have dark alleys."

Well, technically it did, but they were directly behind downtown stores and in residential neighborhoods, all of which would have a lot of traffic, both vehicular and foot, five months out of the year.

Reluctantly, I left Max on my mental suspect list. Down at the bottom, though.

"Mrr!"

"Sorry." I released Eddie from the squeezing hug I'd been giving him. "I asked Sondra if she knew when Mort had started having affairs, if he'd started cheating on her earlier than 1992, but she didn't know."

She'd also said she'd been so young and so stupid that he might have been carrying on even before they got married. So there was that.

"And then there's Duffy," I said, sighing. Duffy Ulrich, who'd recently retired and sold the commercial sign fabrication business she'd started and grown herself to her employees, was a force of nature. Our paths hadn't crossed until she'd become the new Friends of the Library president, but she'd rapidly become one of my favorite people.

About my height, slender enough to be called skinny by some, and with fiery red hair that was even curlier than mine, Duffy had a penchant for wearing clothes in colors there were even brighter than her hair.

A few weeks ago, she'd said she'd had enough of winter and hopped a plane for Florida. She'd texted me that she'd be back in town for the April meeting of the Friends and was still sending me the occasional photo of the tops of her feet up against a seaside beach and blue skies with the message, "Come on down, there's plenty of room in the condo!"

But Sondra had told me why the sheriff's office had talked to Duffy about Cheryl's death. In 1989, Duffy had just started her business. Like many startups, cash had been tight. Duffy, however, was determined to be a success, and to do that she needed employees. One of the people she had hired was Cheryl Webb.

"What Sondra said," I told Eddie, "was that Duffy hired Cheryl part time to answer the phones, take down messages, that kind of thing. But it turned out that Cheryl was also taking deposits from people. In cash. And not turning all of it over to her boss."

"Mrr?"

"Yeah, buddy. Cheryl was stealing. From Duffy."

Chapter Sixteen

The next morning, after a breakfast of buttermilk blueberry pancakes and link sausages cooked by my favorite husband of all time, I kissed him good-bye and wished him luck finishing his friend's plumbing project.

"Going to be another three-trips-to-the-hardware-store day," Rafe said morosely as he zipped his coat. "All we got done yesterday was pulling out the old stuff, thanks to too many years of corrosion."

"Just think of all the good karma you're piling up."

He brightened a bit. "Bob will owe me, that's for sure." He left, speculating out loud on favors ranging from dropping us off at the airport for the 5:45 AM flight to maneuvering a pool table into our basement.

After doing the dishes, I wandered around the house, doing vaguely domestic things like plumping pillows and making sure our books were aligned to the front of their shelves.

An embarrassingly short time later, I'd had enough of having the house to myself. Well, except for Eddie, but he was in the middle of the bed, snoring, so I was alone for all practical purposes. Next I tried reading, but my legs got all restless. I needed to get out and go somewhere, so I put on my coat.

When I opened the back door, I didn't have a destination in mind, but by the time I started my car, thanks to the magic of texting, I knew exactly where I was going, and in just over half an hour, I pulled into the visitor parking lot of the Petoskey hospital.

After missing some (in retrospect glaringly obvious) signage and wandering around in various hallways, I eventually found the recently relocated gift shop. The selection of flowers was depleted, this being a Sunday, but I picked a cheerful mix of freesias and carnations out of the leavings and a cute card to accompany them. The kind young man at the counter lent me a pen to sign the card, and I carried both card and vased flowers up to Alicia Gwaltny's room.

I knocked gently on the door frame and eased inside.

Though it was a two-person room, Alicia was the only occupant. She was in the bed closest to the window and so had a view of Little Traverse Bay. Even though it was another gray and dreary day, the water's expansive blue hue made something inside of me ease, just a little.

Her head was turned to face the window. "Alicia?" I asked.

When there was no response, I noticed that her lime-green-framed glasses were on the hospital table positioned over her lap, and that her breathing was slow and steady.

Quietly, I put the flowers down on the wide windowsill, propped the card up against it, and tiptoed away.

If Alicia had been awake and feeling up to it, I would have asked what she remembered about the GAC. About Cheryl, Gerald, Duffy, Max, Mort, Rick, Jim Kittle, Sabrina, Mr. Goodwin, and Uncle Everett. And I would have asked her thoughts about a connection between the deaths of Cheryl and Gerald.

Instead I whispered, "Sleep tight," and left the room.

Back in Tonedagana County, I drove around for a while, going down roads I'd never traveled before in hopes of finding smoother and faster routes for the bookmobile. After an hour, when my gas tank was dropping under a quarter tank and the only thing of interest I'd seen was a row of flannel long johns hanging from a clothesline like a regiment of floppy red soldiers, I went back to Chilson in time for my appointment with Aunt Frances.

I shucked my boots and coat at the door and waved at Otto, who was hunkered down in the front room with a book and the adorable little gray cat he'd brought to the marriage.

"Good luck," he said, smiling.

"Thanks. I'll need it."

He laughed, but I was dead serious.

I tried not to slink as I walked into the kitchen, which managed to feel sunny and bright even on a dank and dark March day. I found this almost annoying, since I was in a dank and dark mood and would have been okay with matching surroundings.

"Ready when you are," Aunt Frances said.

She was standing at the kitchen island, which looked like a setup for a cooking show. Bowls, utensils, pans, and containers holding food of various shapes and sizes were lined up at the ready, somehow looking a lot like the long johns I'd seen on the clothesline.

I gave it all a baleful glare and plopped myself down in the breakfast nook. "Nope," I said. "I'm not going to ruin any more of your pots or pans."

My aunt did the one eyebrow thing. "Don't tell me you're giving up."

"Not so much giving up as recognizing that cooking isn't my thing. Thanks for trying so hard, but it's time to face facts. They say you should play to your strengths. Another way to say that is don't keep doing things you're horrible at doing, so I'm going to stop pretending I'll ever learn to cook."

Aunt Frances extended her arm with a flourish. "But this, dear niece, isn't about cooking. It's baking."

I shrugged. "Distinction without a difference, isn't it?"

"Don't let Kristen hear you say that," she chided. "There's a world of difference between the two. Cooking is creativity and constant tiny adjustments. Baking is nothing but following directions."

"Yeah?" At some level I'd known that, but since both cooking and baking required washing dishes . . .

"You," my loving aunt said, pointing at me with her index finger, "can follow directions. All it needs is a little focus. Come here," she commanded. "You're going to make drop biscuits."

"I am?"

"You are."

She said this with such confidence that I began to believe her. This belief strengthened through the measuring of the ingredients, the mixing and stirring of them, turning on the oven, dropping the doughy lumps onto the parchment paper-covered sheet pan, sliding them into the oven, and setting the timer.

Then the front doorbell rang.

She went to answer it, and I was left in the kitchen.

Alone.

But surely everything would be fine. The oven timer was on, and I was standing right there. I couldn't possibly mess this one up.

And I didn't.

Until I did.

* * *

"You are pathetic," I said to my car's rearview mirror. Or, more accurately, the part of my face that was reflected in the rearview mirror. The absurdly curly hair, forehead, eyebrows, eyes, and the top half of my nose. All that, plus all of the rest of me, was sad and pathetic.

"The only thing you had to do," I said to myself as I carefully and gingerly started my car, "was take the biscuits out of the oven. A five-year-old could have done it. Easily."

In actual fact, I had taken the pan of biscuits out of the oven a handful of seconds after the timer had beeped. But, because my brain had wandered off and was thinking about Alicia and Gerald and Mort Neely and Jim Kittle and Duffy and Sabrina and Max and Uncle Everett and Mr. Goodwin, what I hadn't remembered was to use potholders. I'd opened the oven door, reached out for the sheet pan, and pulled.

My screeching gasp of pain had coincided with the sheet pan and its load of lovely golden biscuits tumbling to the floor. The pan clattered. The biscuits broke apart. My aunt and Otto came running, and I'd stood there like a toddler, staring at my first-degree burns and saying, "I don't know what happened."

On the plus side, I hadn't ruined any pots or pans. And I'd always been a fast healer, so in a day or two this would be nothing but another Silly Minnie story for my friends and relatives to trot out whenever the occasion demanded.

Then again, it was possible that Aunt Frances and Otto would keep this to themselves, and . . .

"Not a chance," I muttered. Because he was a gentleman, Otto would never say a word, but Aunt Frances would have no such compunctions. The next time my extended family gathered, I would have to smile and endure the auntly embellishments.

Well. That was a problem for another day. And as long as she waited until after Rafe's birthday to share any new Silly Minnie stories, I'd be okay with it.

Also on the plus side of my daily list of accomplishments—not that I had such a list, but it was a fun concept that I should think about implementing—was the idea I'd had about Max. Whether or not he'd been involved with Cheryl's murder was not a question for me to answer. But there was a way that I might be able to establish whether or not he'd had anything to do with Gerald's.

Five minutes later, I pulled into the visitor parking lot at Lake View. It was nearly full. The knowledge that so many people were coming to visit their loved ones on a Sunday afternoon warmed my heart, and I was smiling as I walked into the lobby.

This time, it was noisy with human life in ages ranging from infant on up. Everyone was grouped on the left side of the large room, centered around four middle-aged men wearing flat straw hats, white shirts with black bow ties, and red-and-white striped vests. The attire was a huge hint, but when they started singing "In the Good Old Summertime," I knew for sure that a barbershop quartet would be taking up all the attention in the room for a few minutes.

Serendipity can be a thing.

I eased over to the front desk. This afternoon it was staffed by a young man, but he'd moved to the counter's far end, closer to the action, and far-ish away from the object of my desire.

Smiling blandly at no one, I made my casual way to the sign-out clipboard. As per usual, there was a stack of completed sheets underneath the top one. I'd thought that maybe there would be a sheet a day, and it would be the work of moments to find what I needed, but no. Some sheets covered multiple days, and some days had multiple sheets. Days with crappy weather and weekends, respectively, I hypothesized, but didn't want to take the time to check.

Flipping pages with my ouchy fingers, I made my way back in time to mid-February. Maybe ten names. None of them Max Compton. Or any kind of Max. Or any kind of Compton.

Here was the proof I needed. Max hadn't killed Gerald.

I whooshed out a sigh of relief, pushed the clipboard back home, and edged to the back of the crowd, letting myself enjoy a male quartet version of "Amazing Grace."

As I listened to the music, it belatedly occurred to me that, even if Max had been signed out on the day Gerald died, and even if he had made his way to the little lake house, there was no way that he, in his wheelchair, could have maneuvered onto the frozen lake and pushed Gerald through the ice fishing hole and into the frigid water.

In retrospect, obvious. And not that I'd really thought Max had killed anyone, but it was nice to know for sure that I could shorten the suspect list by one.

One down, lots to go. And my father-in-law was still on the list.

* * *

I got into my car, buckled up, started the engine . . . and sat back.

"Now what do I do?" I asked, my words turning into tiny white clouds. I pretended to be Puff the Magic Dragon for a few more breaths, then remembered what had eventually happened to poor Puff and stopped.

I tapped the steering wheel with my mittened thumbs—not my fingers because they were too tender from the Biscuit Debacle to think about doing such a thing—and thought about what I should do with the rest of my day.

What I needed to do next was make sure Rick could be crossed off the suspect list. And since I couldn't think of a way to do that other than talking to him, I pointed my car in the direction of their house.

"Minnie?" Lois asked, her eyebrows going up the same way her son's did. "What brings you here?"

"Um." I flapped my hands inside my coat pockets, feeling like a little kid who unexpectedly stopped by to ask their friend to come out and play, "Can I come in? For a few minutes?"

"What?" She blinked. "Of course. Sorry. I didn't mean to keep you out in the cold. In you go, that's the way." She closed the front door behind me. "Put your coat and boots any old place. Rick's out, he's helping Al install the ceiling fan for that three-season porch and I was heating water for a cup of tea. Would you like some?"

"Um, sure."

Lois laughed. "You don't sound convinced. I know you're a coffee drinker, but try some of my favorite chamomile. If you don't like it, I can cook up some of that hot chocolate you like."

Five minutes later I was sipping a hot, fragrant herby liquid that wasn't horrible, and it triggered a memory. "My mom used to give me chamomile when I had a sore throat," I said, cupping my hands around the hot mug, being careful to keep my sore fingertips away from the heat.

My mother-in-law laughed again. "Maybe that sent you in the coffee direction. Bad associations."

I'd never thought about it like that. "Speaking of associations," I said, "the other day, when we were talking about the GAC and Cheryl Webb, it seemed like that brought up a lot of bad ones for you."

She didn't say anything for a long moment, then murmured, "Too many."

"If it's okay, could you tell me about it? I didn't know any of this until a couple of weeks ago, and if I know what happened, maybe I can avoid saying the wrong thing."

After another long moment, Lois sighed. "Okay. Let me tell you what I remember, then if you have questions, ask away." She waited until I nodded, then started talking.

"Back in 1990," she said, "Rick had just been promoted to supervisor. He was hyper focused on being the best ever. Intent on following the company's rules, regulations, and policies. Every single one. To the letter."

I squirmed a bit.

Lois nodded. "You're management, so you see where this is going. Rick was so busy being a stickler for the rules that he forgot it's the people who make a company successful. Before he got his act together, he made work life miserable for his entire staff. And that included Cheryl Webb."

"Ah."

My mother-in-law nodded again. "She was part-time, entry-level office staff. He berated her in front of the entire office for clocking in two minutes late, and she quit in a huge huff."

After waiting a beat, I asked, "This was soon before she died?"

"Couple of weeks. And Cheryl Webb spent a lot of that time telling people that she'd make him pay for what he'd done to her."

"But he didn't actually fire her," I said, frowning. "It was corrective action, is all. Not in the best way, but that's not anything close to termination."

My mother-in-law shrugged. "And now you know what Cheryl Webb was like and why the police wanted to talk to him. There was a theory that he killed her because she was going to sue him for wrongful termination and ruin his career. Which would have been ridiculous, but . . ." Her shoulders sagged. "It was a bad time."

"I'm sorry to dredge up all those memories," I said quietly. Then in a desperate move to change the subject, said, "Did I tell you I'm taking cooking lessons from my aunt as a birthday present for Rafe?"

By the end of my tale, Lois was laughing so hard that she was wiping tears from her eyes. That made me feel better, but as I drove home I came to a reluctant conclusion.

Rick was still on the suspect list.

Chapter Seventeen

After a sleep plagued by a long disjointed dream that started with forgetting my high school locker combination after a holiday break (something I'd never done), which morphed into forgetting my passport on a trip to Paris (a place I'd never been), which segued into a pub crawl with Kristen in New Orleans (another place I'd never been), I woke up with an excellent idea.

Rafe eyed me as I bounced into the kitchen. "You're looking perky for a Monday morning."

I beamed. "It's a good day when you know exactly what needs to be done next."

"Mrr."

Eddie, who was sitting like an Egyptian cat statue on the third stool at the kitchen island, obviously agreed with me. The island had been designed to take four stools, but that had always felt a bit crowded. Ever since we'd taken the fourth one to the attic, Eddie had claimed the stool closest to the dining room as his, and we'd learned to accept this as fact and as fate.

After Rafe had trundled off to school—a bit bleary-eyed, because though the plumbing project was complete, it had taken roughly a zillion times longer than he'd expected—I patted Eddie on the head and drove to the library, early even for me.

I was leaving early because I had things to do that were in no way, shape, or form part of my job description, even if you considered the catchall phrase of "other duties as required." And I was driving because, if those things worked out, I might have to go places that my feet didn't have time to walk.

Humming, I bopped into the library, got coffee started, got my computer started, filled my mug with life-affirming liquid, and got to work on my dream-inspired idea of tracking down whoever had been Cheryl Webb's best friend.

It took longer than I'd hoped, but not as long as I'd feared, and before anyone else came into the building, I was making a lunch plan that involved a trek to the far eastern side of Chilson, the part of town that sported a furniture store, a physical therapist, an insurance agent, a long-empty drive-in theater, and an auto parts store.

Terry's Auto Parts, to be precise, because that's where Marcia Keeby worked as store manager, and according to high school yearbooks, social media, and the newspaper articles I'd already copied from the *Gazette*, Marcia and Cheryl had been very close.

The second before I walked in through the front door of Terry's, it occurred to me that a smart person would have come up with a sensible and sensitive way to convince

Marcia to talk to me. But I'd put myself in the same situation more than once, and it had always worked out, so I pulled in a deep breath and opened the door.

Inside, the textured gray floor practically sparkled with cleanliness. The overhead lights shone brightly, and the products on the many shelves were lined up soldier-like. I hadn't a clue what any of the products were, but I appreciated the order and tidiness.

"Almost like a library, isn't it?"

I'd been admiring a long line of brightly colored boxes, each of which surely contained important and expensive items critical to the functioning of internal combustion engines, but I turned and faced the female voice, which belonged to a sixtyish woman with shoulder-length hair that was straight and a lovely shade of dark red. "Um, hi?"

She laughed. "You're Ms. Minnie, the bookmobile librarian, and my granddaughter loves Eddie, the bookmobile cat. Her mom took a picture of her with you and Eddie that she carries with her everywhere she goes."

Light dawned. "You're Megan's Gramma M."

"Marcia Keeby," she said, walking forward with her hand out. "And if you're here for parts for the bookmobile, I'm afraid you've come to the wrong place."

I shook her hand. "Happily, Darren Bryant takes care of all that. No, I'm here for something that has nothing to do with auto parts. It's a . . . personal thing."

She gave me an appraising look. "Let me guess. It's about Cheryl."

I blinked. Couldn't find any words and blinked again.

Marcia laughed again. "You should see your face. Sadly, I'm no mind reader. It's just that I know you've been asking around about the GAC. People talk, you know."

I did indeed. And every so often I could make that work to my advantage. "Is it okay if I ask you a few questions?"

"All these years later and they still don't know who killed Cheryl. It's what I think about, at two in the morning when I can't sleep." She sighed, shaking her head. "Fire away. No guarantee I'm going to remember a thing, but if you can turn up something that helps nail the guy who killed Cheryl, I'm all in."

I murmured my thanks and asked my first question. "Did you know Gerald Arnhold?"

"Knew of him." She pursed her lips, making fine vertical lines all around. "Mostly from Cheryl. She thought he should have been more proactive with the GAC. A lot more. He of all people knew the difference an expansion would make."

I let that point go. Gerald had been staff in the public sector, and staff wasn't supposed to have opinions. "Cheryl and Gerald didn't get along?"

"They got along fine," Marcia said. "Cheryl always wanted more, that's all. More than people were willing to give, sometimes."

"Oh?" I tipped my head. Waiting. Listening.

"Like poor Jim Kittle."

"Her high school boyfriend," I said.

"That's the one." She nodded approvingly. "The story is she broke up with him because he wasn't ambitious enough for her."

"That wasn't true?"

"Wasn't the whole story, that's all. A few weeks before she was killed, Cheryl told me she'd started seeing someone else. That she was just waiting for the right time to break up with Jim."

"Did Jim know about this other guy?" When Marcia shrugged, I asked, "Do you know who it was?"

Marcia shook her head. "Just that he was older."

Well, that was interesting. But what did older mean to someone just out of her teens? Twenty-five? Thirty? Thirty-five?

I was about to ask if she'd told the police any of that when a Santa look-alike in Carhartt overalls barged in through the front door and spied us. "Yo, Keeby!" he boomed. "You finally get that muffler I ordered?"

Marcia rolled her eyes. "'Finally,' he says. Like he didn't just order it on Saturday. Afternoon." She moved off to deal with her customer. I called out a thank-you that she acknowledged with a wave.

I headed outside and started making my way back to the library, but all the while I was thinking about Cheryl's older man.

Did he actually exist? She could have made him up, giving herself a fake reason to break up with Jim. But that seemed unlikely for someone like Cheryl.

So who was he?

Could it have been Gerald?

Or maybe Mort Neely?

But whoever it was, the one person it couldn't have been was my father-in-law.

Could it?

* * *

My overarching goal for the afternoon, other than to bury my fears about what Rick assuredly didn't do in 1990, was to soothe the morass of feelings that were swirling about the library. The disaster with the website was not my fault, but it was my mess to clean up, and I did not want an emotionally drained Graydon to come back to a staff that was prickly, needy, and unhappy.

I'd had a text from Graydon earlier that day that he expected to be home by the weekend, and that he should be back in his office on Monday. But the short sentences he'd typed had also conveyed a bone-deep weariness. Though I could have been reading too much into "Will be really good to get home," I didn't think I was, and since I liked and respected my boss, I wanted him to return to a smoothly functioning workplace.

After shedding coat and boots in my office, I filled my mug with the day's final cup of coffee and stood at the breakroom's window, thinking about how to actually achieve my goal.

"Penny?"

I jumped, and because miracles do happen, I didn't spill any of my coffee. "Hey, Donna. Sorry, what did you say?"

She looked apologetic. "Didn't mean to startle you. I assumed you heard me rummaging through the fridge," she said, hefting what looked like a ham sandwich. "Penny, I said. As in for your thoughts?"

"Oh." I breathed out a small laugh. "Sadly, I don't have many. Not productive ones, at least."

"Welcome to the human race." Donna pulled out a chair, sat at the small table, and patted the back of the chair next to her. "Have a seat, Minnie. You look like you need to talk, and I could use the company."

She didn't need anyone, because I could see her surreptitiously tucking a book under her legs, but showing appreciation of a kind gesture was something my mother had done her best to shoehorn into my character. "Thanks," I said and sat down.

Though I wasn't going to broach the subject of employee morale with her, I could pose questions about the GAC. Sideways ones, anyway. I thought for a moment, then asked, "Did you know Duffy Ulrich before she joined the Friends of the Library?"

Donna, in the midst of chewing a sandwich bite, nodded. "Since she was born. We're cousins."

Would I ever cease being amazed at the familial connections in Chilson of which I wasn't aware? I would not. "Huh. I didn't know that."

She shrugged. "Not a huge surprise. Our mothers are sisters who both got married, so we never had the same last name. And as adults, being cousins isn't much different than being friends."

It was an interesting statement, and someday I'd think about it a little more. Today, though, I wanted to learn more about Duffy.

"What was she like as a kid?" I asked. "Did she have the same kind of fashion sense?"

Donna paused with her sandwich halfway to her mouth. "You know what I remember most? As a baby, her face would get all wound up in a tight little ball and turn bright red when she cried."

"Um, don't all babies do that?"

"Not like Duff." Donna grinned. "She was a champion crier. Could go for hours without taking a breath. And as a toddler, she threw these amazing temper tantrums. Full length, face down on the floor, pounding her fists and feet like her life depended on it."

"But she grew out of that, right?" I asked.

"Oh, sure. Well . . . mostly. She still can't stand bullies. Not that that's a bad thing," Donna added quickly. "It's a good thing, if you ask me. And these days the most she'd do is call someone out. When she was younger, I remember my aunt saying it felt like she was looking for confrontations."

It was now or never. "Like the Great Airport Controversy?" I asked gently, remembering how she'd clammed up about the GAC when I'd broached the subject before.

Donna pulled a piece of crust from her sandwich, peered at it, and dropped it onto her napkin. "Like that," she said evenly.

"Which side was she on?"

"Against."

I waited, but she didn't expand, so I asked, "Was it because you work here that Duffy got interested in joining the Friends?"

Donna snorted. "Hardly," she said and started on a long and wandering story about the amazing English teacher they'd both had in junior high—Mrs. Haggard.

I listened to her fond memories, and when she was done, I thanked her and wandered back to my office, lining up my thoughts.

Duffy had been against the airport expansion. Cheryl had been in favor.

Duffy had a crusade against bullies. Cheryl, by some accounts, could have been construed as a bully. Not to mention the fact that Duffy had fired Cheryl for stealing from her.

I didn't like how any of that was stacking up, but what I really wanted to know was if Duffy had any connection to Gerald beyond what had happened in 1990. And could Duffy have considered Gerald a bully?

I couldn't see it, not by the stretchiest stretch of the imagination, but . . . maybe?

* * *

That night, Rafe spent half of dinnertime trying to explain what had happened that day at the middle school and the other half fielding phone calls and text messages from school board members, teachers, and parents.

"Sorry," he said after he'd hung up for the ten thousandth time. "I know we said no phones at the table, but . . . today . . ."

I forked up a small portion of the leftover mashed potatoes that Lois had forced on me as I'd left her house the day before. "No worries," I said. "I've been learning a lot about calming techniques."

Rafe looked over at Eddie, who was sitting in the exact middle of the wide doorway to the living room. "Think they'll work on him?"

"Nothing works on—"

My critique of our cat was interrupted by the ring of Rafe's phone. He groaned and picked it up. "Evening, Bob. I take it you've heard?" This time he stood and took the conversation into the kitchen.

I heard an odd noise and turned to see what Eddie was doing. As far as I could tell, though, he wasn't doing anything, which couldn't be right.

"Am I wrong?" I asked. "Are the things your dad is doing to calm all those people working on you, too? Although I'm not sure why you'd care much about Rafe reassuring everyone that a bat flying around the school gym during an afternoon assembly hadn't bit anyone, wasn't at all likely to be rabid, and had been put there as a prank by a group of kids who have already been suspended."

Eddie shifted and looked me straight in the eye.

"Okay, sure, it'll take a day or two before the health department knows for sure that the bat wasn't rabid. But after the maintenance staff captured it—in a box, taped up against the ceiling of the classroom they'd chased it into using badminton racquets—the poor thing didn't show any signs of being diseased."

My cat sighed at me.

"Sorry for wasting your time." I rolled my eyes, turned my attention back to my dinner, and muttered, "Just like

I'm wasting my own time if I try to convince Rafe to do anything he doesn't want to do."

As we'd sat down to eat, I'd made one final vague reference to a personal strategic plan. Vague as in that it wasn't a pointed reference, but precise enough that the love of my life absolutely knew what I was talking about. He had, as per my expectation, ignored the reference. Though he was preoccupied with what he was already calling Batgate, he could have acknowledged what I'd put out there.

"And he didn't," I said to Eddie. "Do you think I should try again later? Maybe next year?"

My cat, who was easily winning the one-sided staring contest, heaved a huge kitty sigh, stood, and stalked into the living room, tail twitching back and forth, metronome-style.

I poked at what was left on my plate, but grill pan pork that had turned room temperature wasn't appetizing to me. I got up and carried the dishes into the kitchen, where Rafe was still talking to whoever Bob might be.

Doing the dishes, always a noisy task, while he was on the phone would be rude, so I headed off to find Eddie. He'd looked like he was on a mission, something that was always worrying.

"Yo," I called. "Mr. Eduardo. Where are you?"

Though there was no answering "Mrr," I did hear an odd rustling noise in the study that sounded cat-related. I paused in the doorway and surveyed the scene. Computer, desk, chair, bookshelves, mostly empty filing cabinet.

No cat.

I backed out of the room and stood there. Waiting. Like a cat about to pounce on a mouse, only in reverse.

After waiting for a few beats I got bored, and my attention wandered off. To the events of the day, to Rafe's captured bat, to what I'd heard about Cheryl from Marcia at the auto parts store, and to what I'd learned from Donna about Duffy.

Everything except Rafe's bat started tumbling around in my mind. Marcia said Cheryl had been dating an older man. She'd said older but hadn't said anything about him being married. Then again, would Cheryl have told her best friend that she was committing adultery? And had Cheryl even been telling the truth about the older man? Maybe she'd made it up to ease the breakup with Jim and used the same story with Marcia.

And Duffy. A younger, more temperamental Duffy. Could she have run into Cheryl at a meeting about the GAC and, it being not long after Duffy had fired Cheryl, could the two of them have started arguing, and could that have led to murder?

I rubbed my eyes.

Yes, it was possible that any or all of that had happened. But I liked Duffy. I didn't want her to be a killer. And finding Cheryl's killer was not my remit, as they said on BBC police procedurals. Finding Gerald's killer was the mission I'd tasked myself with, and I knew I should stick to it. Three weeks since his death and I wasn't sure I'd really learned anything.

Then again, I'd started looking into the GAC because Gerald had been the airport director and because a young woman had been murdered. To me, it still seemed reasonable that the murder of the then-airport director, even so many decades later, would have something to do with Cheryl's murder.

"But . . . how?" I murmured. Using my fingers, I counted out the ten names Don Devereaux had given me as the people who'd been questioned more than once about Cheryl: Gerald, Uncle Everett, Rick Niswander, Mr. Goodwin, Mort Neely, Max, Duffy, Sabrina, Linda Kopecky, Jim Kittle.

I studied my extended digits and pulled in one thumb, because Gerald hadn't killed himself. "And not Uncle Everett," I said, because he obviously couldn't have killed Gerald, and pulled in a pinky finger. I'd also eliminated Mr. Goodwin and Max, so I was down to six suspects, five on one hand, one on the other.

"Five and a half?" I murmured, because I couldn't imagine Linda Kopecky killing a spider, let alone a human being. But no. She had to stay, even though it was way unlikely. I assigned her to the remaining pinky. Who should be the thumb? And the index fingers?

I'd just decided Jim Kittle should be the thumb when a whisper of a rattle went across the floor, left to right.

"Hah," I said, shaking the Sabrina index finger at Eddie. "Got you."

A black-and-white feline slinked out from behind the bookcase and bounded after the small object that had become his newest toy.

"Hang on," I said, blocking him with my leg. "Is that a push pin?" I crouched, picked up the sharp-tipped object, and brandished it at Eddie. "This is not a cat toy. It's dangerous and it could hurt you." I stood and reinserted the pin into the tack board that hung next to the computer.

"Mrr!"

"Not. A. Cat. Toy," I repeated, this time at a higher decibel level, just in case he hadn't heard me the first time.

"MRR!"

"Back at you, pal."

He glared at me and stomped out of the room.

Cats.

Chapter Eighteen

The next day was a bookmobile day, which meant that even though the morning sky was dark and cloudy and spitting snow down on us, my heart was singing with happiness and even confidence.

I would figure things out. I would find a way to cure the library staff of its malaise. I would work out who had killed Gerald, and maybe who'd killed Cheryl. I would learn to accept that my husband wouldn't always want the same things I wanted, and I would learn to understand everything my cat was trying to communicate.

"MrrR!"

"Great green gumdrops," Julia said, putting her hands over her ears. "What was that horrific noise?"

"That," I said with conviction, "was the sound of Eddie telling me that he is unhappy with the way his morning kibble bits were mounded in the bowl. And if my performance doesn't improve, he's going to write me up and put it in my personnel file."

"MRR!!"

Both humans winced, and Julia asked dryly, "You sure about that?"

Not in the least, but it didn't do to vocalize doubt when Eddie was in earshot.

Happily, Eddie kept his thoughts to himself the rest of the drive, and we pulled into a gas station parking lot with our eardrums mostly intact. This was our first stop, and it was one that was usually busy due to the many families that were homeschooling their children. This morning, even though we were a few minutes early, there was already an SUV in the lot waiting for us.

Smiling, I parked the bookmobile, anticipating a pile of kids emptying out of the vehicle and racing toward us, their parents calling them back to shut their doors properly and to make sure to hold the hands of their little brother/sister.

Julia nodded at the man climbing out of the SUV. "Isn't that your father-in-law?"

"What?" I looked up, startled, from my efforts to rotate the driver's seat. "Why would Rick be out here?" I peered out the side window, and sure enough, an older version of Rafe was walking toward us. He must have looked on the library's website to find the bookmobile's schedule, but that he'd done so was . . . odd.

"Why doesn't he age?" Julia asked. "He hasn't since he hit fifty, anyway. So unfair."

I locked down the seat in its new position and reached to unlatch the computer table. "Pot. Kettle. Black. You haven't changed since you turned forty."

"Different." She opened Eddie's carrier door. "I work at it. Or did, until I retired. He doesn't. Bet he doesn't even use sunscreen."

I unlocked the side door and pushed it open. "Hey, Rick. Do you use sunscreen?"

My father-in-law didn't blink at the offbeat question as he came aboard. "Not if I can help it. Can't stand the smell of any of that stuff."

"Like I said." Julia nodded. "Unfair."

Rick, because he was a smart man, ignored the background commentary. He reached down to rub Eddie's head, asking, "Minnie, do you have a minute?"

I glanced around at the empty bookmobile. "Sure, until people start showing up."

"Left the engine on," he said, tipping his head in the direction of his SUV.

So, a private minute. I glanced at Julia. "You okay alone?"

"Eddie and I got you covered," she said.

"Mrr," my cat agreed.

Rick went first, holding the door open for me, and we crossed the parking lot to his SUV, which I now noted had the name of his company painted on the door.

"If you ask me," he said, "the unfair thing is that Julia lost out on the lead role for the spring play our senior year."

I did a quick double-take. How had I not known that he and Julia were in the same class? I would never, ever fully grasp the details of the connectedness woven all about me.

We climbed inside the SUV, which was indeed nice and toasty warm.

Rick wasted no time getting to the point. "Lois said you stopped by the house on Sunday afternoon."

"She sent me home with leftover mashed potatoes."

"Wondered where they went." His grunt could have been a recording of Rafe's. "I wanted to talk to you about Cheryl Webb."

"Oh. Um, okay."

He put his hands on the steering wheel, ten and two. After a second, he put his hands on his lap and almost, but not quite, looked at me directly. "Talking about this isn't easy," he muttered. "It was a long time ago, and I don't like to remember it."

"Because of what happened to Cheryl?"

"Horrible thing," he said quietly. "But no."

I waited silently, trying to project patience and compassion while at the same time keeping an eye out for incoming bookmobile visitors.

"It was all new to me," he finally said. "Being a manager. I had no experience leading people, so I thought it was going to be easy. Make people follow the rules. What else did you need to do?"

Though I didn't say any words out loud, my involuntary snort of derision gave away my thoughts.

Rick laughed. "Yeah. I wasn't the brightest bulb in the box. I don't have many regrets, but how I treated people is one of them. Cheryl, for sure. She deserved a reprimand, but she didn't deserve it to be in front of her coworkers, and she didn't deserve my holier-than-thou attitude."

We sat there, looking out the front windshield, thinking our thoughts. Eventually I said, "Thanks for telling me."

He nodded. "There's one good thing that came out of that time. I'm now in a position to make sure anyone in our company that moves into management gets solid training."

As legacies go, there were far worse.

* * *

I opened the door to the bookmobile as Rick pulled out and as a van and an SUV turned into the parking lot. As soon as they were parked, kids piled out, clown car style.

Smiling, I held the door open. "All aboard!" I called. "The bookmobile is ready and waiting for you."

Kids hopped up and in. The last one in the line, a girl of about seven, stopped and looked up at me through absurdly long lashes. "Eddie's here, isn't he?" she asked. "I dreamed last night that he let me pet him."

"Sweetheart," her mother chided. "I told you I couldn't promise anything about Eddie."

"Wise woman," I said, laughing. "You must have cats yourself."

She helped her daughter climb the steps. "Grew up with them, but my husband's allergic."

I almost asked if she'd known that before she married him, but I didn't want to freak her daughter out, so I said, "Eddie's here. Ask Ms. Julia if he's ready to come out and play."

Her head swiveled back to her mother. "After I pet Eddie, can I borrow all the books I can carry?"

"You sure can, honey."

The girl's grin was bright enough to light up the sky, and for the millionth time my mind was boggled at the notion of

Eddie as a reading ambassador. The world was an amazing place, full of wonder and mystery.

"Speaking of mysteries," I said an hour later as we were preparing for our departure, "how is it I never clued into the fact that you and Rick were in the same graduating class?"

Julia squinted at me. "You didn't? Huh." She tapped Eddie's carrier. "Hear that, Sir Edward? Your mom is still learning things."

"And I want to learn more," I said. "Especially stories about Rick in high school. Or even better, middle school. Did you go to the same elementary school?"

"Back in the day," she said, pulling the bungee cord around the rolling chair and up against the back desk, "they called it junior high. Seventh, eighth, ninth grades. And no, we went to different elementaries. I first got to know Rick in band."

My eyes went fake-wide. "You? Were in band? How did that work?"

"Point of fact." She held up an index finger. "My legendary non-musicality is because of my singing voice, not my capacity for playing instruments. I'll have you know that I played a mean clarinet for years and years, and by that I mean four."

"What did Rick play?" I pictured trumpet. Maybe trombone. Possibly percussion.

"Flute."

I laughed. "Cute. No, what did he really play?"

"Flute," she repeated. "Don't ask me why, but his family owned a nice flute. His grandmother played, his uncle played, and then Rick did. I think a downstate nephew has it now. Plays in a community orchestra."

So many things were swirling about me, invisible, but still impacting orbits and trajectories. "Rafe has never said a thing about his dad being in band."

Julia shrugged as we walked forward. "Maybe he doesn't know. High school was a long time ago, and my guess is Rick didn't play much after that. And—gaahh!" She leaped sideways, whipped around, and looked about frantically. "What was that? What was that?"

The white paw that I had been watching as it had snaked out from underneath the passenger's seat, a space I'd always considered too small for a hamster, snaked itself back, Wicked Witch of the East style.

Since I was a horrible person, I laughed out loud. And since I was a deeply horrible person, I didn't feel guilty about it. "That," I said, "would have made an excellent video."

"Titled what?" Julia asked sourly. "'Cat Versus Woman, Cat Wins'?"

"Too predictable. How about 'Watch That Paw'?"

She shook her head. "Boring. I was thinking maybe 'Wait For It,' but that's predictable, too."

Eddie's whiskers appeared from underneath the seat, followed by the rest of him. "You know," I said, watching him. "Videos might be fun. Nothing super serious, just stuff that happens on the bookmobile. Could be a good outreach piece."

"What about our unofficial motto? What happens on the bookmobile stays on the bookmobile."

"Good point." Eddie was thumping his head against my shin. I picked him up and snuggled him close. "Maybe it's not a good idea. Though it could be a good idea for the library. People don't think of libraries as places to laugh, but funny things happen there all the time and it's the funny things that . . ."

"That what?" Julia asked. "You just went somewhere and I'm not with you."

"What?" I blinked at her. "Oh. Nothing."

But it wasn't nothing. At least I hoped not. What my brain had wandered into was a potential solution for the library's morale problem. It would take some string pulling and verbal arm twisting, but I'd finally figured a way out.

Maybe.

* * *

The rest of the day sped by with the speed of a typical book-mobile day—zoom!—and by the time we rolled into Chilson, the light in the sky was nearly gone.

Julia peered upward as we lugged crates of books into the library. "It's not even six. How can it be this dark already?"

I had the answer to her question, but it wasn't one I wanted to share because I'd been hoping like crazy that what I'd seen on my phone five minutes ago was wrong. "Snow," I said, sighing. "There's a big blob of it coming our way."

She gave a snorting laugh. "Welcome to northwest lower Michigan. Winter and three months of tough sledding. Why is it we choose to live here?"

"Because those three months are amazing. And winter isn't so bad."

Julia picked up a final crate of books. "I'm okay with winter in November, December, January, and February, but according to the wall calendar in my kitchen, March is supposed to be lambs and daffodils."

We descended the bookmobile stairs. I shut the door behind us, made sure it was locked, and picked up my last crate. "I think you need a new calendar."

"What I need," she said, "is sunshine. My seasonal light helps a lot, but it's not the same as blue skies and that lovely feeling of radiant heat on your skin." She looked up. "Here comes your snow."

The flakes drifting down were the fat wet ones that would stick to branches and trees, transforming the world into a white wonderland in minutes. It would also mean super slippery driving, so the second we got the crates inside, I told Julia to go on home.

"Your commute is ten times longer than mine, and way hillier. I'll finish up."

She protested, but not very hard, and soon I saw her taillights fade off into the falling snow.

"And now the work begins," I murmured out loud and traipsed over to my car and opened the passenger door.

"Mrr?"

"Yeah, I know this isn't the normal schedule," I said, unbuckling the cat carrier. "Your mom voluntarily stuck herself with the job of checking in all the return books. And because it's cold and dark, I don't want to leave you in the car that whole time."

"Mrr!"

"Yes, I know you have a fur coat and you'd almost certainly be fine, but I'd feel guilty."

"Mrr."

I wasn't sure he'd be so nonchalant about it when he realized he was going to be stuck in the carrier for the next half hour, but that was a problem for half an hour from now.

The task of checking in and reshelving books could be monotonous, but only if you thought of it as checking in and reshelving books. If you thought of it as the story of a book's journey out of the library and into a home and mind, or if you thought of it as the job of reuniting a book with its friends and family, it wasn't a job at all but an exercise in imagination.

Eddie, mercifully, took a nap while I worked, and in not so very long, I was pulling on my coat. "Awake, my friend," I said. "Time to head for home. If we're lucky, Rafe has started cooking and the sum total of my contribution will be washing dishes."

"Mrr," the carrier said sleepily.

"Know how you feel, pal." I picked up the carrier. "If you want to snore through the whole thing, fine by me. Your kibble won't spoil and . . . whoa."

I'd just pushed open the door. The forecast for two to four inches of snow had been wildly inaccurate, because I was looking at five inches, and it was still coming down.

"Pretty," I muttered to myself as I trudged with Eddie to my car. "It's pretty. And at least I'm wearing boots." The thought perked me up, because five inches of snow with no boots would have been zero fun, so I was humming as I started the car, got Eddie inside, and brushed the snow off my car.

I opened the driver's door, sat, knocked my boots together to shake off at least some of the snow, swiveled around, and shut the door. "Ready, Eddie?" He didn't say no, so I slowly eased the car forward, thankful for the hundred millionth time for the invention of snow tires.

We made it out of the employee lot and to the side street and were passing the library when, through the blanket-like snowfall, my attention was caught by a man picking his way gingerly across the main parking lot.

"No boots," I said to Eddie. "Bet he's not happy."

The main library was open for another hour, but with this snow I wasn't surprised that the man's SUV was the only one left in the lot. I hoped he had a snow brush in his vehicle and looked back over my shoulder, just in time to see the man's arms whirl around, his legs churning.

There was only one way for that to end.

I pulled to the side of the road, put the car in park, and ran to him. "Sir? Sir? Are you okay?"

By the time I reached him, the man was sitting up. "Okay? What kind of question is that?" he asked, making his way to his hands and knees. "Of course I'm not okay, I just fell on my—" He stopped suddenly and looked up. "Oh. It's you."

I almost said the same thing. Instead, I leaned down and helped Jim Kittle to his feet. Or rather, tried to help, because he shook off my assistance, grunting that he was perfectly capable of standing up by himself, that he didn't need the help of anyone, let alone a girl.

"Glad you're not hurt," I said politely.

He glared at me. "Why? Worried about your insurance? About negligence? This is a public parking lot. It should be clear."

I wasn't sure how anyone could possibly accomplish that, since it was still coming down like a snow globe, but I did my best to smile. "Good to see you, Jim. Take care driving home."

"You and your little cat, too," he practically snarled.

I'd started walking away but turned back. "I heard that you'd been dating Cheryl Webb back in 1990. And that she broke up with you because she was seeing an older man. Do you know who it was?"

"None of your business," he snapped. "And why do you care? She's been dead for years, the GAC has been over for years, and now I hear Gerald Arnhold is finally dead. Not to speak ill, but sometimes people get what they deserve." He stomped to his car, got inside without brushing off his windshield, and pulled away with his wipers straining against the snow's weight.

Stepping through my own footsteps, I picked my way back to my car, thinking that his reaction had been interesting. Very, very interesting indeed.

A sudden and horrific thought entered my brain. I whirled around and peered through the snow at Jim's SUV. Was that the same one that had almost run me over? Could what I'd assumed was a distracted driver have actually been a murder attempt?

"Don't be silly," I said out loud. "This is Chilson. A happy little summer resort town. We all know each other. People don't kill people here."

Only apparently they did.

Chapter Nineteen

Overnight, the wet heavy snow froze into a solid mass of slipperiness. The roads were clear and plowed, but most of the sidewalks were going to be too treacherous to walk on for days, if not weeks. As I drove the short distance from home to the library, I made a face at the frozen world and started to catch a glimpse of why people went south for the winter.

To help lighten the library mood, that morning I sent an email to everyone working that if they gave me their order for Shomin's and handed over their money, I'd do pickup and delivery. A small flurry of orders came in, so at lunchtime I drove downtown where the roads and the sidewalks were clear of all things slippery.

Shomin's Deli, owned and operated by library patron and my friend Reva Shomin, was one of those places where if you didn't make a concerted effort to try new things, you'd order the same thing over and over again, digging your rut deeper and deeper every time you walked in the door.

Luckily, I was okay with food ruts, so it didn't hurt my feelings at all when Reva called out, "Olives and Swiss cheese on sourdough," the second she saw me.

"Yes," I said, laughing, "but also this." I held out the list.

She took it from me. "You know, you could have ordered this online and saved yourself fifteen minutes," she said as she started entering the order into the register.

"But then I wouldn't have the chance to talk to you."

Reva smiled. "You're the nicest bookmobile librarian I've ever met. Speaking of, how's Eddie doing? The kids and I haven't seen him in ages."

I dangled one of my mittens in the air. "These got covered in cat hair just this morning."

"Fresh Eddie hair." She laughed. "If this wasn't a restaurant, I'd take some of that home for the kids. They'd love it."

Just after I'd handed over the money, the deli's door opened and, without looking, I moved aside to make way for the next customer.

"See you finally got that website thing figured out."

I turned and saw Mort Neely eyeing me. His wife, Lisa, was coming in after him, stomping the snow from her boots on the entry mat. Though there were many things I wanted to say to him, they would all remain unsaid. I was a professional, and it was never a good idea to get into public arguments with anyone, library patrons least of all.

"Hello, Mort," I said politely. "Lisa, how are you?" Mort gave me a grimace and I stiffened, preparing for a verbal attack.

"I need to apologize," he said, giving his wife a sidelong glance.

Wait, what? "Um . . ."

"About that letter to the editor. You saw it, right? How I lambasted the library about that website thing?"

So many things came to mind all at once that my brain got stuck. Jammed tight like a plugged sink that could only be cleared with a huge plunger and a lot of sweaty effort. "Um . . ."

"Honey," Lisa said, patting his arm, "if you're going to talk to Minnie a minute, I'm going to put our order in. I know how you get when you're hungry."

Mort nodded and she moved off. He stepped closer, forcing me to look up at him. I inched backward, but he closed the gap. "Anyway, I'd had a bad day, we've had some family health issues, and my worries manifested in that letter. I emailed it in without thinking things all the way through, and I shouldn't have."

"Okay," I said. "Thanks." I moved backward a second time, but it didn't do any good because he moved, too, looming over me. In the three years that Mort and Lisa had been using the bookmobile, I'd never once realized that Mort had bullying tendencies. I hated bullies with a fierce and abiding passion. Which made me think of something. Last night, I'd gotten quite the reaction from Jim Kittle when I'd irritated him with questions. Now might be an excellent time to learn more.

"Do you remember Gerald Arnhold?" I asked. "From the Great Airport Controversy?"

Mort didn't blink. "Of course I remember."

"You heard he was killed?"

Mort frowned. "Arnhold died ice fishing."

"I heard you were involved with the pro-expansion side of the GAC. That you worked with Cheryl Webb, going door to door."

"Me, Cheryl, and fifty other people. If that expansion had happened, I might not have had to move downstate to get a job. Why are you asking? What does that have to do with Gerry Arnhold?"

"It's just curious. Cheryl's murder back then, and Gerald's murder now, and both of them involved with the GAC."

"There's nothing curious about any of it. She died what, more than thirty-five years ago? And Arnhold's death was an accident. At least that's what I heard," he said. "Didn't know anything about it until we got back the next Saturday. The wife and I were downstate for two weeks, helping with the grandkids."

He pushed past me and sat heavily at a table in the back.

And that, I supposed, was that.

* * *

I walked out of Shomin's carrying two bags filled with carryout containers. The bags, though not heavy, were distracting in that they were emanating a variety of scents, not all of which I could identify.

I sniffed. That one was ham. That one was some kind of drippy cheese. That one was corned beef, and that one was maybe turkey. I sniffed again, trying to isolate more smells.

"Yo. Minnie."

The voice sort of registered, but it was the large shape that made me stop in my tracks. I looked up—way up—to see Mitchell Koyne standing in front of me, next to my car's passenger door.

"Hey, Mitchell," I said. "Do me a favor and open the car door, will you? It's unlocked." My statement was pointless; no one in Chilson locked their vehicles in winter, a fun fact that I would never tell my parents, as they'd be shocked and appalled that I would ever be so careless and trusting.

"Huh? Oh, sure." He swept it open, and as I deposited the bags inside, he asked, "You still looking for a present for Rafe's birthday? Because I think I finally figured out a great one. Took some work, though. He's not an easy guy to shop for."

"I'm finding that out," I said, sighing. "Maybe I should have thought about that before I married him."

"Yeah." Mitchell nodded. "Bianca? I'll never run out of things to get her. And she always knows what to get me. My mom says it's the sign of a good marriage. Like last Christmas, Bee was so cool with the—"

If Mitchell started listing the gifts he'd bought for Bianca, he'd start listing the gifts he'd considered and didn't buy, the gifts he might buy next year, and the gifts she'd bought him, so with no guilt whatsoever I interrupted him mid-sentence. "What is it that you think I should get for Rafe?"

"It's not super expensive," he said.

I laughed. "Don't sound so apologetic. Librarians are very happy to give great presents that don't cost a lot."

"Yeah?" He brightened. "Okay, then. Rafe likes beer, right?" That didn't need a response, but I nodded anyway, and Mitchell nodded along with me. "Right," he said. "So I found this poster of beers from all over the world. Only they're scratch-off."

"Scratch-off? You mean there's a beer smell when you . . ." I made a face. To me, the scent of beer was about as appealing as burned cabbage.

"What? Oh. No. Before you scratch, the beer label is black and white. After you scratch, it's in color. I'll text you a link, but take a look." He pulled out his phone, tapped a few times, and turned it around.

I did see. And I also saw that Rafe would have a great time tracking down all those beers. He would make it into some sort of game, involve friends, and make a ceremony out of the scratching. "That," I said in full honesty, "is an amazingly cool present, and I doubt I ever would have thought of it. Thanks. I owe you."

Mitchell beamed. "You're welcome, and you owe me nothing. This is fun. I should be paying you!" He headed off, back to the toy store I presumed.

I continued to stand on the sidewalk, looking through the car window at the food bags, mentally listing my current life failures.

First, Mitchell came up with better gifts for my beloved than I did.

Second, everyone I'd ever met in my life was a better cook than I was.

Third, that my idea of a personal strategic plan was not, as I'd hoped and dreamed, infusing my husband and our marriage with a sense of purpose.

I stopped counting, because I'd thought of something. There was one thing I could do for Rafe for his birthday that would make him happy—tell him I was abandoning the idea of writing up a strategic plan.

The idea was simultaneously depressing and cheering, but I decided to think about it cheerfully, because if you have the choice, why not be cheerful?

Nodding to myself, I stood up straight, turned, and came an inch away from barging straight into Sabrina.

"Do you ever look where you're going?" she asked.

"Not very often."

"Get yourself into trouble someday, doing that."

It was a statement so true it didn't need any discussion, so I said, "I didn't know Cookie let you out at this hour of the day."

"Not working until three," she said. "Not today, not any Monday for the last month. Got a friend doing chemo in Traverse, and I've been driving her down and back."

I said the things you say in that sort of situation, and she got a sly look on her face. "Her treatments are going so well they're getting shorter. I could probably get back before the lunch rush now, but what Cookie don't know don't hurt him."

After extracting a promise from me that I'd never ever tell Cookie, she went on her way, and I, at long last, got into my car.

But I was whistling, because now I knew there was no way Sabrina had killed Gerald. She was off the suspect list.

* * *

When I was leaving the library that evening, I decided to go the long way home. Getting into food ruts was one thing;

getting into travel ruts was another thing altogether and was something I considered a slippery slope.

Take the same roads day in and day out and what do you see? The same things over and over again. Your mind turns off to your surroundings. You stop paying attention and you turn inward, thinking about the things you need to do and the things you really need to do. You miss things. To combat all that, I liked to take alternate routes whenever I remembered to do so, which admittedly wasn't all that often, but still.

I'd just passed Chilson City Hall and was approaching the Tonedagana County Building when I saw Detective Ash Wolverson walking out the front door of the sheriff's office.

Well, if that wasn't a sign, I didn't know what was.

I slowed and tapped my car's horn, a quick double honk. Ash looked up from picking his way across the asphalt's patchy ice as I pulled into the parking lot and rolled down my window.

"Got a minute?" I asked.

"Depends. Are you going to talk about the wedding?"

"Do you want me to?"

"Not a chance. You know the term bridezilla, right? Don't look like that. I'm not saying Chelsea is. I'm saying our moms have turned into motherzillas."

I tried to picture Lindsey Wolverson, an elegant, urbane woman who'd intimidated the living daylights out of me until I got to know her, as an interfering mother of the groom. "Your mom? Really?"

"Everything was fine," he muttered, "until we told them we didn't want any table decorations. Do we need table decorations? No. Do we want them? No. But apparently Chels and I can't get married without having some table doodads."

I was pretty sure that being classified as a zilla took more than having an opinion about reception decorations, but I let it go. "I was wondering if I could talk to you about Cheryl Webb's murder."

Ash pulled up his coat sleeve and glanced at his watch. "I have a few minutes. I can't tell you anything, though, since it's still an open investigation."

How could I not know, since between him and Hal Inwood I'd been told a zillion times?

I parked my car and, since the sun was going down, taking the thirty-degree temperature down with it, we went inside and settled ourselves in his small office.

"What's up?" He leaned back in his chair, putting his hands behind his head and his feet up on his desk.

I looked pointedly at the bottom of his shoes. "I take it the sheriff isn't around?" Sheriff Richardson wasn't exactly a stickler for spit and polish, but I had a feeling that the placement of Ash's feet would not meet with her approval.

"She left half an hour ago for a county board meeting. So do you have something to tell me about the Cheryl Webb case, or are you just going to ask questions I won't answer?"

Probably both. I sat on the front edge of the chair. "You knew that Jim Kittle was dating Cheryl, right? But that she broke up with him not long before she was killed?"

Ash yawned though his nod. "Sure. Back then, he was . . . well, let's just say he was investigated heavily."

"But did you know *why* Cheryl broke up with him?"

"What?" He frowned. "What do you mean, why?"

"Exactly that."

"Kittle was looked into. Inside, outside, top, and bottom. If he did it, there was no proof." His feet came down and he started to stand. "Now, if you don't mind, I have a fiancée who's waiting for— "

"Cheryl was seeing an older man."

Ash sat down hard. "She was what?"

"That's why she broke up with Jim. She was seeing someone else. Someone older."

"According to who?"

I repeated what Marcia had told me, word for word, or at least as close as I could remember.

"Huh." Ash picked up a pen. "Who told you this? Marcia Keeby . . . okay, thanks. I'll go back and look at the notes, see if that was in there. It probably was, but sometimes things get missed." He paused, then said, "Thanks, Minnie."

* * *

Later that night, sitting on the couch with the two males in my life, I patted my cat on the head and said, "He actually thanked me, can you believe it?" Eddie stopped purring. "Not you, silly," I murmured reassuringly. "Ash. Ash thanked me. I would never expect any thanks from you." Half a heartbeat later, Eddie started purring again.

The love of my life, who was far more interested in thumbing through the television offerings than in anything I was doing, said, "He does that at least once a year. Now that's what I'm talking about." He sat back, smiling.

I glanced at the television. Apparently what he was talking about was a baseball game. "It's the middle of March. There is still snow on the ground. Why is there baseball?"

"Spring training," he said, in a "duh" tone of voice. "And that's Florida. No snow, see?"

He pointed at the green grass and blue skies. I did indeed see, but that didn't explain why it was on our television. "If I recall correctly, the spring training games have zero impact on the regular season games."

Rafe, not looking away from the screen, patted my knee. "Knew you'd catch on eventually."

"But if . . ." I let my question trail off into nothingness. Clearly, I did not understand sports. If I pressed, he would tell me that watching these games was a rite of spring. Or that it was interesting to watch the young players. Or that he wanted to see how what's-his-name was hitting now that he was recovered from some icky injury the year before.

"Just half an hour," he said. "Then we can do whatever."

I patted his knee. "Yes, dear," I said, and reached for my tablet, knowing that his version of half an hour was fluid, depending wholly and completely on who was at bat and in what part of the inning the game happened to be thirty minutes from now.

After spending a few minutes on email, I turned the tablet a little bit away from Rafe and ordered Mitchell's gift suggestion. The email reply assured me that it would be delivered to the library long before Rafe's birthday, and my only problem would be remembering to bring it home to wrap before the day.

With my chores done, there were still twenty minutes left in the theoretical half hour. Since I needed something to occupy my mind, I decided to write actual notes of the things I'd recently learned.

Mort Neely. He'd apologized for hating on the library's website, which was nice, but if he hadn't gone off the rails about it in the first place, the apology wouldn't have been necessary. Anyway, he'd said he and Lisa had been downstate the day Gerald died, helping out with their grandchildren, so he was out as a suspect.

Sabrina. Though she'd never been on my list of people I wanted to be when I grew up, it might be time to revise things. Anyone who volunteered to drive a friend to Traverse and back for months on end—in the winter—was a good person, even if she was sometimes gruff around the edges. And it was hard to come up with a more solid alibi than chemotherapy, so Sabrina was also out.

What else had I learned? Mostly that Jim Kittle was still touchy about . . . well, okay, he was always touchy about pretty much everything, but he'd flared up like a rocket when I'd asked him about Cheryl breaking up with him for an older man.

So. I'd eliminated two suspects. Who was left? Sliding a glance at Rafe, I took my hands off the tiny keyboard, because some things shouldn't be written down. I ran through the four names in my head: Rick Niswander. Duffy Ulrich. Linda Kopecky. Jim Kittle. My father-in-law, the Friends of the Library president, a library board member, and a top contender for crankiest library patron.

As I thought about the names, I started to get a tight twisty feeling in my stomach. Of course I wanted to find out who'd killed Gerald. Of course I wanted whoever did it to pay for their crime. But I absolutely did not want Gerald's killer to have been three of those four people.

"Stop that," I murmured.

Rafe nudged me. "I know, right? That ump is either blind or this is the first baseball game he's ever seen."

It was so weird when my internal monologue meshed with my husband's viewing experience. I nudged him back and pulled out my phone. While I'd learned a lot about Duffy's past, I hadn't done anything to find out if she'd known Gerald outside of the GAC (he was pro, she was con), if she'd had any contact with him since 1990, and if she'd been anywhere close to Gerald's little lake house on the day he'd died.

Duffy and I had long ago exchanged cell numbers, and to date, all of our text exchanges had been about the Friends, coordinating meetings and events and all the activities that the Friends of the Library helped with. This would not be that. This was going to be a jump into vastly different territory.

I stared at the small screen, thinking. Came up with an idea. Thought some more. Realized the idea was pretty stupid. Squinched up my face in an attempt to wring more thoughts out of my brain but gave it and started typing.

Minnie: *Sorry to bother you with something that's not about the Friends, but I was wondering if you remembered Gerald Arnhold. He died about three weeks ago, and I'm thinking about helping the family put together memories for a service this summer.*

I waited, but there was no immediate response. Well, that was to be expected. It was an odd question, and I didn't know her well enough to know whether or not she was the respond-right-away-to-text-messages kind of person, or if she was a I'll-respond-later type of person.

Hoping I hadn't damaged my relationship with Duffy, I put my phone down and did my best to be interested in baseball. I could do it for ten minutes, couldn't I? It turned out that I could, and the promised half hour was ticking down to zero when my phone pinged.

Duffy: *I considered that man dead years ago.*

I watched the dots blink and waited for a second sentence. Something that explained her statement, that indicated she'd been making a joke that turned out to not be funny. Something. Anything.

But the dots disappeared.

And didn't come back.

Chapter Twenty

The next day was a bookmobile day, but because of Graydon's continuing absence, I was going to have to take care of business in the building and entrust the outreach enterprise to Julia and Rila in my absence.

In a fun twist of serendipity, Rila had recently obtained her commercial driver's license and had taken the bookmobile out on enough roads for her to be comfortable driving. Though having a CDL was not technically a requirement to drive the vehicle, back in the days when I was trying to convince my then-boss to approve the concept, one of the arguments that had helped him say yes was going above and beyond for every safety procedure I could find.

Because according to everyone, the bookmobile wasn't the bookmobile without Eddie, I handed his carrier over to Julia, saying, "And don't you dare give him treats every time he asks."

"Yes, Mom," she said to me. To Eddie, she stage whispered, "What she doesn't know isn't going to hurt her."

"Mrr!"

I waved them off, confident that everything was going to be fine but wishing I could go with them. Strongmindedly, I turned away before their taillights were out of sight and headed for the building. Inside, I divested myself of coat and boots, made my way to the coffeepot, and had just pushed the happy-making Go button when my cell rang.

"Hey," Rafe said.

"Hey yourself. You know, one of these days I'm going to remember to make a special ringtone for you. If I ever get around to it, what do you want it to be?"

My husband's response was immediate. "Snare drum roll followed by a cymbal crash."

"Really? I was thinking the rubber ducky song." I hummed the tune.

"That works, too," he said. "But I did call for a reason, one that has nothing to do with ducks, rubber or otherwise."

"Oh. Right." My stomach clenched tight. "Is everyone okay?"

"What? Why wouldn't they be? Why, have you heard something?"

This conversation was taking an odd turn, and it was my fault for leading us astray with the ringtone side issue. "No, all good," I said cheerfully. "What's up?"

"It's that personal strategic plan thing."

"Don't worry about it," I said. "Yes, I was making kind of a fuss about it, but it's not a big deal. You don't want to do it, and I'm okay with it. I'm the one who's interested in doing one, and I still can."

"Okay, but I'm doing it, too."

"You . . . are?"

"I can see this is something you care about, so I'm in. But there's one thing."

My singing heart didn't care about that caveat. "Whatever you want."

"No paperwork."

And just like that, the song my heart was warbling went from a theme of rainbows, puppies, and kittens to the theme to the movie *Jaws*. "No what?" I asked, because surely he couldn't have said what I thought he'd said.

"No paperwork. And that includes handwritten, typewritten, and especially anything on a spreadsheet."

"But . . . how . . ." After stammering out thosc two words, I couldn't think of any more to say, so I stopped trying.

"You're the smart one," he said. "You'll figure something out."

He said a quick good-bye, and I stared at my phone, which was suddenly less a communication device and more an expensive rectangle of uselessness.

No documentation? How was that supposed to work? And how could he put the smart label on me? I didn't want that kind of pressure, not this early in our marriage. Maybe in a few years, but not now, for crying out loud.

I filled my coffee mug. "If I'm so smart," I muttered to myself, "why can't I manage to cook anything that has more than three ingredients? If I'm so smart, why did I have to ask Mitchell for present ideas? If I'm so smart, why can't I figure out what happened to Gerald? If I'm so smart, why did I leave my takeout lunch on the roof of the car last month? If I'm so smart, why—"

Knock knock knock!

The rapping noise was coming from the front door, a door that very clearly stated the library's opening time, which was more than an hour from now.

I squashed a shameful temptation to ignore the noise, and mug in hand, went to the lobby and pushed open the door just wide enough for my head. "Sorry," I said, "but the library doesn't—" I stopped. "Pam? What are you doing here?"

Pam Fazio bounced up and down on her toes. "Can I use one of your public computers? Something's wrong with mine, and if I don't finalize my order from this one company by ten, I lose the sale price, and twenty-five percent off isn't nothing."

I pushed the door open. "Twenty-five percent is a solid reason for early entry, and if that's not in the library handbook, it should be."

"You're the best." Pam stomped wet snow off her boots as we walked through the lobby. "I owe you one."

I wondered if this itchy feeling was how Mitchell had felt the day before when I'd thanked him. "Thank the coffee," I said, holding up my mug. "So maybe that's what your store should sell. Coffee beans." I laughed.

Pam came to an abrupt halt and stared at me. "Out of the mouths of librarians. Coffee beans. No one else downtown sells them."

"I was joking," I said weakly.

Pam was speedwalking past me, on her way to the closest computer. "Glass containers," she said. "Tall round ones, like old candy jars in a general store. I have a sideboard in the back I can bring out for the display. I'll have to move something, maybe a couple of somethings, but that's okay. A little moving around could be just the ticket."

Her words caught at me. A little moving around. Maybe that's what I needed to do with how I was thinking about Gerald's death.

Only . . . how?

* * *

The rest of that morning, I buried myself in the things that needed doing before Graydon got back. Not that I'd been slacking, but now that his return was imminent, I realized two things. One, I wanted Graydon to come back to a library in tip-top condition inside and out. Two, I was seriously looking forward to his return so I could get back to focusing on my own job.

"Focus," I murmured every time I started to get sidetracked by something shiny, and I repeated it so many times that it actually started to work.

At half past noon, I pushed back from my desk extremely satisfied with my morning's work. The next board meeting packet was done, the April schedule was finalized, and my solution to the website drama was underway.

"Just goes to show," I told Holly, "staying focused is the key to success."

We were sitting in the kitchen. I was eating reheated pasta leftovers, and Holly was forking up a salad mixture that was almost too pretty to eat. At least three different greens, carrots, zucchini, red peppers, cauliflower, hard-boiled egg, and feta cheese, all topped with a light vinaigrette.

"Take this." I pointed at her lunch, then mine. "I hardly think about food at all and am happy to eat whatever I can grab. You have growing children that need proper nutrition, and so you're focused on that."

Holly glanced at my plate, which to my way of thinking included vegetables because, tomato sauce. "Adults need nutrition, too, you know."

"Not my point."

"Which is? Sorry, I lost track."

Oh, the serendipity of conversation. "That keeping on track, staying focused, is the way to get things done."

My good friend gave me a "duh" look. "You're just learning that now? How old are you?"

Apparently not old enough to keep from sharing my internal narrative with coworkers was the obvious response, but instead of answering I redirected. "Where are you and Brian taking the kids for spring break this year? You told me, but I don't remember. Colorado, was it?"

Holly brightened. "Close, but not quite." She started telling me about the plan to fly to Salt Lake City to meet Brian, then driving up to Park City to ski.

After my lunch dishes were washed, dried, and returned to my backpack, I sat down at my desk. "Focus," I said to my computer screen.

There were four names still on my suspect list. How could I eliminate some of them? By focusing on finding alibis. How could I find the alibis for any of the four?

"By focusing," I said quietly, hoping that repeating the words over and over again would help me get somewhere. It didn't, so I got out pen and paper and started writing initials. RN, for Rick Niswander. DU, Duffy Ulrich. LK, Linda Kopecky. JK, Jim Kittle.

RN. DU. LK. JK.

I stared at the letters until my eyes started drying out, which didn't help me focus at all.

Sighing, I pushed back and thought about the four of them. I knew very little about Linda, even though she was a board member. I'd met Duffy less than a year before, and though I'd known Jim Kittle ever since I'd moved Up North, it was more professional acquaintance than anything else. I didn't know if he was married, if he had children, or the name of his favorite Chilson restaurant.

However, I did know a fair number of things about Rick. His wife. Offspring. What truck he drove. Where he worked. What he liked to do in his off hours. What he—

My thoughts came to a screeching halt.

Where he worked sometimes impacted what he did in his off hours. The other day he'd mentioned having to attend a County Board of Commissioners meeting, something about needing their approval for an easement to a substation his company wanted to construct. When were . . .

I sat up, brought my computer screen to life, zipped to the county's website, started looking at their board meeting schedule, yes, there had been a morning board meeting the day Gerald died.

A few clicks later, I found the meeting packet, and sure enough, first on the agenda was Easement Request—Northern Energies. Below the listing were the small words "Presentation by Rick Niswander." Another couple of clicks and I opened the link to the meeting's video.

And there Rick was, looking relaxed and confident sitting in the front row of the audience right at the meeting start time.

The Board of Commissioners met in Chilson, practically on the other side of the county from Gerald's little lake house. No way could Rick have had the time to kill Gerald, motor across the county, and show up to a board meeting by eight thirty. He didn't do it. Not that I'd really suspected him, but it was lovely to have proof.

Humming happily, I picked up my pen and crossed out Rick's initials.

Down to three.

* * *

Eliminating Rick from the suspect list for absolutely sure made me so happy that my afternoon flew past almost as quickly as a bookmobile day did. Thanks to the ongoing miracle of cell phones, Julia kept me up-to-date on their whereabouts. She also sent photos.

Eddie sleeping in the cat carrier, Eddie sprawled across the lap of a grinning gap-toothed urchin, Eddie sitting on the driver's seat, looking as if he was ready to start the engine and drive off, Rila and Eddie waving good-bye at the third-grade class where Julia had just done a story hour.

She texted me when they'd entered the Chilson city limits, and I was waiting as Rila drove in and parked in the back lot as smoothly as if she'd been doing it for years.

"Good thing I don't get stage fright," she said as she handed down a crate of books into my outstretched hands. When I looked puzzled, she laughed. "I'm talking about you. You were standing there watching me. I've never done this by myself."

"Oh." I blinked. "Sorry. Didn't think of it like that."

She smiled. "Well, you can be intimidating. Not," she hastened to say when she saw the stunned look on my face, "that you intend to. It's just that you're so good at this, it makes me a little nervous to have you watching me."

"Huh," I told Eddie after I'd been shooed away and he and I were driving home. "Who would have thunk it? I can be intimidating."

"Mrr," he said through a yawn, which I interpreted as "Maybe to a human. Not to a cat."

"Fair," I said. "We all know that cats are superior beings. The big question for you, then, is why do you let us run the world?" He made no response. I glanced over and saw him looking straight at me, eyes wide open, gaze intent.

I looked away and shifted in my seat. Yes, I anthropomorphized many conversations with Eddie, but that look clearly said, "What makes you think cats aren't already running the world?"

"Whatever," I said, because what I needed to focus on wasn't feline world domination, but the three suspects left on my list. I tapped my mittened fingers on the steering wheel and decided to think through what I knew about Duffy, Jim, and Linda in my head in alphabetical order.

Duffy had been a successful business owner, now retired. She was full of energy. She'd taken on the role of Friends of the Library president, and . . .

I frowned. And what else? Someone like Duffy would surely be doing far more than one thing in her retirement. What else was she doing? Renovating her house? Gardening? Writing a book? Playing an instrument?

It was easy to picture the colorful Duffy playing lead guitar in a band, so I wished it could be true. But Chilson was a small town and surely I would have heard about something like that.

Then again, maybe she kept it a secret because . . . because her family didn't approve. Maybe she only played gigs that were out of town to preserve her secret, and maybe . . .

I rolled my eyes at myself. It was a fun idea, but way outside the realm of likelihood. What I needed was to talk to someone who knew Duffy. Ideally, someone who could provide her with a rock-solid alibi so I could cross her name off my list and move on.

Pam Fazio knew Duffy, but only from the Friends, so she probably didn't know her all that well. Julia also knew Duffy, but though they'd been close in high school, I wasn't sure if they'd reconnected much since Julia had moved back to Chilson.

I ran through the other names in my head, but it wasn't until I pulled into the garage that my brain synapses finally did their thing.

"Aunt Frances," I told Eddie as I lugged his carrier into the house. "Remember? Last year when I first met Duffy, she said she knew Aunt Frances. I asked her how, and she told me to ask my aunt, but I don't think I ever did. Now's the time, yes?"

"Mrr," he said sleepily.

"Glad you agree." I set the carrier on the kitchen floor and opened the wire door. Eddie, instead of leaping out like a normal cat, curled himself into a tiny ball and started snoring.

"Hope you don't stay awake all night tonight," I said, but I said it quietly so I wouldn't disturb him.

Rafe had texted me that he had some Batgate fallout to deal with and that he'd bring home takeout, so after changing into my comfy loose leggings and oversized sweatshirt, I flopped on the couch and called my aunt's cell phone.

"Hey," I said when she answered. "You busy?"

"Doing dinner dishes, so depends on your point of view."

I almost asked what she and Otto had made for dinner, but I didn't want to get cooking envy. "Duffy Ulrich," I said. "A while back, she said to ask you how you two know each other, and I forgot until now."

My elegant aunt gave a snorting laugh. "Oh, she did, did she? Kind of her to let me tell the story my way."

"There's a story?" I put my feet up on the coffee table. "Do tell."

"Once upon a time," she said, "there was a chamber of commerce golf outing."

I frowned. "You don't golf."

"Not after that outing, I don't," she said darkly, then launched into a long and rambling tale that started with her name and Duffy's name being drawn as partners ("My name from the novice bucket, hers from the experienced bucket") and ending with the two of them coming in dead last thanks to my aunt's complete lack of golfing ability, and finishing with the two of them becoming friends for life.

"Huh," I said. "Guess I didn't know that Duffy golfed, either."

"She's a nut for it. If she'd taken it a little more seriously, she could have gone pro. And now that she's retired, she's having fun traveling around, doing pro-am tournaments. You know, professionals pairing up with amateurs? Matter of fact, she was down in Florida just a few weeks ago, playing in one. A Valentine's weekend thing, I believe."

We chatted a bit longer, and when we hung up, I lunged for my tablet, fired up the search engine, and started typing.

Sure enough, there'd been a pro-am tournament in central Florida on the weekend of Valentine's Day. It had been rained out on Sunday, so they'd finished the tournament on Monday, the day that Gerald had been killed. The tournament had a Facebook site, and there were dozens of photos. Duffy, with her mop of wild red hair and vertical efficiency, was easy to spot.

This was proof. Duffy was in Florida that day. She couldn't have killed Gerald. Which left two suspects: Linda Kopecky and Jim Kittle.

And of the two, one was far more likely than the other.

Chapter Twenty-One

The next day was the happy combination of being Friday and being a bookmobile day. And, since I'd been so amazingly productive the day before, I was able to drive off into the wild blue yonder with a light heart and a clear conscience.

"Maybe that's why it was so easy for me to focus yesterday," I said to Julia. "Motivation."

She gave me a look that felt a lot like the "duh" look Holly had given me the day before, the one that again made me think I should really keep more of my thoughts to myself.

Luckily, I'd made the inane comment just as massive snowflakes started smacking against the windshield, so it was easy to redirect the topic to the ever popular one of Northern Michigan weather patterns.

That particular topic ended up as the trend of the morning. Every person who came aboard commented about the snow, a handful positive, but most negative, along the lines of "I know it's still March, and getting snow until mid-April is expected up here, but geez, I'm getting tired of this."

One of the few who didn't mind was a new-ish bookmobile patron, Lanelle Westphal. She was a few years younger than me and had recently moved Up North with her husband and their two tiny humans. Her husband was working at the Petoskey hospital as an operations manager, and she was miraculously managing to juggle kid caretaking with a part-time remote job of design engineering for a major car company.

"Isn't it pretty out there?" A smiling Lanelle tucked her straight dark blond hair behind her ears as she watched her offspring arrow toward Eddie. "I love the way snow looks on the pine trees."

I smiled back. "And I love your attitude. Everyone else today has been grouchy about it."

"I'm saving my grouchiness for tomorrow." Her laugh turned into a sigh. "I've been avoiding doing something because it's going to make me sad, and being sad always makes me grumpy." Lanelle brightened. "On the plus side, I'll have an entire day without anyone tugging at my pant legs."

"Always a silver lining," I said, nodding, "if you look hard enough."

She gave me an odd look. "That's what Uncle Gerald always said."

"Sounds like a smart man."

"He was. But . . . you knew him. He's the one who told me about the bookmobile in the first place. And Eddie."

Light dawned. "Gerald Arnhold was your uncle?"

"Great uncle, technically. My parents brought us up here all the time as kids. Those summers are one of the reasons I wanted my husband to apply for that job in Petoskey."

I wondered how I hadn't known Lanelle was Gerald's great-niece, but not for very long. Gerald never talked about his family, and I suppose there was no real reason for Lanelle to say anything about it.

"And," she said quietly, "I've been wanting to talk to you and Julia. To say I'm sorry you had to find him, but also, thank you." Her voice went higher at the end of her sentence, making it almost a question.

"Your uncle was a very nice man," I said, smiling sadly. "We miss him."

Lanelle sighed. "Thanks. We do, too. It's going to be hard, sorting out the things in his house, making all those decisions. The biggest decision I've made so far is to turn off the water heater, because I could just hear Uncle Gerald saying 'No sense spending that money when no one's in the house.'"

Without thinking too much, I jumped in. "Would you like some help? I'd be happy to come out."

"Oh. No. That's super nice of you, but I couldn't ask you to do that."

"Sure you can," I said. "My husband's going to be helping a friend with a plumbing repair"—at least I assumed he would be—"and I don't have anything else I have to do." I could see her wavering. "I'd like to do this one last thing for Gerald," I said quietly. "Please let me help."

"If you're sure . . ."

I was. We arranged a time, Lanelle said she'd bring lunch, I said I'd bring coffee, and the deal was finalized with an exchange of cell numbers.

"What was that all about?" Julia asked when we were on the road again. "With Lanelle." When I told her, she gave me an arch look. "Let me guess. In addition to cleaning and boxing things up, you're going to try and find clues."

"Is that a problem?"

"No," she said. "Just . . . be careful."

I tried to do the one eyebrow thing. "Of what? Lanelle?"

"Not sure," she said. "I have a feeling, that's all."

"A good one or a bad one?" I asked, trying not to laugh. The last time Julia had had a feeling it turned out to be an allergic reaction to the capers her husband had added to the mayonnaise he'd slathered on her ham sandwich.

She shrugged and didn't say. She still wasn't saying much when we pulled into the next stop, where a small cluster of cars was waiting for us. We weren't late, but this stop was known for its avid readers, and they liked to have as much time as they could on the bookmobile, making their reading choices. As we came to a stop, people started climbing out of their cars, and I noted that one of them was Lisa Neely.

After she was on board and had petted Eddie sufficiently, I asked, "No husband today?"

"It's his turn for downstate grandkid duty," she said cheerfully. "Our daughter and son-in-law have needed help the last few weeks. Their new baby has been in the hospital—she's out of the woods, now, thank heavens—so us four grandparents have been taking turns, sitting with the other kids."

"Glad to hear things are getting better," I said, thinking fast. "That's a lot of stress. How long has this been going on?"

Lisa hmm'd. "It's what, almost the middle of March now? The baby was born on the seventeenth of February, so going on a month."

Something wasn't adding up. "At Shomin's the other day, Mort said you were both downstate the weekend of Valentine's Day." Or words to that effect.

"No, we didn't go down until Molly was in labor, and that was the sixteenth," Lisa said, frowning. "You must have heard him wrong."

Not a chance. "Probably." I smiled.

Lisa moved off to peruse the New Fiction section, and I watched her go, wondering about her husband. Had Mort merely been mistaken about the dates, or had he lied? And if he'd lied, why?

I sighed.

Back to three suspects.

* * *

The sun made an actual appearance the next morning, something I took to be a good omen for the day ahead.

"Because why not?" I asked.

It was a question asked of Eddie, who I'd thought was waiting patiently for me to put my empty oatmeal bowl on the floor so he could lick up the few molecules of milk I left behind.

"Mrr," he said, but his voice came from a distance.

"Where are you?"

Something skittered across the floor from the dining room into the kitchen.

I slid off the stool. "Thanks." I bent to pick up a paper-wrapped straw. "Good of you to clean up after me," I said, hoping that the straw was a leftover from a recent takeout order and not from, say, last summer. "You're the best."

"Mrr!"

"'You're welcome' would be the correct response." I tossed the straw into the trash and popped my dishes into the dishwasher. Rafe had already left, not, as I'd supposed, to help Bob with his plumbing project ("What? No, we finished that last week. Didn't I tell you?") but to help his buddy Tank drywall the ceiling of his workshop.

"This is the last Saturday," he'd told me as he'd kissed me good-bye. "Well, maybe one more. Then our weekends are free from here on out, so start thinking of fun things to do."

It was an interesting opportunity, and I thought about it the entire drive out to Gerald's little lake house. When I pulled in, Lanelle was already there, and when I walked in with a big thermal jug, she was seated at the kitchen table.

She looked up from the piles and piles of paper. "Please tell me that's coffee."

I hefted the jug. "All for us." With my other hand, I hefted a canvas bag. "Sugar, cream, mugs, and snacks."

"You," Lanelle said fervently, "are my favorite person and I want to be you when I grow up."

Laughing, I said, "That's something I think about other people all the time."

"No way." Lanelle got up and pushed aside the boxes sitting on the laminate kitchen counter, making room for the coffee and its fixings. "How could you want to be anyone else other than the bookmobile lady and Eddie's mom?"

It was a lovely thing to say, and I told her so as we filled our mugs. "But I suppose we should plan our day. Unless you've figured that out already?"

Lanelle blew across the top of her steaming liquid. "Nope. I started with the paperwork because of bills, is all. I put flat boxes, packaging tape, papers, and some moving blankets in the living room, but . . ." She took a long look around the kitchen and blew out a long breath. "There's just so much."

I added cream to my coffee. "Cleaning out the house of a loved one isn't easy. Have you ever done it before?" She shook her head. "Okay. How about this?" I asked, and offered to sort through the things in Gerald's bedroom. I had no idea why, but for me it had always been the shoes that were the most emotionally difficult personal item to deal with, and I'd be happy to spare her that pain. Plus, I wouldn't mind avoiding the kitchen, because that's where Gerald stored the cat treats he'd bought especially for Eddie.

"You'd do that?" The relief in her voice was clear.

"Absolutely no problem. Anything that's in good condition I'll keep for donations, everything else I'll bag up for hauling away. Unless there's something of his you'd like to keep as a memento? No? Okay, then I'll get started."

She eyed the paper-covered table. "I should get back to that."

"You know," I said, "you don't have to work on those here. We could put the papers in a box and put it in your car to go through at your own house."

Lanelle grinned. “And that’s why you’re my role model. You’re always thinking.”

“Oh, the pressure,” I said. “Please don’t.” Especially since my idea for tidying the papers had an underlying ulterior motive of getting a look at everything.

But after the box was filled and escorted outside, the only things I’d seen had been personal papers: bills, bank statements, and insurance policies. And the only things I’d learned were that Gerald’s bill-paying habits had been exemplary and that he could have done Facebook Reels on how to be organized.

After refilling my coffee mug, I left Lanelle to start sorting the kitchen and went down the hall to Gerald’s bedroom.

The door was closed. I put my hand on the knob and turned. Inside, the room was dark and empty of life, just as it had been when Julia and I had peeked in that sad day. I flicked the switch and blinked at the sudden blaze of light that filled the room.

Double bed with a dark plaid bedspread. Nightstand with lamp and reading glasses on top. Four-drawer dresser with nothing on top except a small tray filled with coins and a flattish wooden box.

I lifted the lid. Cuff links. Lapel pins. A dress watch. Things the family might want?

Maybe. I shut the lid, sighed, and got to work.

* * *

It turned out that Gerald had been as organized with his clothing as he’d been with his paperwork, so it didn’t take me long to grasp his system. Dress clothes in the bottom drawer and on the left side of the closet. Non-dressy clothes to wear in public in the next-to-bottom drawer and on the right side of the closet. Everyday and work clothes in the next-to-top drawer; socks, underwear, and pajamas in the top drawer. Extra sheets and blankets were in the closet on the shelf above the clothes rod.

I taped up a couple of the boxes Lanelle had brought, labeled them "Donation: Clothes" and "Donation: Bedding" and filled them up. The paint-spattered work clothes and the worn shoes I put in a garbage bag.

The entire effort took less than an hour, and the room, which had never felt very personal to begin with, was almost oppressively impersonal when I'd finished.

I hauled everything out to the living room and stacked the boxes along the wall where Lanelle had started piling the kitchen things. I told her I'd left the coins and the cuff link box behind. "Do you want me to start on the office?" I asked. Because surely that was where I'd learn something useful.

She was looking at a set of nested mixing bowls. "Uncle Gerald used these to make Christmas cookies. His grandmother's recipe."

"They were excellent," I said. "He always had a plate for us."

Her smile was watery. "I'm really . . . really going to miss him."

At that moment, if I'd been face to face with whoever had killed Gerald, I might have strangled them with my bare hands. I gave Lanelle a quick hug, and murmured that I'd be in the office, sorting out personal things from the business things.

Fifteen minutes later, I found something extremely interesting.

And five minutes after that, I found the jackpot.

* * *

As soon as I got home, I uploaded all the photos I'd taken of Gerald's papers and printed them out. I was still in our little office, reading them, when I heard the back door open and shut. There was a slight pause, then I heard stocking footsteps coming my way.

"In here," I called. "And I have a lot to tell you, so buckle up."

Rafe's voice floated toward me. "I'm covered in drywall dust. I left my pants and shirt by the door and I need to shower before I do anything," he said, his voice getting farther and farther away as he climbed the stairs. "Be back down in a few."

Though that took the wind out of my investigative sails, I did appreciate that he'd taken off his filthy clothes at the back door and not tracked drywall dust all through the house.

Since I was trying to be a kind and considerate wife, I got up, took his dust-laden clothes downstairs at arm's length, and put them in the washing machine on super-duper mode, but on an hour delay to make sure he was out of the shower. I returned to the office, collected the papers, and went into my favorite kitchen drawer—the one that held the takeout menus—because no way would either one of us be feeling like cooking dinner.

An eternity later, Rafe came into the kitchen and right away noted the array of takeout menus. Some of that might have had to do with the fact that I was waving them in front of his face, but he was the best of husbands, so instead of commenting, he took the Fat Boys menu from my hand, asked what I wanted, and made the phone call.

I managed to wait until our sub sandwiches were gone—yes, mostly because I didn't want to get any goo on anything important, but still—and pushed the papers under Rafe's nose while I tidied up the sandwich wrappers and poured the adult beverages.

Rafe read through everything once, then a second time. Though I did my best to tamp down my impatience, I was pretty sure I did a very good job. My husband, however, was excellent at ignoring my physical hurry-up cues and took his time.

At long last, he looked up. "Where did you find these?"

That was his question?

"In Gerald's study," I said. "In two different filing cabinets. The drawer those came out of"—I pointed at the small pile—"was the bottom drawer, which was labeled 'Former Clients.' That other pile was in the drawer marked 'Active,' and it was in a file at the very front of the drawer, and the file itself didn't have any label, but it was a bright red file folder."

Rafe looked at the small stack, the one from the Former Clients drawer. He rubbed his chin, all sandpapery bristly since he hadn't shaved that morning. "If Gerald still had active clients, isn't their paperwork their property? And shouldn't it be going to their new accountant?"

"Sure," I said, and told him what I'd learned that morning. "Lanelle's mom is executor of the estate. She's dealing with all that. But since Lanelle lives here, she was tasked with the sorting. And since I have more administrative experience than she does, I volunteered to deal with the office."

"Okay. So this"—he tapped the small pile—"isn't confidential, or anything."

I resisted the urge to squirm. "Not sure. But all that is twenty years old. And to me, it shows a motive for murder." Rafe put his hand on the papers. I wanted to pull his hand away, to keep him away from the ickiness inside. I didn't, because he would have thought I was even wackier than he'd previously thought.

"Okay," he said again. "Once upon a time, for one year and one year only, Jim Kittle was a client of Gerald's."

"Jim's company," I clarified.

"Right. Jim's company, Precision Metal Solutions. That one year, Gerald did the income taxes for Precision. While running the calculations, he found numerous errors in bookkeeping and reporting. The errors had resulted in underreporting to the IRS, and quarterly payments that were thousands of dollars less than they should have been."

I nodded. "That letter on top tells Jim that the company owes the IRS thousands and thousands of dollars more than they'd estimated. According to the year-end report, Precision lost money that year. A lot of money."

Muttering something derogatory about people who thought they could get away with breaking the law, Rafe pushed the small pile away and drew the larger stack toward us. "This is the stuff I don't get," he said.

I blinked. "What part?"

"All of it. There's a lot of work here. Years and years of notes, but it's just a bunch of notes. Basically nothing but ramblings on eight-and-a-half-by-eleven yellow pads."

His comment cut at me. "They're dated," I said. "And they were filed by year." Rafe gave me a "so what" look. "That matters," I said patiently, "because it shows intent."

"Of what?"

I couldn't believe he was being so obtuse. Then I remembered that he'd been hanging drywall all day. The poor man was probably exhausted, and here I was thumping him for not instantly grasping something I'd been thinking about for hours.

I went to the refrigerator for another beverage for the male human in the house. He made noises of appreciation, and I sat back down. "Years and years of notes, like you said, starting right after he moved to the little lake house."

Rafe popped the top of his beer. "And?"

"And look what he wrote those first few years." For whatever reason, Gerald had put down comments on the first day of every month. "About the GAC, about his role in pushing for the airport expansion, about the division in the town. About Cheryl's murder."

"Okay." Rafe took a long drink. "Still. I don't see the point."

I was sure I was right about this. "Gerald blamed himself. For everything. He'd been the original impetus for the expansion, so to him it only followed that the GAC was his fault. That Cheryl's death was his fault."

Rafe, who'd been about to take another drink, froze with the can halfway up. "Oh," he said.

"It's the only thing that explains all this." I waved at the tall stack. "After those first few years, he spent the next decade or so writing about ways to end the community division." His best idea had been a new project that everyone could rally around. Unfortunately, he hadn't been able to think of a realistic one.

"And then," Rafe said slowly, "he began his own investigation into Cheryl's murder."

"Exactly. With his own version of note taking."

"Okay, I get it." My husband nodded. "These were his personal notes. Most of it was in his head, so he didn't need to write down full explanations. I can see doing that."

Of course he could. "Anyway," I said, "his last notes were the first of February. And he was killed on the fifteenth."

Rafe put his beer down. "He was close. To figuring it out. At least it sure seemed like it. I mean, what was it he wrote that last time, that he needed one more piece of information?"

"Doesn't mean he was close to getting it," I said.

"Or that he even knew how to. Either way, if the killer knew that Gerald was doing this work . . ."

We sat in a silence that was uninterrupted except for a soft "Mrr," from Eddie, who was standing on his back paws, his nose stuck into my elbow. I picked him up and tried to settle him on my lap, but he seemed more interested in what might be in the pocket of my sweatpants. He was so weird.

Rafe gave the paper stack a long look. "Did you tell Lanelle about any of this?"

"Not yet. She knows Julia and I are the ones that found Gerald, but that's it. I think anything else should come from the sheriff's office."

"Yeah," he said. "You're probably right. Speaking of that . . ."

I rubbed my eyes and looked at the wall clock. Almost ten o'clock. "I'll talk to Ash tomorrow."

"In the morning?"

I nodded. "First thing."

Chapter Twenty-Two

If I'd been thinking things all the way through, I would have anticipated Ash's response and prepared myself.

"You did what?" he asked, his voice rising to a near-shout at the end.

I could feel myself prickling so I took a calming breath, just like the management articles recommended. "It's not like I was being sneaky about anything."

"You took pictures of private documents without permission," he said flatly.

"Do you want to know this or not?" I glared at him. The four of us—Ash, his fiancée Chelsea, Rafe, and myself—were sitting at the Round Table. A new twentysomething waitress had poured our coffee and, wonder of wonders, had let us order our own breakfasts. As soon as she'd left, I'd decided it was time to broach the subject of what I'd learned the previous day.

When we'd sat down, I'd maneuvered to sit across from Ash, with the goal of making this conversation easier. In retrospect, that had been a mistake.

Ash glared right back. "I can't act on information that was obtained illegally."

"I was helping a friend! There was nothing illegal about this!"

"Minnie?" Rafe murmured.

I whipped around to face the love of my life, ready and willing to snap at him. Luckily, before a word came out of my mouth, I registered an expression on his face that I'd never seen before. Concern mixed with an apprehension that looked very close to fear.

A zillion thoughts ran through my head in a fraction of a second, most of which could be distilled down to three things: If I let my current anger rise to the surface, it could permanently damage my friendship with Ash. It could damage the friendship that Chelsea and I were developing. And it had the potential to change my marriage, and not in a good way.

So instead of lashing out at Detective Wolverson, I squeezed Rafe's arm lightly and took a deep breath. "Right," I said. "Sorry. It's just . . ." Just what? I shook my head.

Ash gave one of those shrugs that communicated great discomfort with the emotional level. "Don't worry about it. You're invested in this, and you want to see it come to a conclusion."

"Thanks. But . . . can I tell you what I found? A summary, that's all. Thirty-thousand-foot-level stuff. Nothing specific, nothing that couldn't have been learned a number of other ways," I said, and hoped he wouldn't ask what any of those ways might be.

Chelsea leaned, elbows on the table. "Tell me, and if he happens to overhear, that's not your fault, is it?"

Her fiancé rolled his eyes. "Chels, you know that's—"

"Excellent idea," I said. "First off, I've already learned that Jim Kittle hated Gerald." I told them what had happened when I was leaving the library the other night, something I suddenly realized I hadn't told Rafe. Oops. "Maybe his anger was because he blamed Gerald for Cheryl's murder, indirectly anyway. Maybe he'd been stewing about it for years."

Ash held up eight fingers. "That's how many times you used the word 'maybe' in the last thirty seconds."

I ignored his hyperbole. "Yesterday I learned that Gerald did the income taxes for Jim's company. He found some errors that meant the company owned thousands of dollars more in taxes than they'd anticipated."

For the first time, Ash looked interested in what I was saying.

"So," I went on, "maybe, just maybe, Jim hired Gerald to do his company's taxes to get closer to Gerald. To work with him, to find out what he knew about Cheryl, but before that happened, Gerald found out about the taxes."

"That," Ash said slowly, "is interesting."

I nodded. "Isn't it, though? And Gerald was writing notes about—"

Ash held up a hand. "Hang on. I want to establish the timeline. Cheryl Webb was killed during the Great Airport Controversy and the airport expansion efforts died with her. Soon after that, Gerald Arnhold bought that place on the lake, left his job as airport manager, and started a small accounting firm that he operated out of his new house."

He waited for my nod, then kept going. "Meanwhile, Jim Kittle is busy starting his company. Years later he brings his company's tax business to Gerald, who promptly tells him they're doing it wrong and that they owe a ton of money." When I nodded again, he asked, "Was that this year's taxes, or last year's?"

"Neither," I said. "It was five years ago."

And, just like that, Ash's interest vanished. He sat back against the back of the booth with a slight *thump*. "Five years," he said in a tone that indicated he never wanted to talk about this again. Ever. "So why, pray tell, would he wait that long to kill Gerald Arnhold?"

"I don't know," I said. "Maybe it took him that long to decide to do it. Or maybe it took him that long to get up the courage. Or maybe it took him that long to figure out how to do it."

"Again with the maybes." Ash's smile was barely big enough to fit the definition. "Minnie, I trust your instincts. I believe it's possible that Gerald Arnhold was murdered. And believe me, I would love to arrest Cheryl Webb's killer. But this? This isn't anything close to probable cause. It's not actionable."

Of course it wasn't. I'd known that since he'd thumped himself against the seat back. And, in my heart of hearts, I'd known it since yesterday.

All of which meant one thing: I needed to find some hard evidence.

Luckily, I had an excellent idea of how to do that.

* * *

A couple of hours later, I was running my fingers around the outside door trim, looking for Gerald's house key.

"Come on," I muttered. "You were there yesterday and I watched when Lanelle put you back and—hah! Got you!" I took the key off the nail and unlocked the side door.

Inside, the house felt . . . empty. I shivered, and it was only partly because the thermostat had been turned down to the just-warm-enough-to-keep-the-pipes-from-freezing temperature of fifty degrees.

After we'd returned home from the Round Table, I'd told Rafe I wanted to take a quick trip to Gerald's house to take a final look. He'd snorted and said not a chance.

"You're forbidding me?" My voice went up half an octave.

Rafe's arms went around me. "Wouldn't dream of it," he murmured into my hair. "What I meant to say was there's not a chance you're going out there without asking Lanelle, and without me going with you."

And so I'd asked Lanelle, saying I had a few free hours and I'd be happy to continue the boxing up and that my husband would be coming with me and he could work on the basement, a space we hadn't ventured into the previous day.

"You've already done so much. Are you sure?" she'd asked.

I was, but now that I was looking around at the mess we'd left behind, I wasn't so sure. "A work in progress," I said to the piles of boxes strewn all over, and tried not to look at the kitchen table, the place where Gerald and Julia and I had inhaled too many cups of coffee to count. We'd talked about books, TV shows, movies, and the state of the world. We'd also talked about cats, because Gerald liked Eddie and Eddie liked Gerald.

But that was all over. I clenched my fists. And it was gone because someone—

No. Channel the anger. Get to work. Focus.

I had some time to myself, because just before Rafe and I had left, he'd had a call from the school superintendent, a.k.a. his boss, who volun-told him to meet with one last set of parents about Batgate. He'd reluctantly agreed, and knowing that I had no inclination whatsoever to delay my departure for Gerald's little lake house, he made me vow to be careful and to keep my phone with me. Since the only time I didn't have my phone with me was in the shower, that was an easy promise, and on the drive over I made sure it was charged to the tippy top.

I turned the thermostat all the way up to sixty-five. While I was waiting for the house to warm up, I brewed a pot of coffee. It was only after I'd poured coffee into the travel mug I'd brought in from my car and added cream from yesterday's small jug that I realized Lanelle had already packed up the utensils.

"Rats," I said. Not a big deal, but still. I opened drawers and cabinets. Empty, empty, empty . . . but there, in the very back of a drawer, was a single plastic straw. Perfect. I happily stirred my coffee, then, since I didn't want to start a new bag of kitchen garbage, slid the straw into my pants pocket to take home. I spent an obligatory hour sorting, boxing, and labeling the contents of the living room, the bathroom, and two hall closets. Then I headed to the office.

Though the house had warmed up, this room still felt cold. Maybe because it was a corner room, maybe because it had west-facing windows and the west was where most of our wind and weather came from, maybe because this was where Gerald had sat and thought about the sad events of the GAC and—

"Again with the maybes," I said out loud, rolling my eyes at myself because what was I doing quoting Ash? What I should be doing was taking advantage of the time I had available.

I sat on the worn office chair and determinedly didn't think about the hours that Gerald must have spent in this very spot. What I wanted to think about was the most efficient way of looking through Gerald's files, and this time with a narrow purpose: finding any mention of Jim Kittle, Linda Kopecky, or Mort Neely.

To help me focus, I put my phone on the desk and set it to play calming music. Once the soothing spa sounds were in my head, I got to work.

I'd hoped the task would be fast and easy. It was not. Because instead of what I'd hoped to find—folders filed alphabetically by client last names—I instead found a confusing mix that made no sense at all. Not at first, anyway. As I kept looking, however, I realized that the files were indeed alphabetical, but also by year and type of job; bookkeeping, personal income taxes, sole proprietorship income taxes, corporate income taxes, small business audits, larger business audits, and nonprofit audits.

These were Gerald's files, and he'd grown them himself over the years, so he apparently had no need to label the drawers. Not what I would have done, but to each their own.

I hunted around, found a pad of sticky notes and a marker, and soon each drawer had a small square yellow label.

Progress. I rubbed my hands. Definitely progress.

Since there was no reason to dive into the business drawers unless I had to, I started flicking through the personal income taxes files, figuring that was where there'd be the largest number of clients, because basically everybody had to file income taxes.

"H, I, J, K," I murmured in the alphabet song chant, going through the years quickly. This year, five years ago, ten years ago, thirty years ago—no Linda Kopecky. There were, however, many files were labeled Neely. Mort and Lisa Neely, specifically.

Every time I came across a Neely file, I piled it on the desk. By the time I came to the end of the personal income tax drawers, the pile was high enough for me to start worrying about its stability.

And just as I had that thought, the folders cascaded to the floor, papers flying left, right, and center.

"Well, rats," I muttered, and got down onto my hands and knees to clean up my mess. As I did, I felt more than heard the back door open and close.

"Rafe?" I called over my shoulder. "I'm back here." The footsteps approached and I kept talking. "Linda was never a client of Gerald's. I don't think she knew him at all, so she's off the suspect list, not that she was a serious contender."

The footsteps slowed but continued to grow closer.

"So we're down to Jim Kittle and Mort Neely." I realized the pads were out of order and sat back on my heels to sort them by date. "Remember that Jim Kittle's company was a client, but five years ago? So sort of a motive, but maybe not as strong as it could be? Well, Mort and Lisa Neely were active clients, and have been for years, even though they lived downstate most of that time. Which I can see because it's easier to email documents than to change tax professionals and—"

A thick softness dropped over my head, turning my world dark and small.

My hands flew up. A blanket? Why was there a blanket over my head? I tried to pull it off but couldn't find my way out. "Rafe Niswander, if you think this is funny, you're wrong. Take this off right now."

"Not a chance."

Every muscle in my body clenched with an intense fear.

Because that voice wasn't Rafe's.

Chapter Twenty-Three

Abject fear made me freeze like thc proverbial deer in the headlights. I didn't move. Couldn't move, really. None of the hide, fight, or flight trainings we'd gone through at the library entered my tiny little head. Not that any of those scenarios had any relationship to this particular situation, but you'd have thought I'd be able to dredge up something at least indirectly useful.

My mouth opened and I heard a faint squeaky noise coming out of it.

Wait. Was I *whimpering*?

No. I was not. I would not. I could figure a way out of this. I always had and I always would.

My brain kicked into gear and I thought of a way forward. "Hey," I said as casually as possible. "You know it's Minnie, right? Minnie Hamil-, I mean Minnie Niswander? I have permission to be here. You don't have to call nine-one-one or anything. I'm helping Lanelle, that's Gerald's niece—well, great-niece technically—do the sorting and cleaning. There's a lot to do yet, you know, and I need to get going. Plus it's getting stuffy under here."

Then, at long last, my body was able to move. I flailed my arms, trying to get the blanket off my head. The footsteps, which must have moved away during my temporary panic, came running back and suddenly my arms were pinned to my sides. "Oh, no you don't," a deep voice snarled.

I twisted and turned and tried to get away. "Yes, I . . . do," I insisted, panting out the words. "I abso . . . lutely . . . do."

There was no other choice for me. I had to get away. This man had probably killed Cheryl and had certainly killed Gerald. Clearly, I was next in line, and this wasn't a line anyone wanted to be in, let alone be at the front of.

And I couldn't let him kill me. There were too many things on my to-do list. I'd never finished the personal strategic plan, for one thing. I still had to finish resurrecting the library's reputation post–website debacle. Plus there was all sorts of places I wanted to go. I hadn't ever been to Borobudur. Or Angkor Wat. Or attended the Songkran Festival. Plus Rafe's birthday was just around the corner. Me dying now would probably put a huge damper on that, and who would make sure he got the cool poster that was sitting in my library office?

"Hold. Still," he said.

Which had to be the stupidest thing I'd ever heard anyone say. Why on earth would I want to make it easier for someone to kill me?

So I did the opposite of holding still. In one burst, I used all the strength my legs had to push myself up. The back of my head connected with something hard and sharp and my cry of pain coincided with a male grunt.

His grip on my arms tightened. "You're making it worse," he said.

I didn't see how. He was already planning to kill me. How much worse could it get? Okay, drawn-out pain and agony before the death part would absolutely be worse.

"You know," I said, still trying for casual, "my husband will be here soon." At least I hoped he would be. "We can work this out. You leave now, and I'll stay here under the blanket. I promise I won't come out, or even peek, until I count to one hundred. Slowly."

As a foray into release negotiations, I'd thought it was excellent start, but my captor ignored me. Completely. And I hated being ignored as much as Eddie hated being ignored.

I tried to think what Eddie would do in a situation like this. Hissing, spitting, growling, and using his pointy teeth and claws. If I had teeth and claws like him, I'd absolutely be using them, but I didn't, so I had to think of another way out.

"Listen," I said. "Like I said, my husband will be here soon. So why don't—"

"Shut up!"

An explosion of light filled my head.

Noises.

Metallic clanking something heavy something sliding something . . . someone . . . anyone . . . Rafe . . .

And everything went black.

* * *

When my brain started up again, my first conscious thought was how cold and wet my back felt. Then I registered that my feet were higher than the rest of me. Then that my head was pounding with pain so intense that, if I'd been asked, I would have said it was nine point nine on the one to ten scale, with ten being painful and agonizing death, so I was saving that.

I tried to lift my arms but found I couldn't. What had happened? Was I paralyzed? And where was I, anyway?

"Stupid women," someone muttered.

My eyes finally focused. Gray. The only thing I saw was gray. Was I going blind, with gray being the first phase of blindness?

I blinked. Nothing changed. Blinked again. Again nothing changed. But I did wake up enough to understand that I was seeing the sky. A March sky with such thick cloud cover that it seems like the sun never really came up, or if it did, it didn't feel up to doing a very good job.

I was seeing the sky, and I was seeing the sky because my captor was dragging me through the snow, feet first.

Think. I had to think.

I wasn't dead yet—at least I didn't think I was—so there were still opportunities to get out of this alive.

"So stupid," he said, and dropped my feet.

Instinctively, I closed my eyes. I didn't have many advantages right then, in fact I couldn't think of a single one, but there was no way it would be beneficial to me if he knew I was awake. He'd probably just whack me again with whatever it was he'd whacked me with before, and that wasn't anything I was interested in.

"If women could only keep their mouths shut," he said, "I wouldn't have to do this. Wouldn't have had to do any of it."

My fuzzy brain tried to identify the voice. Jim Kittle? Mort Neely? Somebody else?

"And I got to tell you, none of this is easy."

There was a weirdly hollow squelchy thump, a noise that sounded familiar and unfamiliar at the same time. There was a second thump, then another and another and another, all accompanied by a callous narration.

"I thought about picking up a chainsaw for the February job, but didn't want to leave a paper trail."

Thump.

"All this chopping is harder than I thought it would be. I mean, I knew it was going to be tough back in February."

Thump.

"But you wouldn't know it was the middle of March by the thickness of this stuff."

Thump.

"Sure, it's handy having the ice around, but a boat would have done the trick just as well."

Though the thumps and the dialogue continued, I wasn't paying as much attention as I could have. I was far too busy being terrified because my concussed head had finally figured out the obvious. I'd been dragged onto the ice. This guy was chopping a hole in it, and when it was big enough, he was going to shove me down it, like Veruca Salt in *Charlie and the Chocolate Factory*. It had turned out okay for her in the end, though, which gave me some hope.

"Wish I didn't have to do this," he said.

I was quite sure he *didn't* have to do it, but I was also sure he wasn't going to listen to anything I had to say.

"If you hadn't talked to Lisa, everything would have been fine. But no, you had to find out that I wasn't downstate over Valentine's Day.

Downstate. Grandkids. Lisa.

Thump.

"Maybe it serves me right for volunteering information," Mort Neely said. "You'd think I'd know better. My dad always said that was what the army taught him, not to volunteer for anything."

There was a quieter *thump.*

"You know, I think that's big enough," Mort said. "You're smaller than Arnhold. A hole that size should do the trick."

This was it. My moment of opportunity. I'd been keeping still as a statue because trying to inch away from a man wielding an axe had seem supremely stupid, even for me. My window of opportunity, however, was about to slam shut. It was now or never.

I pulled my feet to my chest and rolled onto my side, away from Mort. With momentum on my side, I kept rolling, up and onto my knees. I sprang to my feet and took one running step.

Two running steps.

I was doing it. I was getting away! I was—

Large black spots blossomed in front of me. Dizziness whirled around me. My running steps slowed to a fast walk. A stagger.

No no no. I had to move. Had to run. Had to get away . . .

"So stupid." A panting Mort grabbed my arms and hauled me around roughly. "I should have tied you up. You know, I had my right knee replaced just last year, and I swear if I messed it up running after you, you're going to pay for it."

I wasn't sure how that was going to work if I was dead. I tried to tell him so, but my words came out in a stammer of syllables that didn't make any sense.

"No idea what you're trying to say."

His words came out short and gasping. Either the short sprint chasing me down had tired him out, or it had been the chopping. He didn't sound good. His heavy breathing actually indicated that he could be a good candidate for a heart attack, something that I normally wouldn't wish on anyone, but in this case would be a serendipitous event approaching miracle status.

"Nope," he said, yanking me with him. "Still can't make it out. Not that it matters, nothing you can say is going to make any difference, and there's nothing I'm going to pass along to whoever. For obvious reasons."

He chuckled, but I barely heard him because I was too busy kicking and hitting and screaming. Or trying to, because none of my body parts seemed to be working properly.

"Ah, cut that out." He tightened his hold on me. "You're just making this harder. I am sorry about this, but you left me no choice. Okay, here we are. They say after that first breath, that drowning is like falling asleep. So sweet dreams, Minnie."

He nudged the back of my knees. My feet were going to hit the water first.

Waterproof boots, my muzzy brain thought. They'll save me!

But no, I'd taken off my boots once the house had warmed up. I'd been working in my stocking feet ever since I'd gone into the office, and I was sure that one sock had a hole in it. If they ever found my body, my mother was going to be so embarrassed.

"Get . . . in!" Mort nudged me again, and there was nothing I could do to stop him.

I went in.

Hard and fast and deep.

The water was more than cold. Shockingly cold. Deathly cold. So cold it was—if I believed in anthropomorphizing inanimate objects and in this case I absolutely did—a malevolent force intent on sucking the life force out of me.

Hypothermia. It was a thing. Water this cold? If I was unlucky, I'd start to get symptoms in two minutes. If I was lucky, I'd get maybe five. Unconscious in fifteen minutes. But it was going to be a close contest as to what killed me first, hypothermia or plain old drowning. How long could I hold my breath until my lungs were so starved for something that they pulled in water? And how long would I last after that?

In one of the first aid training courses I'd taken, the instructor had been keen on teaching us wilderness survival techniques. After we'd told her that we didn't need to spend time on how to survive in the desert, given that we lived in Michigan, she'd quickly pivoted to giving us tips on surviving in cold weather.

At this particular moment in what might be (but I hoped wasn't) a relatively short life, I could have absolutely used

Top Five Tips on How to Survive Being Tossed Into a Frozen Lake After Being Whacked on the Head. Sadly, all I could remember was there was something called the rule of threes. But three what?

I looked up through the murky light, for once not caring about the horrific possibilities that could happen when swimming while wearing contacts.

Briefly, I considered counting seconds down from three minutes, just to know how much time I might have left, but discarded the idea faster than it had come to me. Doing math was not how I wanted to spend my final moments. Not that these would be my final moments, though, because I was going to figure a way out of this.

Wasn't I?

Up there, in the lightest part of the murk, was Mort Neely. He'd still be up there, waiting. If I resurfaced, he'd just hold my head under until . . . well, until he didn't need to. If I waited down here, I'd run out of air at roughly the same time the hypothermia started to seriously kick in.

Not that it wasn't already. My toes were already in the numb stage, and my fingers weren't far behind, and . . .

. . . and I hit bottom. Literally and figuratively, I supposed, and the thought almost made me smile. Then, because I could still find something funny minutes before my probable death, I decided that I was proud of myself. Finding humor in almost everything was a good thing. It meant optimism and creativity and that's what it took to get through life.

Short as it might be.

My lungs were a tight burn of oxygen-depleted pain. Since the only way out was up, I pushed my feet against the mucky lake bottom—a type of surface I normally avoided because eww—and rose back up to the underside of the ice, trying very very *very* hard not to panic, because I knew that would not serve me well. I had to stay calm, had to think, had to be smart.

Then the top of my wounded head bumped against the underside of the ice and pain was the only thing in my world.

There was no water.

No ice.

No darkness.

No fear of drowning.

No fears at all, only an explosion of excruciating pain that would have taken my breath away if I'd had any extra. It was only by the grace of all that is good in the world that I didn't reflexively shriek in agony and suck in a killing glug of lake water. Instead, some atavistic survival instinct kept my mouth shut.

The pain also focused me. Maybe the water wasn't quite as cold as I'd thought, because though my toes were icy blocks, I could still waggle my fingers. That made breathing priority one. How I was going to wriggle myself out of the water and up onto the slippery ice was priority number two, but I would worry about that later.

If Mort was up there—I pushed away images of Arctic hunters poised with a harpoon in hand, waiting patiently for a seal to surface—I was doomed. But if he'd watched me drop down and walked away, maybe . . . maybe . . .

I kicked with sluggish legs and waved my arms about me, keeping them moving and keeping myself close to the underside of the ice, thinking very hard about how to save myself and not, absolutely not, thinking about claustrophobia and that Gerald had been down here not that long ago, but thinking about how much longer I could go without breathing and how to—

"You are so stupid," I said out loud. Well, not out loud out loud, but in my head. I kept kicking, slapped my pants pockets with hands that were starting to lose all feeling, and felt nothing.

No no no. It had to be there. I couldn't have lost it, not when Mort was hauling me out of the house or dragging me across the ice or dumping me into the water. It had to be there. Had to had to had to . . .

And then I found it. The plastic straw I'd used to stir the cream into my coffee. All I had to do was get one end into my mouth and the other out of the water and I'd be able to breathe.

If my brain had been working properly, I'd have known that this was impossible. I mean, honestly, even if my entire self hadn't been nearly numb, in what world would I have been able to tread water at just the right height *and* hold the straw at just the right height?

But I tried. As carefully as I could, I tried, and after three attempts of sucking in air and getting water instead, I let the straw slip through my fingers and watched it go down down down to the lake bottom. Part of me was ashamed that littering might be the last thing I did, but the rest of me was busy, because my frozen brain had remembered something important.

The Swiss Army not-a-knife.

My oxygen-starved thoughts raced around inside my skull.

Hah. Who needed a straw, anyway? I had the best tool in the world in my front pants pocket. A plan, Watson, I had a plan!

Without pausing to try to remember if hallucinations were a symptom of hypothermia, because what was the point really, I tried with frozen fingers to get the small red tool out of my pocket.

It barely moved.

Think, Minnie. Think.

But all I could think about was how badly I needed to breathe, and there was nothing for me to breathe except water, and that didn't bode well for my future.

So instead of thinking, I kept trying. Using my fingers. Using the heel of my hand. Pushing and pulling and wedging the tool higher and higher until . . . yes!

What little sensation remained in my fingers felt the tool's end slide out of my pocket. I grabbed, pulled, and—

No!

In slow motion, it fell out of my hand.

Chapter Twenty-Four

End over end, the tool did a breathtakingly slow spin down toward the bottom of the lake.

The panic that hadn't ever been far away roared loudly in my ears. Instinctively I pulled up my knees hard and fast. One of them hit the tool. It did a patient U-turn and came back toward my hand.

This time I held on tight. No drops. No fumbles.

I used my teeth to pull open the multi-purpose tool.

If Mort was up there, maybe I'd stab him, which I'd actually be okay with. If he wasn't there . . . please please please let him not be there.

As hard as I could, I scissor-kicked. At the same time, using every ounce of oxygen I had left in my body—which was none, but I had to try as there were no options left—I arced my arm out of the water and stabbed the ice with the tool's tip.

It held.

Then it pulled free and I started sliding back down into the depths.

No no no! I'm not ready! This can't be my time, I have too much living to do!

Gasping in what air I could, I gave another kick—*not my final kick please don't let it be my last ever*—held tight, and plunged the tool into the ice.

This time it held.

I kicked and wriggled and rolled my way out of the water. Flat out on the ice, eyes up to the still-gray sky, I heaved in breath after breath, pulling in the air I'd always assumed would be there for me. Never again would I take it for granted. Every morning, noon, and night I would bless the air around me and my loved ones, thanking it for giving us life.

My breaths slowed to a normal respiratory rate and my thoughts moved past Immediate Survival and into How to Make Sure You Stay Alive.

I rolled onto my hands and knees, summoning the strength and will to stand. And capacity, because none of my body parts were working properly, and the shivers I'd so far been able to ignore were reaching previously unheard of levels.

Two threats. First was hypothermia. Second was Mort.

Though he hadn't been standing over the hole he'd chopped in the ice, waiting for me to surface so he could shove me back under for the final time, he couldn't be far away because I wasn't that good at holding my breath.

My fingers might as well have been blocks of wood for all the feeling they had in them, so I pushed myself up to kneeling with the heels of my hands.

Dizziness sparked in and out of my vision. I blinked once, twice, and the third time my eyes cleared and I could see that I was alone on the ice. This was a big win for Minnie, and I would have cheered myself if I hadn't been so busy shivering and trying to stay alive.

Staying alive. Yes. I needed to get on that. Right now.

I tried to stand, but the sparkles started to take over and I went back to kneeling. Fine. I could crawl away from that gaping hole. I wasn't proud, not about this anyway.

On hands and knees, I started shuffling across the ice. One inch . . . two inches . . . every fraction of a foot was a victory. I was doing it! I was getting away!

A shiver vibrated through my entire body and I fell on my face, crying out as my chin cracked on the ice.

"You have got to be kidding me," Mort Neely said.

Right. I'd been so focused on surviving the first threat of hypothermia that I'd forgotten about the second threat. I pushed myself back to my knees and looked up toward Gerald's house.

Mort was traipsing down the snowy hillside, muttering dark things about women who won't stay put.

I scrambled to my feet. Fell down. Got up again. Fell. Got to my knees and struggled to stand, thoughts whirling and colliding and not being helpful at all.

No no no. Mort Neely was *not* going to throw me in the water again. I could get away. I could do it. I would do it. I would find a way to survive, and I would get Ash to put Mort Neely in handcuffs and lock him away forever and—

And that's when I heard a distant noise; the glorious rattling racket that could only be a car part in dire need of replacement. Time-wise, Mort could easily stuff me back into the ice, walk up to the house, and then casually tell Rafe that he had no idea where I was, but that he was afraid something horrible had happened to me. The two men would search the house, and eventually, when it was far too late, I'd be found.

But maybe, just maybe that wouldn't happen. I had an idea, and it was a good one. Maybe.

"H-hear th-that? It's a truck m-muffler th-that needs replacing," I called. "It's m-my husband. H-he'll b-be looking f-for me."

Mort went still.

"Have y-you m-met Rafe?" I asked. "He's t-taller than you. Thirty years younger. A-about the s-same weight, b-but way m-more muscle than f-fat. If I were you, I'd—"

Mort, bully that he was, did what I'd hoped.

He turned and ran.

Moments later, I heard his car start. Tires screeched on the concrete pad in front of the garage, and he roared off.

A loud and familiar horn blare made me close my eyes, but there was no crash. I breathed a deep relieved breath. Rafe was okay. I was okay. We were both okay. Everything was going to be fine.

"R-Rafe!" I called out, but it was a weak effort. I didn't have the strength to do more. "Rafe," I called again, and kept crawling off the ice. I had to keep moving. Had to get to warm. Threat number two was gone, but hypothermia was still a very real danger.

"R-Rafe," I whispered.

Find me. Help me. I need you.

"Minnie!" Footsteps scudded down the snowy hillside and his arms were around me, pulling me to my feet, pulling me close. "What the . . . never mind. Let's get you inside and into the shower—"

"N-no h-hot water," I croaked.

Rafe cursed. "Right. Hang on." Still holding onto me, he pulled his phone from his pocket and dialed 911.

My ears knew that he was talking to someone, but none of the one-sided conversation made sense, so I decided to focus on walking. One foot in front of the other, just like the Winter Warlock. Or was that the Snow Miser?

I shook my head, trying to crowd out the cobwebby scraps of ancient Christmas specials, wondering why on earth those had surfaced out of my deep gray matter at that particular moment.

"Okay." Rafe slipped his phone away. "Here's what we're going to do."

He said more words. Lots of them. None of them registered. But I didn't care, because Rafe was there. He was going to figure this out. His turn, right? I'd figured out who killed Gerald and Cheryl and—

"M-Mort," I whispered.

"What?" My beloved bent his head to me. "I'm getting you to the truck. It's warm and there are blankets."

"M-Mort," I repeated. "N-Neely."

Rafe's grip on me tightened. "Mort Neely," he said in a tone of voice I'd never once heard him use. "Is that who did this to you?"

I nodded. Tried to, anyway. "H-have p-proof." I felt more than saw Rafe look in the direction Mort had fled. "Don't," I said. "H-he c-can't run f-forever."

"He'll wish he had," Rafe muttered. He scooped me up into his arms and carried me up the hill and into his truck, which I was pretty sure he was telling me was still warm as he buckled me in. I believed him because he wouldn't lie to me, but the warmth didn't do anything to get rid of the bone-rattling shaking that was taking me over.

"S-sorry," I said as he buckled me in. "C-can't d-do th-that mys-self."

He kissed the top of my head and reached for the ancient sleeping bag that he kept behind the front seats. He tucked it around me, kissed me again, and shut my door.

Panic flared.

He was leaving? Don't go! No no no . . .

The driver's door opened. He climbed in, started the engine, and my brief panic attack faded.

"It won't be long," he said. "Just stay awake, okay? They'll meet us, but dispatch said to keep you awake."

Or that was at least what I thought I heard him say, because my ears weren't hearing very well. I tried to make my eyes focus on him, but they really didn't want to. A nap. That's what I needed. Just a short nap until we got to wherever we were going. Or a long nap. Long would be okay.

"Minnie! Wake up!"

Rafe's voice came somewhere far, far in the distance. Which didn't make sense, because last I knew he was sitting right next to me. But it would all be okay after I got some sleep. Nice, deep sleep.

"Minerva Joy Hamilton!"

I opened my eyes a fraction and looked for my mother. But it was my husband. What was he doing, calling me by my maiden name? He was so silly . . .

The truck's horn blared, a noise that normally made me jump out of my skin. This time it just made me smile.

Silly Rafe . . .

Brakes squealed. Doors opened and shut and opened.

"She's wet all the way through," a distant Rafe said. "I covered her up, but I didn't have any way to get her warm."

"You did fine," an unfamiliar voice said. "We got this, okay?"

Hands unbuckled me, eased me out of the seat, carried me, and put me on something long and horizontal. What was the word? Gurgle. No, that wasn't right. Gurney. That was it. I felt Rafe at my side and batted at him with an unfeeling hand. "Not-a-knife saved my life," I said, then giggled at the unintentional rhyme.

"Shhhh." Rafe put his hand on my forehead. "You're going to be okay. I'm not leaving you. Bonus of the marriage thing is I get to ride in the ambulance."

Of course I was going to be okay. I hadn't pulled myself out of near freezing water, dragged my hypothermic self across the ice, and scared off Mort Neely just to die anyway.

I opened my eyes, and Rafe's face swam into focus. On my left and right were two uniformed EMTs busy doing their jobs, something that I hoped involved letting me go back to sleep. But before I did that, there was one thing I had to say.

"P-pock . . ." Nope. Too much trouble to get out the two syllables. It would have to wait until I woke up. Over the top of me, Rafe and the EMTs exchanged a glance.

Rafe leaned close. "What was that?"

Great. Now they were concerned for my mental state. Nice. "Pockets," I said, clearly and firmly.

And closed my eyes.

Chapter Twenty Five

"Seriously?" Aunt Frances asked. "Pockets?"

"They saved my life," I said indignantly.

She laughed. "Good thing, because you never would have lived down having your final word be 'pockets.'"

I rolled my eyes. "Seems like you'd be nicer to someone who's still in the hospital."

"Only because your discharge is taking forever."

It was Monday afternoon, almost exactly twenty-four hours after my freezing plunge. My recovery from hypothermia had been rapid, and the doctors didn't think there'd be any lingering impacts. Though the crack to my head had caused me to have multiple scans in long noisy metal tubes, the resulting pretty pictures had reassured the white-coated people.

That night, Rafe had taken a long list of post-trauma instructions home with him—"I'll tape it to the bathroom mirror," he'd said grimly—and I'd promised everyone that came into my room that I'd be a model patient. The janitor had seemed to believe me, although I wasn't sure anyone else had.

I'd been kept in the hospital overnight, and I was now waiting for paperwork and for Rafe to return from retrieving our vehicles from Gerald's little lake house with the help of a couple of his buddies.

In the meantime, my loving aunt was keeping me company. That was her story, anyway. To me, it felt more like I was being criticized for things outside of my control, so I reminded her of that.

"You're right. I'm sorry," she said contritely. "It's just . . ." She stopped. Cleared her throat. "It's just that you came close to dying, and I don't want to think about that. Much easier to make fun of you for your theoretical final words."

I waited a few beats for the emotion in the room to settle down. "I know," I said. "And to some extent I agree, but I also want to emphasize the importance of pockets in my survival. All pants should have them."

Aunt Frances leaned against the wall and slid her hands into her own pockets. "Agreed. What are we going to do about it?"

We were brainstorming language for legislation when Ash walked in. My aunt and I grinned at each other and continued our conversation.

"It also has to include a ban on the fake ones," I said firmly.

"Absolutely." My aunt nodded. "And every single one has to be useful, so we need to include a depth requirement."

"Front and back?"

We considered the question as Ash eyed us warily. "Just the fronts," I finally said. "Unless we want to include both when it's first introduced, with the intent to be negotiated down."

This, for some reason, struck us as hilarious and Aunt Frances and I burst out laughing.

Ash shook his head. "I am not going to ask," he said, then gave me a look. "You ready to go?"

The EMTs had cut off all my cold and wet clothing in their first aid efforts, so I was dressed in the clothes Rafe had brought from home that morning; baggy old leggings and one of his ancient MSU hoodie sweatshirts. "Almost." I was sitting on the bed, trying to be patient. "Waiting for paperwork. And Rafe."

"Do you want to do this here or at the sheriff's office?" he asked.

"If you want it done today," my aunt said, "you're doing it here. This one is headed straight home."

"Works for me." Ash pulled the wheeled hospital tray around and put a pile of papers on it. "I have a couple of questions for you," he said, flipping through the stack.

I kicked my heels against the bed. "Did you find the fireplace poker?"

"Right where you said it was."

Cool. The night before, after I'd been warmed up and while we were waiting for the results of my scan, I'd guessed that Mort had used the fireplace tool to hit me on the head. I'd heard it clatter to the floor and heard it slide away after he kicked it.

"Which reminds me." He reached into his coat pocket and held out my phone. "This was on the desk."

My aunt snatched it away before my fingers could take hold. "Oh, no you don't. Not until you get some sleep. And if you start arguing with me, I'll get your parents up here. Your mom wanted to drive north last night, so you can thank me now or later for talking her out of that."

I immediately tucked my hands under my armpits. "Thank you now," I said, "and later." I loved my mother, but she could be . . . a bit much. I looked up at Ash. "Have you had time to look for fingerprints? On the poker?" Because another thing I'd remembered was that Mort hadn't been wearing any gloves.

"It's in evidence," he said. "They did find some black curly hair on it, though."

I patted my own, careful to avoid touching the tender areas of my skull. "Bet it looked a lot like this."

Ash shrugged. "Testing takes time. If there are fingerprints or DNA, the techs will find them."

What they had found already was Mort Neely. Last night, as soon as my shivers had stopped and I could string words into a reasonable sentence, Ash and Detective Inwood had appeared in the ICU. For once, they'd taken lots of notes when I'd talked. An alert had gone out quickly, and a couple of hours later, a state police trooper had pulled him over on I-94, not far from the Indiana border.

He'd claimed he'd been driving to Chicago to visit a very sick friend. The trooper, however, hadn't cared, and Mort was now a guest in the Tonedagana County Jail.

"Okay," Ash said, clicking a pen. "As close as you can remember, what exactly did Mr. Neely say about Cheryl

Wood? And about Gerald Arnhold? And are you okay with me recording this?"

I blew out a breath. I'd known this was going to happen. I was going to have to relive those eternal minutes on the ice over and over again. While answering Ash's questions. While answering Hal Inwood's questions. While answering questions from the prosecuting attorney, defense attorney, and eventually a judge.

It was going to be a long road, and I might as well get used to it, because not only had I been an eyewitness to Mort's confessions, I was also accusing Mort of attempted murder.

"Not sure I can remember word for word," I said. "This will be a lot of paraphrasing."

Ash nodded. "Understood."

"Okay, then." After pulling in a breath of air—happy, life-giving, easy to access air that I had already restarted taking for granted in spite of my fervent vow less than twenty-four hours earlier—I nodded to Ash that it was okay to push the Record button on his phone, and started talking.

I told him that Mort had said he'd killed Cheryl because she was threatening to tell his then-wife about their affair.

"The thing is," Mort had said as he'd pulled a mostly-limp Minnie across the ice, "I'm a problem solver. She was a problem, and I solved it. Same thing with Arnhold, and with you. Would have been a lot easier for both of us if I'd been able to take care of you with my SUV that day, but no. And if you'd all just kept your mouths shut, I wouldn't have had to kill anyone."

I'd wanted to tell him that blaming the victim was the refuge of scoundrels, but I'd been too busy trying to stay alive, struggling as much as I could, and asking a single question. "Why?"

"What is it with the questions?" he'd groused. "Why can't people mind their own business? Why did Arnhold care who killed Cheryl? He caught me off guard, that day I was dropping off the stuff for income taxes. Asking me about Cheryl and that night? How could I have been prepared for a question like that, right out of the blue, after all these years? I stammered out something, and he let it go, but I know he suspected something, so that was a problem for me to deal with. And really it's all Lisa's fault. She deals with the income taxes. I should never have been there in the first place."

Which was what Gerald had written on his yellow pad. When I'd first read them, I hadn't understood what he'd meant, but that one additional piece of information had made everything click into place.

Ash, who was scribbling down notes, caught up with me. "Anything else?"

"Not that I can think of." Nothing except a set of memories that would never completely fade, including but not limited to the horrific knowledge that I'd come within inches of a watery death, and the soul-crushing helpless feeling of being dragged across the ice. I also had the feeling that, for a long, long time, it would be difficult for me to sit with my back to a door.

Counterpoint, though, was the knowledge that I'd survived, and that I'd done it by myself. Or could have done it by myself, because I'd already been developing an escape plan when Rafe had shown up. I was glad I hadn't had to implement the plan, because it had involved thumbs (mine) and eyeballs (his), but I was sure it would have worked.

"Question." Aunt Frances held up her index finger. "Minnie had a head wound and hypothermia. Isn't a defense attorney going to poke holes in everything she says?"

My eyes widened. She was right. Why hadn't I thought about that? Of course they would. I'd watched enough courtroom dramas to know it was going to be brutal. Would I be able to take it? Would I break down on the stand, sobbing? Would my temper flare? Would I say snarky things that would damage the case?

"I don't know if I can do this," I said, my voice tight.

"Sure you can. Don't worry." Ash lightly punched my shoulder. "You'll get plenty of help from the prosecutor's office. But asking those questions is the defense's job. It's our job, and the prosecutor's job, to make sure we have evidence to refute everything the defense puts forward. And we will."

His confidence reassured me. And, as it turned out, he was right. The fine folks at the prosecutor's office prepped me thoroughly, there was plenty of evidence, and Mort was convicted and sentenced.

In the trial, Mort claimed that killing both Cheryl and Gerald had been accidents. No one, not even his own attorney, gave the impression that they believed him, especially when he admitted to moving Cheryl's body from the motel room where he'd killed her, out to the airport to intentionally mislead the police. Which it had. And had continued to do for years.

But that was all much later. That afternoon, in the hospital, I was coming to realize that the only thing I wanted was to go home and take a nap with a fuzzy blanket and an even fuzzier feline.

"Look at her," Aunt Frances said. "She's fading."

I sat upright. "I'm fine."

"Don't be stupid," my loving aunt said. "You're not. Ash here is done, isn't he?" She gave him a hard look.

"Yes, ma'am." He turned off his phone and slid his notepad into his shirt pocket. "Glad you're okay, Minnie. It would have been . . . it's just . . . well, I'm glad you're okay."

I squinted at him. "What, no lectures on how stupid I was to be out there alone in the first place? No berating me for doing work that's the role of law enforcement?"

He grinned. "That's Hal's job. I'm sure he'll get around to it soon enough."

"Good to have something to look forward to," I muttered, and in doing so realized that my aunt was right. I was tired, down to the marrow of my bones. I closed my eyes, just for a minute. I'd open them after a short rest.

"Get that girl home," I heard Aunt Frances say, and suddenly Rafe was there, helping me to my feet, out of the hospital and the hospital smell, and home where I knew what everything was and where everything was and where I could sleep sleep sleep . . .

* * *

A few days later, when I didn't feel dizzy standing up and when napping held little allure, I went back to the library. Since I wasn't sure I was up to driving, Rafe dropped me off at the back door, where Holly met me and, over my objections, took my backpack away and shadowed me down the hall, eyeing me as if I might fall apart if a slight breeze came along.

Since I needed coffee before even thinking about tackling my email, my first stop was the break room. I walked in, smiled at the container of brownies on the table, then stopped short.

There was a huge banner hanging on the wall. "Welcome Back" it proclaimed in big bold letters, but directly after the "K" of "Back," an 11 × 17 piece of paper was taped to it that said "Minnie!"

"It's Graydon's name underneath," Holly said, smirking the tiniest bit. "Kind of a twofer, right? But I made the brownies just for you."

I stared at the banner. Of course Graydon was back. He'd come home over the weekend, and Rafe had called him Sunday night to tell him I wouldn't be in for a few days. "How is he?"

"Better than you, probably." Our boss came into the break room. "My dad is much better, they're all moved in, and I even found them a breakfast place that makes hash browns just the way they like them. Do you want to talk in your office or in mine?"

Well, that didn't sound good. I felt Holly's concerned glance. "In mine, please." Because unpleasant conversations were best held on home turf.

Graydon looked from me to Holly and back to me. "I must have been gone long enough to lose basic management skills. There's nothing wrong. I just need to hear from

Minnie how things went while I was gone. The board has already told me you did wonderfully, but I want a debrief straight from you."

"The board thinks I did okay?" I blinked. "Really?"

Holly rolled her eyes. "You can be so stupid," she said, but then gave me a quick one-armed hug. "We're really glad you're back home, safe and sound," she whispered.

I moved my lunch from backpack to refrigerator, filled a mug with happiness, and, after a quick stop at my office to drop off extraneous items, Graydon and I went up to the second floor because he said he had Cookie Tom cookies up there.

"You are the best boss ever," I said, taking an oatmeal raisin to start and plopping into the chair across from him.

"Glad you grasp that." He took a snickerdoodle. "So. Tell me what happened the last few weeks."

"Do you want the short or the long version?"

He nodded at the cookie pile. "We have provisions."

Long version it was. I settled back, started at the beginning, and didn't stop talking until after I explained my solution to the general unhappiness that had pervaded the library staff in the wake of the website debacle.

"It took a few conversations to convince Erik," I said, "but once he was on board, he and his team came up with an outstandingly funny video apology."

Though I'd missed the launch because Erik had set it up to be released on Monday morning, I'd set up delayed emails and social media posts to point library staff toward the video, and people were finding it so funny that it was becoming almost famous in library land. Because that had been my revelation on the bookmobile, that humor brings people together. The text messages I'd received from library staff had encouraged me to think it had been a success, and Graydon's nod assured me.

"Nicely done," he said. "I don't think I would ever have come up with that idea."

My insides glowed from the praise, but I had to ask the question I'd wanted to ask for weeks but hadn't because I hadn't wanted to bother him and I'd wanted to deal with it myself. "What would you have done?"

He smiled. "No idea. That's part of the fun of management, you know. Everybody's approach is different. And there's no one perfect way to do it. There are just too many variables."

Rats. Here I'd thought that someday I'd learn the secret.

"And now I have to ask," he said. "How are you? Rafe told me what happened. If you need more time off, take it."

"No," I said slowly, "I think I'm good."

He reached for the last cookie, chocolate chip, split it in half, and pushed the slightly larger half my way. "Not just talking about physical health, Minnie. Trauma takes its toll in all sorts of way."

Truly, he was the best boss. "I know," I said. "Thanks for caring. And I promise that if I need more time, I'll take it."

I went back to my office to work on emails—the happiest one being from Wanda at Honey Hollow, telling me that Alicia was recovering from her stroke and was coming back home soon—but a couple of hours later, when I'd been staring at my computer screen doing absolutely nothing for ten straight minutes, I realized that Graydon was right. I needed more time. Time doing what, though? I didn't think that more time sitting at home would help.

I picked up the phone, made a few calls, got a recommendation, and made an appointment with a therapist. As I hung up the phone, I felt something inside of me loosen, something I hadn't known had been tight.

"Progress," I said out loud. Because even though I hadn't met my therapist yet, I was sure I was moving in the right direction. Healing from trauma took time, and assistance from a professional would help.

Another thing that would help would be time with friends and family. Most of my friends were at work, but there was a family member just down the road.

I woke up my phone.

Me: *Are you busy? I'd like to stop by.*

Aunt Frances: *Now?*

Me: *If that's okay.*

Aunt Frances: *Of course it is. And if you show up in eleven minutes, I'll have a fresh batch of lemon bars for you to try.*

It took me a little longer than eleven minutes, but the lemon bars were still warm when we sat down in the breakfast nook. "Cheers," my aunt said, holding her square in toasting position. We air-tinked and bit into the yumminess.

Since one wasn't enough, we ate a second, and as we were polishing off the final crumbs, my aunt said, "I have something for you. Don't move."

She left the room. I heard her murmuring something to Otto, who was ensconced in their study, reading, and she came back with a three-ring binder that she handed to me.

I read the title out loud. "Minnie's Triumphs."

"It's a cookbook," she said.

I opened the cover and scanned over the two recipes she'd included. "Good thing I don't have feelings," I said, "because this makes me look like a tremendous failure."

"What? No!" Aunt Frances looked stricken. "Not what I meant. What I meant is there's room to add recipes. Dozens of them. You'll get the hang of it, you just need time to find your way, that's all."

More advice about time. Interesting.

We spent the rest of the afternoon talking idly about this and that, and when Rafe picked me up, both my aunt and Otto gave me solid hugs as I was heading out the door.

"Kind of weird," I said as I buckled myself in. "We're not usually a hugging kind of family."

"They were worried about you." Rafe slid me a look. "So was I. So was everybody."

"Yeah." I sighed. "Sorry about that."

"Not your fault. By the way, I have an idea."

"If you're going to say Fat Boys, I'm good with pizza."

He laughed. "Not that kind of idea. I'll show you when we get home."

It was after we'd eaten our dinner (Rafe-made calzones accompanied by Minnie-assembled salads) and done the dishes that Rafe took me by the hand and led me to the living room.

"Eddie," he said, "gave me the idea."

"Really?"

My reaction must have been loud, because it woke our furry friend, who'd been sleeping in the middle of the coffee table. He gave me a look.

"Sorry, buddy," I said, scooping him up and cuddling him close. "I didn't mean it." I had, but he didn't need to know that. "You're the best, smartest, prettiest Eddie ever."

"Mrr," he said, clearly agreeing with me.

"Exactly." Rafe nodded. "He has agendas and plans, but he doesn't write them down, does he?"

"No thumbs," I said, holding up a white paw.

"So we can take a lesson from Eddie and not write down our plans. Our strategic plan."

I had no idea where he was going with this. "Um . . ."

"Look." He pointed at the fireplace mantel. The night before, the mantel had held a collection of miscellaneous objects that had accumulated there mostly because it had looked lonely. Now, it was empty. "We'll put things here that represent a goal. When we reach it, we can move whatever it is somewhere else."

This was brilliant. "Like a ceramic pig," I said.

"A pig?" He frowned.

"To symbolize a piggy bank. Goal of saving money."

His expression cleared. "Got it. And a book, because you've always said someday you want to write one."

"A wine glass, because we want to go to France."

"Clock, because I want to start running again, and get my 5K time under twenty-two minutes."

Our ideas started spinning out thick and fast. We were excited and energized and—

"Mrr!"

We looked at Eddie, who was giving us the kind of glare that only a cat can.

"Right," Rafe said. "How about a glass cat? Because maybe a companion would make this one less goofy."

I kissed the top of Eddie's head. "Your dad is joking. We don't want you to change. Not a single bit."

"No?" Rafe's eyebrows went up. "Because I'd be okay if he didn't shed as much."

My heart went mushy, and I knew without a doubt that I was the luckiest person in the world, because this man, this wonderful man, loved me. And my boss and coworkers cared about me enough to make me brownies, buy me cookies, and tape my name onto a banner. And my aunt loved me so much that she would never give up nurturing my cooking efforts. And there'd been so many friends and family members reaching out the last few days to see how I was doing that I'd started to tear up whenever my cell dinged.

"Plus there's you," I whispered to Eddie.

His ears twitched as if he were actually listening to what I was saying, so I went on telling him the truth. "You make life more fun. More interesting. More full. And I hope that you feel the same way."

Eddie twisted his head around to look up at me.

And winked.